To mar
Best wishes.

OPTIMUS 4

Ross G. Gaehring

OPTIMUS 4
Copyright 2007 by Ross Gaehring

Ross G. Gaehring

ALL RIGHTS RESERVED
No part of this book may be reproduced or transmitted in any form or by any means, electronic or mechanical, including photocopying, recording, or by any information storage and retrieval system, without permission in writing from the author, except in the case of brief quotations embodied in reviews.

Cover Art:
Kelly Kabell

Publisher's Note:
This is a work of fiction. All names, characters, places, and events are the work of the author's imagination.
Any resemblance to real persons, places, or events is coincidental.

Solstice Publishing - www.solsticepublishing.com

Copyright 2014
Ross Gaehring

Thanks to my Lord, for giving me the inspiration to write Optimus 4, and to my beautiful wife Susan and children Ashley, Anthony, Ryan and Byran for their loving support, without which this novel could not have been completed.

In a real dark night of the soul it is always three o'clock in the morning, day after day.

--- F. Scott Fitzgerald

Let's pray that the human race never escapes Earth to spread its iniquity elsewhere.

---C.S. Lewis

CHAPTER ONE

Detroit Michigan: December 5th, 2063.

The holo-com in the ancient Daimler-Benz blared incessant government propaganda, made even more repulsive thanks to a tiny holographic DJ who babbled on in the "1970s top 40 AM radio" voice favored by America's dictator. Only the Great General George Brinton McLellan and certain eminent scientists in Psychological Operations could tell you exactly why such an archaic style of communication remained so popular.

"Hi y'all! This is DJ Jazzy J coming to you on Armed Forces Comm-Rad 1. Hope you're having an absolutely fantastic morning no matter what part of the Grand Old Republic you're tuning in from! This next one is going out to all you brave troops in our cities continuing the fight for truth, justice and the American Way against those cowardly anarchist traitors. Here it is-a real classic for your listening enjoyment-one of our Glorious Leader General McLellan's all-time favorites-The Beastie Boys, You Gotta Fight…"

"Turn that shit off! I'm tryin' to sleep, dammit!" grunted the still-groggy Special Forces trooper sitting in the passenger seat. Sergeant Danny Trumbell stretched his powerfully built frame like an angry grizzly bear roused from hibernation. With scraggly hair, unshaven face, and crazy eyes, he could have been kin to a savage from another era.

The Daimler's driver, Captain Alan Haig, glanced over and smirked. Trumbell was an annoying son of a bitch but his renowned combat skills would definitely be an asset on this assignment.

The captain's chiseled and weathered features, always deadly serious, became even more severe as he recalled the details concerning their being ordered into a probable suicide mission. The initial briefing with 1st Division's intelligence chief, Colonel Baldwin had been quick and to the point. Someone important (possibly the General himself) wanted Special Forces to retrieve an ex-Navy pilot from the burning cauldron of what used to be known as Detroit before it was declared a dead city. Detroit was the third metropolitan area to gain that dubious label.

At least the briefing provided some much needed entertainment, especially when it came to the VIP's bio.

The guy's name was Commander Rance Edwards. Ancestors included an aristocratic Wehrmacht General who fought on the Eastern Front in the Second World War, a 1940s swashbuckling Hollywood movie star, one of the Sioux Indian chiefs who defeated Custer, an Ottoman sultan and a Jewish freedom fighter who later became active in Israeli politics in the 60s and 70s.

Unbelievable. He'd love to be a fly on the wall during this guy's family reunions.

Commander Edwards had been a hotshot Navy fighter pilot. Went to Annapolis but didn't reveal any exceptional talents until the brief Euro–American war thrust him into the American consciousness as the only notable quasi hero in that entire ill-fated affair. Flying an F-22 off the USS *Washington* (later sunk during a naval debacle now known as the Battle of the North Sea), he shot down ten Euro fighters over northern Germany before a Robotic Hunter-Killer unit finally took him down. Edwards sustained life-threatening injuries on bail out, and spent a month in hospital before being flown to the US after the peace accord between World Leader Antonio Lanza and the General ended the war and brought the isolationist United States into the new world order. Of course, General McLellan tried to put the best spin on things and briefly turned Edwards into The Great American Hero. Problem was hero boy didn't want to play the game. Even though the left side of his face had been severely disfigured, he refused to get reconstruction to be aesthetically appealing for the propaganda campaign. He resigned his commission and broke up with long-time girlfriend Lieutenant Commander Christine St. James.

Edwards was now apparently completely devoted to his cancer-afflicted father. According to Intel gathered before the Detroit situation became totally chaotic, he might be visiting his dad at one of the city's hospitals. This target wouldn't be easy to find. Normally, locating anyone was simple. You just needed to do a mind interface scan of the military database and find the targets GPS signature via the chip implanted in their hand or forehead. Although still imperfect, this technique of mentally linking with the global consciousness of the Supernet had become increasingly important, especially for a totalitarian regime wanting to track every citizen. Unfortunately for the two Special Forces troopers assigned to find him, Edwards seemed to be one of the few crazies who didn't have an implant, even if the penalty for not having one often meant receiving a free bullet courtesy of the Security Ministry.

Intel also indicated he and his father might belong to one of those damn Christian cult groups that in spite of the government's best efforts somehow avoided complete elimination. Apparently the bastards didn't believe in getting chips. They would have no alternative but to find Edwards the old fashioned way and The New God Lanza only knew how bad things were in Detroit, or more correctly Dead City 3 at this moment…

Haig's thoughts were interrupted as they pulled up to the army checkpoint, code named Joy Division. Two mean looking MP's leveled their M-30's at the decrepit looking old Daimler before approaching. One of them pointed his scanner at the center of Haig's forehead and read the holographic images that danced in the air displaying data from a microscopic info chip planted just under the skin.

Somebody nearby was playing "Good" by Better Than Ezra.

"Sorry Captain. Had to make sure. The damned radicals hit us with a guerrilla attack earlier today and we took some pretty heavy casualties. Our orders are to give you any necessary support but I have to advise you for the record that I don't recommend going into that hellhole. The situation is…"

Haig cut him off.

"I appreciate the concern Sergeant, but we've got a mission to complete. Now if you'll kindly get the hell out of our way and raise the gate we can get on with it." The MP's just shook their heads as the Daimler hummed by them. You didn't argue with Special Forces troops... not if you wanted to stay healthy that is.

Other than having to bypass a few crude roadblocks thrown up during the recent hostilities they didn't encounter any visible signs of trouble. Even so, a peaceful appearance didn't guarantee the surrounding buildings weren't full of fanatics just itching for a chance to hit them with an RPG or some other nasty surprise. Not exactly the way he wanted to test the integrity of the Daimlers hidden composite armor plating.

In spite of the savage fighting and obvious anti-Government sentiment in this area, a propaganda billboard along the freeway popped out of the vanishing morning mist, appearing nearly intact. The stylized picture reminded Haig of images circa the 1960's glorifying Egyptian President Gamal Abdel Nasser he once observed in a history studies holo documentary. It depicted an unrealistically youthful, beaming General McLellan, resplendent in a Five Star General's uniform shaking hands with the World Leader, Antonio Lanza. Lanza looked handsome as always, with his slicked back hair, vintage Ray-Ban sunglasses and brilliant smile mimicking some Italian movie star from the mid-20th century. The caption emblazoned across the poster declared "Together we can achieve the impossible!"

Yeah right, thought Haig as they drove past. Lately, the world felt like it was careening down a slippery downward slope, the descent of which no one, McLellan and Lanza included seemed capable of stopping or even slowing down for that matter. The recent Russo/Islamic/Afro/Israeli nuclear war circulated fallout over an already toxic planet, making many contaminated areas uninhabitable. The Russian/Arab/African confederacy had made a dramatic but reckless grab for Israel, launching a joint land invasion in hopes of ridding the world once and for all of the troublesome Israeli's. Not to mention seizing all of that tiny countries valuable oil and mineral rights in the process. The Russian leader Alexander Mikhail Gromeko obviously miscalculated thinking that Benevolent Dictator Lanza would not interfere in such a blatant violation of his celebrated Middle East non-aggression pact. Sudden destruction met eighty percent of the Russian led land forces, being nuked into oblivion before they got anywhere close to Israel. Nuclear warheads also hit a few large Arab cities, most notably Damascus. The Russians annihilated Madrid, Copenhagen, Dresden, Milan and Marseilles in retaliation, but somehow the world stopped on the very brink of complete nuclear extermination.

The crazy thing was many Israelis insisted the One True God deserved the credit for their salvation from Russia, claiming Lanza (that damned Roman as some Jews called him) had nothing to do with saving them. "Fire from God" they called it. A usually reliable, high level CIA analyst that Haig knew swore up and down the Israelis were right, saying only a few European nukes were launched that day even though most credible sources applauded Lanza on his great victory. Once such a stupid rumor got going it usually gained its own momentum, becoming impossible to stop. Almost all of the Jewish people now worshiped their "God" and even more disturbing, many were also becoming converts of the hated Christian sect.

Apparently Lanza planned on taking drastic steps to straighten out the Israelis, moving his headquarters from New Babylon to the Jewish Temple in Jerusalem rebuilt several years before (actually one of the chief catalysts behind the recent war) and installing himself as the new Godhead. After all, he, World Leader Antonio Lanza best typified the True Doctrine of how all men are God and God is in all men. How else to explain his meteoric rise from a poor neighborhood in Naples to Emperor of the entire planet? What other possible explanation could there be for his miraculous healing from the seemingly fatal assassination attempt back in 2059 when a Christian fundamentalist shot him in the head before a horrified world live on holovision?

As Pope Gregory XVII lovingly taught, no longer were corrupt false religions like Christianity needed. Such primitive creeds caused nothing but pain and suffering throughout mankind's history and it would soon be time for the human race to transcend into the next level, becoming the Gods destiny always intended them to be.

His Teachings of Love released all mankind from feelings of guilt caused by the outdated belief systems of the past, most especially Christianity, allowing human beings to express themselves sexually in any way they wished. Goddess of Love Sensual Worship gatherings, although at first causing some controversy had now become an established feature of all New Church services, an innovation that allowed human sexuality to be celebrated and embraced.

Adoring, hysterical crowds idolized the Pope wherever he went, his popularity almost reaching the paramount level of Leader Lanza's.

The Beloved One, Pope Gregory had nearly been killed by an IED several months ago while on an official Papal visit to Jerusalem. On the evening of the assassination attempt, an obviously shaken Pope explained to the world that while lying stunned after the explosion, his Spirit Guides blessed him with a great vision. These "Masters" as the metaphysical beings called themselves, revealed to him the time had now arrived for the Great Leader Lanza to install himself in the New Jerusalem Temple as the Great Savior of the World. The advanced spiritual teachers of ancient wisdom explained to the Pope that by worshipping Lanza as the new ideal, all mankind could then make the leap into the new consciousness and become as Gods themselves. This "paradigm shift" would usher in an age of peace and harmony ending war and strife forever.

After Pope Gregory finished giving his important message, Antonio Lanza himself spoke humbly to the World, thanking the Pope for all of his tireless work and sacrifices made for the noble cause of humanism. The Man of Destiny then went on to say that although he felt inadequate to accept the burden fate had thrust upon him, he knew some causes were much more important than the selfish needs of any one individual. If accepting the worship of all human beings meant everyone on earth could make the spiritual revolution the Pope spoke of possible, then he would be more than willing to face this, his greatest challenge. To aid in this devotion, holographic, interactive images of himself would be placed in all major population centers including most notably, a huge 666-meter replication near Jerusalem. Lanza called upon all true citizens to carry on the fight against the hate filled troublemakers and dissenters such as Christians and Old Catholics idiotically trying to prevent the New World Order. He also swore that the persons responsible for the assassination attempt on the Pope would face immediate justice. Two eccentric, itinerate Jewish Christian preachers of iniquity soon confessed to the crime, being killed in the street like the subversive dogs they were. The world convulsed in a great month long celebration after World Comm broadcast the live execution coverage. Even Haig, usually not a very sociable man, indulged in celebratory drug use and recreational sex with one of the many females freely offering themselves after worship service at the local New Church.

Haig remained constantly thankful of mankind's progression to this new age of enlightenment when it came to sex and religion. If only the entire world would fall into line and follow Lanza's orders, then Pope Gregory's doctrine of the coming glorious age of harmony and love would truly become a reality. Soldiers like he and Sergeant Trumbell would of course be put out of business – but Haig considered the sacrifice of his lifelong military career a small price to pay for the more important cause of peace.

Other than the evil backwards Christians, the only substantial roadblock to world peace now came from the always-troublesome Chinese Asian Federation. Sensing a power vacuum after the defeat of the Russian/Arab/African Confederacy, the Chinese leadership decided to do some very alarming saber rattling by putting a large portion of their two hundred million-troop military on maneuvers. The East also demanded major, audacious concessions from Lanza and the World Empire.

One of the main points of contention quickly became chip implantation. As the Great Leader explained to the world in his famous Amsterdam address of 2059, insertion of microscopic data chips containing personal and financial information into all citizens had been determined by most economists to be the only efficient way to structure the foundation of a global economy. The unified new monetary unit of world credits would replace all national currencies. Initially this program encountered resistance in certain areas of the world, most notably in the Middle East, Africa and China. Although they modified the recipients DNA, some people erroneously thought these chips were developed from alien technology, another silly rumor. Most dissenters found themselves enthusiastically "persuaded" by the Security Forces to participate in the plan. Those who did not willingly partake received a death sentence under section 168; subsection B of the World Constitution (Threats to World Security).

China somehow remained different however. Even now, over three years after the program began, less than half of the Chinese population had chips. Rumors about these implanted micro devices causing incurable infections in certain cases certainly did not help them get many volunteers. Haig knew from experience how the stories about those illnesses could not be dismissed as mere gossip. One of his best friends in the Special Forces contracted so called "chip disease." He lingered in agony for weeks until finally dying, most of his brain eaten away. A kindly Army doctor tried to euthanize him but even massive doses of a morphine derivative would not take the poor Trooper out of his misery. The doctor gave a vague explanation about how these super infections rendered medications ineffective in certain cases but Haig knew medical types tended to spout nonsense when they actually had no rational explanation for something so completely baffling. Of course the Government clamped down, with anyone talking about these troubling "incidents" promptly being shot by the Ministry of Security. Haig's chip hadn't caused him any issues…so far.

So many problems. Even though Haig remained unquestionably loyal to Antonio Lanza and the New World Order it made a person look back longingly at the simpler days when Dictator General George McLellan still remained the USA's lone leader. McLellan would always be known as the heroic savior of the United States in the dark days following the terrorist nuking of Washington D.C. in 2019. With the chain of command irrevocably broken and various factions in the Federal Government and military fighting for power the situation threatened to turn into a nation shattering civil war. At that pivotal moment McLellan, a relatively low ranking Army Brigadier General and a group of Colonels staged a coup de tat, seizing control of key government and military installations. He instituted martial law and established an interim Military Junta to rule the nation. The Junta swiftly dissolved as General McLellan eliminated the other high-ranking members of the emergency government, appointing himself Supreme Military Commander. The General made it clear that his absolute rule would only be temporary and that free elections would of course be held once the "situation stabilized". To no one's great surprise the situation never did stabilize to the Generals satisfaction and he gradually evolved into the very first American dictator. The most disquieting thing about that whole episode of American history were always the rumors, never proven of course that the General himself masterminded the nuclear destruction of Washington in order to seize power. In order to calm the populace the New American Security Forces organized a show trial of Arab "terrorists" before most citizens gradually settled back into something approaching normalcy.

    Almost fifty years had now passed since this single most significant event in American history, making the Glorious General, as the more affectionate citizenry called him, well over one hundred years old. His smiling, iconic countenance became the only leadership image the majority of people had ever really known. That probably explained why nearly everyone loved McLellan like he was their eccentric old Grandfather.

    His latest obsessive peculiarity caused him to order that all communication systems broadcast Comm-Rad 1, which started playing music from his younger years in the late 20th century. According to the velvet voiced Dictator in his latest address, the American people needed revitalization by audibly reminding them of the nation's glory days. More likely thought Haig; it would remind the General of his glory days as a horny little teenager. Yes, the old-fashioned music tended to be annoying but most people, other than radicals in the large cities just shook their heads, followed orders and listened to the shit. Haig once over heard two Intel techs talking about some supposed profound psychological effect involved in this program but he'd be damned if he could see it. (Or more accurately, hear it).

In spite of everything the citizens of the U.S did owe the General a debt of gratitude they could never repay. By withdrawing the United States into a long overdue ultra-patriotic and strictly isolationist guiding principle, he re-established American pride when the nation faced complete ruin. His unopposed, but for the most part solid leadership lasted a half-century until finally with no other options available he brought the U.S of A into the New World Order. He needed to unify with Leader Lanza after being backed into a corner by the disastrous Euro-American war.

No one really blamed him for the recent misfortunes even though living conditions for nearly everyone in the country continued to worsen. Shortages of food and medical supplies as well as the deteriorating situation in American cities were difficulties that even General McLellan and Leader Lanza hadn't yet been able to improve. Although the problems seemed insurmountable, a great number of citizens still retained a child-like faith the General could somehow supply a miraculous, last minute deliverance. Some high-ranking people even spoke in hushed tones about a secret project, code named Optimus, apparently in the works for the past twenty years and now nearing completion. No one could ever explain the details of this scheme but many agreed that it probably meant salvation for the United States, possibly even for the whole world. A few also alleged that the General offered the unconditional surrender of America in return for Lanza's agreement that Optimus be allowed to continue without interference from the Europeans. If true, then obviously this unknown Optimus thing must be of enormous freakin' importance.

    Of course, it didn't really matter what Haig or any other American citizen thought about the dictator selling out their country. Even though the General recently reached his own personal centenary and acted like a foolish adolescent at times, no one dared to question anything he did. Haig shivered when he remembered the coup attempt of 2045. A number of dissenters in the military attempted a rebellion, falsely believing the General's age made him weak and ripe for overthrow. Like an aging medieval Knight having to engage in one last crusade, he personally took command of the Government troops, methodically and ruthlessly crushing the revolt. Haig, only twelve at the time, never forgot the continuous news coverage broadcast on all media outlets showing the execution by firing squad of all the officers involved. Even so, the bulk of American citizens continued to be dedicated to the General, many saying the Rebels deserved what they had received. No one ever attempted an uprising again (at least until the recent problems with Christian radicals) or underestimated the General... except at their own peril.

    As they now entered a very dangerous area, Haig snapped out of these irrelevant thoughts of the past and back into his normal state of instant combat readiness. Anyone in his line of work who didn't focus on their work promptly wound up dead. It may now have become a hackneyed cliché but like the old saying said, they had a job to complete and as a professional soldier Haig meant to finish that assignment...or die trying.

CHAPTER 2

"Good morning America! Hello to all you Comm-Rad 1 fans out there. You just heard a traditional favorite of all us Italian Americans, "Volare" by Dean Martin. Before that we played the greatest pop song of all time, "Be My Baby" by the Ronettes. Dig that wall of sound! Coming up next we've got a very special musical treat, possibly the greatest singer of the 20th century. This one is dedicated to our Glorious Leader General George McLellan. Here we go... the immortal Frank Sinatra from 1965 singing "Strangers in the Night." Enjoy ...Benevolent General...grandfather of the American People... enjoy ..."

The General slumbered in his quarters but the song-*that* song began to rouse him. Images from a distant time almost a century ago flashed through his mind. They weren't distinct memories, more like still photos and impressions really (after all he was only two years old in 1965). He did remember sitting in between his parents in the front seat of the black 1963 Lincoln Continental. He still had old tattered photos of the car. George's father, an executive with the Hell Cat Aircraft Company, loved the Lincoln, keeping it until 1969 when he traded it in on a brand new Buick Electra 225. Listening to the music McClellan's thoughts continued to drift back to that day in 1965, sitting beside his vibrant father and striking blonde haired beauty of a mother. He could recall Sinatra playing on the radio, his old man turning up the volume, both adults looking at each other and laughing. Little Georgie McLellan also started to laugh the way a child will when they don't necessarily understand why Mom and Dad are so happy but just because they feel the love and security from parents who love each other. The image of daddy grinning at him, taking a strong hand and mussing his hair remained vividly etched into his memory. The General luxuriated in a state somewhere between sleep and wakefulness, thinking of those far off childhood recollections of a time and place long ago departed. "I hope you're proud dad...proud of what I've done...of ...who I am..." he muttered as he slowly fell back into unconsciousness, numb to the cares of his other reality, the world of an old man he sometimes didn't recognize when he looked in the mirror.

    Captain Alan Haig and Sergeant Danny Trumbel scanned the holographic imaging for heat signatures from potential insurgents as they guided the Daimler down I-75. Their sensors picked up a few possible hostiles as they passed piles of rubble. Unfortunately the scanner didn't work too well through solid objects, making it difficult to assess the threat level.
    In the Special Forces, operatives enjoyed a fair amount of autonomy when planning missions. Even so, Colonel Baldwin bluntly told Haig that he was "a nutcase" when the Captain insisted on using the Daimler for a ground retrieval. Haig told his superior he thought a stealthy ground operation stood more chance of success as reports said the insurgents were shooting the hell out of any aircraft sent over Detroit. Haig didn't relish the thought of landing at all major hospitals in Detroit and having every idiot with an old AK-47 take pot shots at them as they searched for their target. If they knew Edwards exact location, then it would be a simple matter of getting in and out before the radicals knew what happened. Besides, the Daimler, although looking on the outside like some clapped out old junker, boasted more advanced technology than most Air Force fighters. All of that high tech stuff was all well and good but the most important feature from Haig's always practical viewpoint had to be the lightweight composite armor supposedly capable of withstanding an anti-tank round. Supposedly being the key word.

Finally the two of them reached a compromise. Colonel Baldwin agreed to allow Haig and Trumbell attempt a ground entry into Detroit, but once they found the Navy pilot have a heavy lift VTOL evacuate them and the car by air. Haig, usually too independent for his own good, reluctantly agreed... only because he respected Colonel Baldwin as an Intel Commander.

As they motored down the freeway, Haig wondered to himself again for at least the hundredth time why the powers to be wanted this guy so damn bad.

Suddenly, the intangible thoughts of "why" they found themselves on the mission quickly became secondary to the much more pertinent "how" not to die. A radical on the roadway ahead of them had fired off a shoulder launched King Stinger V missile. In the first second after the weapons launch, the auto's defensive systems sensed the threat and took action. Searching its Supernet database for the schematics of all missiles made in the last one hundred years, the vehicles Artificial Intelligence CPU sent an electronic signal that detonated the Stinger about twenty-five meters from the Daimler. Even though it wasn't a direct hit, the enormous explosive power of the warhead (roughly equivalent to a 20th century cruise missile) stopped their auto like it slammed into a brick wall. The blast, while taxing the structural integrity of the car, did not harm the occupants or any vital components thanks to its highly advanced battle armor. Although uninjured, the almost instantaneous deceleration stunned Haig and Trumbell.

After they recovered their senses, Haig inched the Daimler forward. Everything seemed to work okay as they drove over a red smudge of human blood and tissue on the road surface. It was all that remained of their attacker after the vehicles autodef system fired a self-directed ten second burst from concealed fifty caliber twin Gatling guns.

Haig felt relief when the expected second detonation never came. The militia member apparently worked alone rather than being part of a larger ambushing team.

Trumbell prepared their weapons and gear for an immediate exit in case the Daimler became incapacitated but they encountered no further problems for the next five kilometers.

One of the Daimlers alarms began chirping, alerting them to a roadblock and concentration of approximately fifty anarchists blocking their path a few hundred meters ahead. Small arms fire started pinging off of the Daimlers armor. Haig pulled off onto the first available exit, giving them a bit of limited protection from direct attack.

Even if the cars twin fifties could easily destroy the force manning the barricade, Haig's years of battle experience made him willing to bet that there were probably more missiles ready to be launched at them. Too many being fired at the same time could overwhelm their vehicles defensive countermeasures, which left them with only one alternative: Call in the cavalry.

Haig, like all operatives, remained under standing orders to only use standard mental communication techniques with the Government Issue NSA/CIA telepaths to call for help but he knew that would not work today. Too much adrenaline now pumped through his body for him to relax enough to be able to transmit effectively. That left only voice or text communication which although scrambled could possibly be intercepted by the enemy. Haig hesitated only briefly before muttering, "Screw it" and activating the military S.O.S voice channel.

"Wildcat one calling Eagle one," he said, feeling stupid using the somewhat hokey sounding call signals.

The calm Midwestern sounding female voice responded almost immediately,

"Hello Wildcat one, this is Eagle. How may we help you?"

"I have a rat at DT54-38 requiring nontoxic extermination," said Haig, his response giving the location of the problem and requesting a non-nuclear solution.

"Roger, rat zapper on the way. You have yourself a nice day now," said the Air Force control officer as she signed off.

Within one minute the low rumble of U.S Air Force F-22s mushroomed into a thunder that shook the Daimler as two jets flew over at low altitude and launched their air strike. The radicals attempt to scatter came too late as a fireball engulfed their position.

"Right on!" Trumbell shouted, shaking his fist in the air as the magnesium/hydrogen fueled explosion consumed everything blocking their path.

It took ten minutes for the blast area to cool down enough for them to proceed with unnecessary caution, scattered piles of ashes being the only tangible reminder of the militia members and their roadblock. As Haig had hoped, the rebel forces avoided making any more attacks and they made good progress, soon approaching the first hospital on their route: The Ford Medical Centre.

Haig and Trumbell had been briefed on possible conditions at a large hospital in a "dead city" like Detroit, but nothing could have prepared them for what awaited them after they parked the Daimler and approached the front entrance. Rotting corpses littered the formerly well-manicured lawn and sidewalks near the doorway, obviously overflow patients from the inundated medical center. As they entered the lobby area with weapons drawn, the smell of death became overwhelming even for battle-hardened veterans like the two Special Forces troopers. Emergency power globes cast a ghostly light on a sickening, horrific scene. Their weapons were unnecessary as only the dead and dying occupied this area, a few of the still living crying out for help that would never come. If Edwards had the misfortune to be among these people then they were already too late.

The troopers proceeded towards the operating theatres and ICU, now stuffed full of desperately ill patients. They questioned the few harried medical professionals remaining on site, showing the holo-pic of Edwards but no one could remember anyone matching his description.

It took the rest of that day to do a somewhat thorough check of the patients, as well as the assorted squatters, scavengers and cannibals who now populated the hospital but they did not find Commander Edwards. As the very dangerous night hours now approached Haig and Trumbell found a secure area in a now unused maintenance room to bed down on some old mattresses for the night. Not ideal but safer than possibly needing to fight their way from the exit back to the vehicle. They didn't worry about the Daimler parked outside, knowing any fool stupid enough to go near it would be electrocuted, burned, shot or a combination of all three by the cars shielding systems.

After a restive night of taking turns on watch, the two Special Forces soldiers went out to continue on their journey to the next hospital. Sure enough, several bodies lay lifeless near the car, foolish thieves unsuccessful at their attempt to steal the average looking but lethal old Benz.

As they pulled onto the cratered remains of the M-10 towards I-94, a few sniper bullets bounced off the composite armor but Haig and Trumbell paid little attention, being more preoccupied with the huge plumes of smoke rising from uncontrolled fires in downtown Detroit.

The immediate vicinity of the next stop on the route, the Hutzel Hospital didn't look to be too badly damaged, seemingly unaffected by the violence affecting most of the city. Nearing the hospital parking lot they again saw corpses near the front entrance although far fewer than at Ford Medical Center. The dead were stacked neatly as though waiting for disposal. Haig and Trumbell glanced at each other as they exited the car and drew their weapons. Being professional soldiers, both silently knew a semblance of order at this hospital could either be a good thing or a very, very bad thing. The people here might have a security force or even National Guard remnants protecting them from looters. Semi confident that any remaining security would have enough courtesy to ask questions before opening fire, Haig decided the only thing to be done was to boldly proceed into the building. Of course being bold might also lead to some major gunplay and a lot of people dying. After all, they were undercover on this mission and looked like any other rag tag refuges except perhaps for their unmistakable professional military bearing. Only one way to find out for sure…

"Freeze! Drop your weapons now!" someone screamed as they entered the semi darkness of the lobby.

"Hold on buddy. Let's talk about this," said Haig, attempting to buy some time until his eyes adjusted and he could see what they were up against. He shook his head at his own stupidity. Damn rookie mistake not wearing night vision gear.

"I said…drop your weapons!" the unknown voice screamed out, this time even more vehemently.

Haig began to make out the man behind the voice and assessed the threat level: African American male, mid-thirties wearing a hospital security guard uniform and aiming an ancient AR-15 at them. The man came across as an unprofessional in the business of killing. Not a serious threat. Under normal circumstances Haig would have eliminated such a nuisance like the guard without a moment's hesitation. Something this time however told him he should try and reason with this man. His assistance could save them some much-needed time.

"My name is Haig. Captain Haig. This is Sergeant Trumbell. We're United States Special Forces Troopers… we need… your help."

The man's forceful reply snapped back at Haig. "You expect me to believe that white boy? If that's true then why the hell aint you wearin' uniforms?"

"Were undercover," said the trooper, looking directly into the guard's eyes. "Would you wear an army uniform out there?"

"Even if you is army, give me one good reason why I shouldn't plug you right now. The government and army left us on our own and people is dyin'. I don't owes you nothin' man!" spat the security guard.

If nothing else, thought Haig, this guy had courage. "Look, I can help you. You need medical supplies and troops to protect this place? I can supply you with whatever you need-just name it," said the Captain, lying convincingly enough to fool anyone who didn't know him well.

"Now I'm going to slowly reach into my shirt pocket to get my holo-ID and gently... very gently toss it over to you."

So far so good thought Haig as the security guard bent and picked up the ID and then carefully activated it, examining the holographic picture while trying at the same time to keep a close eye on the two troopers.

Obviously somewhat convinced by the holo-image but still wary, the security guard simply asked, "What you want?"

Haig smiled. "Before I explain could you please stop aiming your weapon at me? You probably don't need any more patients. Am I right? Officer..."

"Johnson. Sean Johnson," the officer said as he lowered the weapon. "I just hope you weren't lyin' about all those promises you made."

"Do I look like I would lie to you Officer Johnson? No wait. Don't answer that," said Haig, grinning. "Seriously though, we do need your help finding someone." The smile disappeared as he turned on and then handed over the small holo-likeness of Commander Edwards. "Have you seen this man?"

As soon as Officer Johnson looked at the image Haig knew immediately by the look on his face that the answer was a "yes." Even though the security guards expression continued to be obvious, he still made a determined attempt to protect the man. "Sorry. Never seen this dude before." He pressed the off button and passed the holo-imager back.

Okay, thought Haig, time to stop this game. "I know you've seen this man so stop lying to protect him. All I can tell you is our orders are not to harm him, just to keep him safe. If you bring us to Edwards right now, nobody will get hurt. Now…if you don't cooperate with us…we'll start shooting the living shit out of this hospital and everyone in it until we do find him and a lot of innocent people are going to die…starting with you. Nothing personal, just part of the job. You have five seconds to make your decision. Five, Four…"

Johnson just glanced back and forth at the two troopers, assessing his chances. He may have been a brave man but he wasn't a fool. He simply said, "Follow me," turned around and began walking down the hall. Haig and Trumbell followed weapons at the ready.

As they walked toward the surgical inpatient ward, Haig realized that their initial assessment about the hospital had been correct: in spite of the chaos reigning in greater Detroit, things remained very organized here. They barely noticed any smell of decay and although stretchers and beds crowded the halls, the patients occupying them seemed to be receiving a measure of care from an assortment of nurses, orderlies and people in civilian clothing. Some gave Haig and Trumbell curious stares but because of Officer Johnson no one challenged their presence, at least not until they neared the operating rooms.

A surgeon, his surgical gown soaked with blood, pushed through the swinging doors and immediately stopped when he noticed Johnson and the two shabbily dressed men approaching with weapons drawn. "Johnson! You know the rules. No civilians are allowed in this area-I don't give a shit if they have guns or not. Get them the hell out of here!"

Haig was impressed, the doctor had chutzpah. He might even regret having to kill Doc if he became too much of an annoyance.

"Sorry Dr. Malvo," said Officer Johnson. "These dudes are U.S. Army Special Forces. Theys uh… lookin' for Mistah Edwards. Thought I'd let you talk to 'em. Maybe you can explain how important Rance is around here. Him and his friends that is."

Dr. Malvo gave them a cold appraising stare. "U.S. Army eh? Well you listen here. I want you to get on the comm with your boss. I don't care if you have to talk to General McLellan himself. We desperately need medical supplies, equipment and doctors. I've been using surgical techniques that have been unknown for at least the last fifty years. Now do something damn it! There are probably a hundred patients that will die by tomorrow unless we get…"

Haig stopped the tirade by raising his H&K 45 and pointing the laser sight directly at the surgeon's forehead. "No Doctor, you need to listen to me. General McLellan has declared Detroit a Dead City. That means no further resources will be wasted on saving people who are already under a death sentence. There's absolutely nothing I, or anyone else for that matter, can do about it. Since that little delusion is now over I'd appreciate your assistance in the urgent matter at hand. Bring me to Edwards. If you don't, we'll begin executing your precious patients."

"Just a minute," said Dr. Malvo. "Rance Edwards and his friends are about the only thing holding this hellhole together. I know you're most likely under orders to kill him because he's a Christian. Look, I can understand that. I used to feel the same way about them myself but my opinion has completely changed in the past month. These are genuinely good people who are sacrificing their lives to help us." Malvo paused to wipe the sweat away from his forehead. "I also think a lot of the propaganda we've been fed about Christians is pure bullshit. The point is I need Rance here. You can shoot me if you want but I won't tell you where he is."

Haig didn't say anything. He just nodded to Trumbell who walked down the hall to a stretcher holding the nearest patient, a middle aged man who appeared to be in a comatose state. The Sergeant calmly pressed the barrel of his .44 caliber handgun directly against the man's temple and pulled the trigger, the deafening explosion blowing a large spray of blood and brain tissue against the wall.

A few screams punctuated the silence that followed.

Haig pointed his weapon at Johnson's head. "Don't …try it!" Bringing his attention back to the surgeon, he said "Okay Doc. It's totally up to you. Should I tell the good sergeant here to whack another patient or are you going to have Officer Johnson show us where your little buddy Rance Edwards is?"

If looks could kill, the glare that Dr. Malvo gave Haig would have caused an instant coronary. Never taking his eyes off the Captain he replied, "Do what he asks Officer." Johnson didn't say anything but infinite sadness clouded his face as he proceeded towards the stairwell area with Haig and Trumbell following. The surgeon, knowing his compliance had probably condemned a good man to death, watched them leave and then went back into the operating theatre to continue the now seemingly futile business of saving lives.

The Troopers went to the third floor with Johnson into what in better days once housed the holistic healing department. The Officer poked his head into several open doorways, inquiring about Edwards.

Finally they found someone who remembered seeing him, directing them to one of the patient rooms. As they entered, Haig noticed that the space originally intended for a single person now held six individuals. "Inside Out" by Eve 6 played softly in the background. His attention focused on one of the beds where a man, his back turned to them, seemed to be providing care to a patient. The caregiver looked trim but solidly built, approximately 6'3", wearing a plain white cotton shirt and denim blue jeans. Even without seeing his face, Haig knew they had found their quarry. He just needed to confirm the obvious ... "Mr. Rance Edwards? Or should I say Commander Edwards?"

Edwards slowly turned towards them, showing the left side of his face first. Haig stared at the former Navy pilot, momentarily speechless. This man did have charisma, a leadership presence that his average looking holo-pic did not begin to hint at. The fierce blue eyes locked onto his as if to say, "Yes and who the hell are you?" Haig managed to break his gaze away in order to examine the rest of the features of this commanding man. Three jagged scars from the war injury ran down the left side of his once almost too handsome face, which although disfiguring for anyone else, only added a more distinguished, martial quality to Edwards. The darkly tanned skin hinted at his interesting ancestry, the brown hair beginning to gray much too early for a man still in his early thirties. Haig, himself an expert at assessing threats knew he had already been evaluated and then dismissed as insignificant by another professional when Edwards turned his back to continue caring for the patient.

It took Haig a few seconds to decide how best to approach the problem of persuading Edwards to willingly come along with them. Getting his agreement would certainly be much easier than forcing him to come along against his will. Although knowing they could do it the hard way if they had no other option, he also sensed that

Edwards, known to be a master of Wing Chun Kung Fu was not a man to be trifled with and would be quite dangerous when cornered. Haig decided to try the good old loyalty and duty ploy.

"Commander Edwards, I have orders to bring you safely to a location near Grand Rapids Michigan where you will then be transferred to the custody of General Singh, Commander of the 23rd Air Strike Wing. Your immediate reactivation into the United States Military is to follow. I cannot provide any further information except to tell you that this is a matter of extreme national importance."

Edwards didn't stop helping the patient, but did respond. "What I'm doing now is also a matter of extreme importance."

"Commander, I am delivering a direct order from High Command, possibly from General McLellan himself. I know you'd prefer to not leave your father here but it can't be helped. We will give you time to say your goodbyes. Now if you would-"

"My father is dead," interrupted Edwards, turning around to face Haig. "He died two weeks ago. I decided to stay on and help my fellow Christians provide care to the sick. I'm sure you're well aware that I'm a follower of Jesus Christ. Correct?"

Haig gave a nod in the affirmative before Edwards continued. "Since I'm a believer, my decision to accept or decline these orders you're delivering must be based on the Word of God. Now, if my reactivation into the military depends on a chip implantation, you need to be aware that I'll never have this procedure done. Scripture makes it very clear that this implant is the mark of the Beast that Christians can't accept under any circumstances. Philippians tells us that 'to live is Christ and to die is gain' so I'd gladly accept death before receiving this mark, which symbolizes worship of the Beast. We also recognize World

Leader Lanza as being this Beast or Antichrist foretold by the Book of Revelation."

Edwards paused, trying to think the matter through before continuing. "This poses an interesting question: If I accept these orders am I then a follower of the Antichrist since the United States is now a satellite member of Lanza's Global Community?" Edwards sounded like an intellectually superior professor making a subtle point to a slightly dim-witted theology class, not surprising since his profile indicated he had an IQ of 142.

"Some may argue that it would. However, if what you've said is true and General George McLellan himself might be the one issuing my orders, then I really need to give this careful consideration. I met McLellan after the war. To my knowledge the old man isn't a believer, and I haven't agreed with many of his policies, but he's definitely an independent man of strong convictions as well as the leader of my country."

Rance paused, glancing upwards, as if he was waiting for divine direction before continuing.

"To avoid any action that might be contrary to God's will, the answer to important decisions should always be found in the Bible. Since Romans states that 'Everyone must submit themselves to the governing authorities' I'll go with you willingly on one condition: there will be no persecution of the other Christians that remain here." Rance flashed a boyish grin. "I think you probably know I could make your life just a touch difficult if you reject my terms."

Haig was more than willing to make that minor concession. After all, everyone remaining in Detroit most likely faced a death sentence anyway. "You have my word. We won't report finding any other…cult members at this location. As for the implantation, that will be up to you to discuss with High Command. Time is a definite factor though, so if you can quickly say your goodbyes I'll arrange for immediate transport."

Fifteen minutes later they boarded an Air Force VTOL, the nervous pilot wasting no time getting out of the Detroit area before some rebels surface to air missile brought them down in a flaming mass of wreckage.

They made the flight without any mishaps and soon landed at General Singh's temporary headquarters outside of Grand Rapids Michigan. Edwards then found himself in the care of six burly Air Force Security Specialists who brusquely shoved him into a briefing room for an "information session" with Singh.

Thankful the mission was over, Captain Haig and Sergeant Trumbull proceeded to the base bar where they promptly got drunk, smoked some good Jamaican ganja cigars and forgot all about that damn Christian war hero.

Chapter 3

"This is Doctor Luv here on Comm-Rad 1 talkin' to all you luvahs listenin' out there. You just heard "What Is Life" by George Harrison and some "Aqualung" from Jethro Tull. Sometime in the next hour I'm gonna play you "Wild World" from Cat Stevens but up next I've got one of the greatest luv songs of all time, a tune that also happens to be a favorite of the Great General. From the dynamic duo of Burt Bacharach and Hal David..."The Look of Love"...Comm-Rad 1 Your Luv Channel..."

The General never forgot that mid-December day in 1970. He remembered going to LAX with his parents and three year old sister where they boarded a humungous new Boeing 747. The McLellan family awaited departure on their long anticipated family vacation to Hawaii. As they found their seats a stewardess bent down very close to him and smiled, asking his parents the name of this handsome young man sitting next to them. He remembered the smell of this beautiful ladies perfume, looking into her eyes, noticing the dark clumped mascara on her eyelashes. The Bacharach song "The Look of Love" played faintly over the planes sound system. She disappeared to another part of the plane after winking at him, George's mother making an idle comment to his dad about how Pan Am hired very friendly stewardesses. A mere trivial moment for them - his folks would never know the importance their young son placed on this casual contact, how all of his interpersonal relationships with females were vividly, psychically imprinted by that brief connection. Now he recognized his three failed marriages, many mistresses, and countless casual liaisons with women as nothing more than tragically doomed attempts to capture emotions experienced so briefly during that vaporous long vanished instant.

Memories were a funny thing. He remembered this experience from ninety-three years ago better than he could recall what he had for dinner yesterday...

Rance Edwards sat alone in the sparsely decorated conference room in General Singh's temporary headquarters. The solidly built brick building used to contain Federal Government offices at some point, judging by the old framed photographs of General McLellan and former President Ronald Reagan that hung on one wall. Reagan's image often bedecked Government bureaus since McLellan regarded the man as a super patriot, underappreciated during his own era.

Rance thought about the possible reasons why he found himself here awaiting reactivation into the military. Various scenarios ran through his head but none of them made any real sense. The powers to be obviously knew of his Christian faith, apparently willing to overlook that glaring truth if they now wanted him back in the Armed Forces so bad.

It all made him very curious indeed. People of his faith had become the most hated group of all time, hunted and exterminated at every opportunity as well as being the scapegoat for most of the world's problems. Even though the General sometimes gave nominal lip service to preserving the rights of all citizens, including Christians, his treatment of this minority group was almost as savage as that practiced in the rest of the Community of Nations under World Leader Antonio Lanza. Believers could count on imprisonment as a near certainty with brutal torture and interrogation of detainees being very common. Even so, executions were not automatic as in Europe where Christians found themselves sent to thinly veiled extermination factories the New BBC and other European propaganda agencies referred to as "re-education camps." Most people knew the truth about what happened to the missing, but since the practice mainly affected a despised hate group called Christians, no one really lost too much sleep over it. Besides, as Lanza's propaganda machine constantly drilled into the population, if the cult members simply ceased their senseless and stubborn resistance to world peace there would be no need to detain them for their own protection. In Europe, actually most of the world, anyone alleged to be a member of this "repulsive organization" immediately found themselves held for questioning by the ruthless security forces. Following interrogation by the political officer, if any suspicion still existed the prisoner might be a Christian or even merely sympathetic to this group, they were given three chances to renounce their "God" Jesus Christ and to pledge allegiance to the True God Antonio Lanza. As an additional act of loyalty, the suspect also needed to provide the names of at least three other people who might be Christians. If the three opportunities to accept True Salvation were rejected and the detainee still insisted on allegiance to their outmoded, pagan Deity, they would immediately be sent to the camps. The State used some inmates as forced labor but most usually faced an immediate death penalty. Those killed could be considered lucky as the Government worked slaves to near death before finally guillotining the worn out human husks when no longer of any use to the World Community. Rance feared that with the United States now a member of Lanza's empire, believers here would also share this gruesome fate.

As bad as things sometimes became under General McClellan's independent rule at least the old dictator did not play favorites. Yes, Christians were persecuted, but no more than any other group perceived as "radical" and a possible threat to the ultra-paranoid American regime.

The authorities detained Rance on two occasions, with his history as a former war hero not earning him any favors. During the last incarceration a dozen sadistic prison guards attacked him with batons. After taking out six of his attackers, he then received an even more severe beating for daring to fight back, suffering a concussion, a bruised kidney and cracked ribs. Rance never learned why he found himself being released after only a few days, both times unceremoniously getting dumped in a back alley. He suspected the reason had something to do with someone higher up the chain of command learning about his war record and not wanting a potential "embarrassment" incarcerated in their interment center. Most of the fellow members of his home Church had also been arrested.

    Then came his father's illness, Errol Edwards's being diagnosed with a form of aggressive mutated carcinoma, unable to get treatment because he did not have a chip. For three months the cancer continued to ravage his body, until Rance heard a rumor that some big city hospitals now gave ineligible people basic medical treatment and may be able to help.

    After a dangerous journey from Lansing to Detroit, Rance eventually found the Hutzel hospital and compassionate care for his father. Unfortunately, because of the late delay in receiving appropriate treatment, doctors diagnosed the elder Edwards normally curable malignancy as being too far advanced to treat effectively. Now facing an imminent demise and feeling unsure where his eternal soul would go upon death, he allowed his son to lead him through the Sinners Prayer. With Rance's gentle guidance, his father thanked the Savior for dying on the cross for his sins and then invited Jesus Christ to come into his heart, accepting Him as his personal Lord and Savior. Errol Edwards died of his illness less than two months later. Rance thanked God for the assurance found in God's Word that he would meet him again and also for the doctors and nurses at the Hutzel for making his dad's last days as comfortable as possible. The environment could not exactly have been considered friendly towards Christians but the administration made a fair and determined effort to help everyone they could regardless of beliefs. Rance and a few fellow believers began helping the overwhelmed staff during the desperate days leading up to Detroit being declared a "Dead City." As word of the Christian presence at the hospital spread throughout Detroit, Hutzel became an oasis of peace as more people sharing the Faith began to find their way to the building. Because of the heroic efforts expended by the Christians in helping to keep the Health Center open, they earned the grudging respect of most staff and patients. Rance had been fully prepared to stay and to die if necessary helping these people wholeheartedly as the Apostle Paul spoke of in Ephesians 6:7.

Then, totally unexpectedly the Lord God demonstrated His enigmatic omnipotence by taking him from that situation and putting him here, facing what he knew not. Because of that uncertainty weighing upon him he decided to do the only thing he could do under the circumstances: he prayed.

Right there in the conference room he knelt down in communion with his God. He could not have cared one little bit if General Singh came into the room at that very moment or if surveillance techs happened to be monitoring him (which they most likely were). Rance only knew he needed to submit all his cares to a much higher authority than a mere worldly General.

"Lord, I come to you in prayer. Dear God, I pray that your Kingdom comes quickly before any more lives are lost on this evil world. I ask you for strength and wisdom to discern your purpose in all things. I don't know your reasons for bringing me here, but I do know you remain firmly in control of everything and everyone. As King David said in the 40th Psalm, I desire to do your will and ask that your love and your truth always protect me. I submit myself to you Lord. I ask these things in the name of Jesus Christ... Amen."

General Rajinder Singh came into the room a few minutes after Rance had finished his prayer. Surprisingly, for such an important officer, he was alone without any security or even an aide. Even though not yet officially back in the military, Rance stood to attention and saluted. Singh did not bother returning the salute, snapping a quick "At ease!" and sitting heavily in one of the conference chairs.

They just sat there a few moments, studying each other across the table. Although Rance had never met Rajinder Singh, sometimes affectionately called "Raj" by his subordinates, he knew a few things about the celebrated Commander of the 22nd Air Strike Wing. The mustachioed, distinguished looking General Singh came from a famous Sikh family with a long history of illustrious service in the Indian Army. Young Rajinder immigrated to the United States early in the 21st century with his military engineer father and biologist mother. After scraping through West Point, he turned his back on the long family tradition of serving in the army and transferred to the US Air Force where the rest as they say is history. He proved to be one of General McClellan's ablest and most loyal officers, qualities of great importance during the recent "troubles."

The fierce fighting in Detroit had decimated the Second Army with Lieutenant General Jackson and his staff officers being killed by a stolen battlefield size nuclear weapon. Because of these catastrophic losses, various Army and National Guard remnants became part of Singh's US Air Force command (in the chaotic American Military of 2063, the line between the different services often became quite blurred anyway). These combat ravaged fragments, ranging from platoon to battalion size as well as some armored units, were now getting reorganized into Division strength and prepared for what appeared to be the next theatre of operations against the anarchist forces: Chicago.

The Sikh-American General looked exhausted; the leathery wrinkled face and emaciated body reminding Rance of his father's appearance just before he died. General Singh's voice sounded weary as he began speaking with a distinctive upper crust Indo American accent.

"Welcome Commander Edwards. It's a pleasure to finally meet you. I'm well aware of your exploits during the war – at least someone taught those bloody European bastards a lesson they won't soon forget. I know you're probably curious as to why you've been brought here. I'll try and explain what I can, although even I too am limited about what my orders allow me to tell you. First of all, your reactivation: Effective immediately you are conscripted back into the Military of the United States of America with a rank of Brigadier General. Yes, I agree. That is an unusual rank for a former Navy officer but let's just say it certainly wasn't my decision."

Rance tried to make sense out of these somewhat baffling orders being conveyed by General Singh. His promotion to Brigadier General rather than the corresponding Navy rank of Rear Admiral pointed to the involvement of a person with a rather bizarre way of doing things: General George McLellan.

Singh coughed a few times before continuing. "I'm also aware of your peculiar taste in religion, but don't worry. I have no orders to force you to get a chip. It may surprise you to know that most senior U.S military commanders do not have them implanted either... anyway; you are to be immediately brought by an F-22 trainer to Peterson Air Force Base. You will then be transported by an X-36 shuttle to…to an orbital platform where you will be given further instructions. Those are all of your official orders," said Singh as he focused his gaze on Rance. "Now, off the record I wanted to ask you something. What do you know about the Optimus Project?"

Rance didn't answer immediately. Although it had been almost two years since he left the Navy, even then there were numerous theories about Optimus and speculation, sometimes quite fanciful about what it may be. The ready room on board the USS *Washington* always bred various wild rumors but as far as Rance could tell these contained very little hard fact.

"Just the usual gossip sir. Truthfully, I have absolutely no idea what Optimus is."

General Singh paused as if carefully searching for the words that he could or possibly should say next. "Son, all I can tell you is this. You are about to become one of the few individuals on Earth who is ever going to find out exactly what the word Optimus means. In some ways I envy you - in other ways I pity you."

General Singh had a faraway look in his eyes as he got up from the table and left the conference room, leaving Rance alone to try and make sense of it all.

Within a few minutes the security team hustled Rance out to the landing pad where a VTOL transport sat, warmed up and waiting to transfer him to Selfridge, a Michigan Air National Guard base. The crew of the aircraft as well as the men escorting him meant business, not saying one word to Rance on the short flight. His efforts to make small talk were met only with polite smiles and nods. Rance didn't take it personally however. He knew to them he was only a very important piece of meat they were under orders to escort safely to the Air National Guard base. The team's responsibility for his safety would then be transferred to someone else and they could breathe a huge sigh of relief. Allowing Rance to be killed probably meant their sure deaths, as a mission failure, especially in an operation protecting a VIP was not looked upon very sympathetically in the U.S military.

If they were, God forbid shot down by a radical missile on this flight and crash landed in hostile territory, Rance knew the men entrusted with his safety would without any hesitation sacrifice their own lives to protect him. That may have been one of the main reasons why the tense looks on all of Air Force Security Team members noticeably eased as they safely landed at Selfridge.

The former backwoods Air National Guard base now bustled with U.S Air Force activity, having become the main air support hub in anti-radical militia efforts in the Michigan region. The familiar rumble of F-22's landing and taking off assaulted Rance's ears as the security team brought him to one of the Air Force buildings, transferring his custody to a waiting U.S.A.F General.

Even though Base Commander Michael Maltin outranked his guest, the tanned and silver haired Air Force General and his staff received Rance like a conquering hero. He enjoyed Cuban Salsa music, (a tribute to another famous ancestor), refreshments and a delicious meal all the while being peppered with questions about his legendary exploits in the Euro-American war. Rance, as always remained humble. He explained how possible divine intervention, not to mention the known superiority of his F-22 over the European Dassault-Dornier Omega fighter, played a major role in being able to shoot down the ten opposition fighters.

After goodbyes and handshakes all around, General Maltin introduced him to Lieutenant Colonel John Williams. Almost unknown to the general public, this heroic pilot shot down three European fighters over the Persian Gulf on the last day of the Euro-American War. Williams, who with his blonde crew cut and all American good looks could have been in an old Air Force recruiting poster, would be piloting the F-22 trainer bringing him to Peterson Air Force base. Rance sat in the trainee seat, a place he hadn't occupied since he was finishing his pilot's training in the Navy.

"Sorry General Edwards," said Williams through the intercom as he and Rance readied themselves for takeoff. "I know you would have loved to fly this baby but General Maltin felt it would be better if I took the controls since you haven't flown in a while."

"That's okay Colonel," said Rance as he went through his checklist. "You won't be getting any complaints from me. My last flight was…slightly…eventful. I don't know what your beliefs are Williams but if you don't mind, I'd like to say a little prayer before takeoff."

Somewhat taken aback, Lieutenant Colonel Williams paused before saying; "You go right ahead Sir. First though, I just wanted to say what an honor it's been to meet you and have the privilege of flying you to your destination."

Rance appreciated the pilot's sincerity. "The pleasure is all mine Colonel. Now the prayer:"

"Dear Heavenly Father, we come to You in prayer and ask for Your protection on this flight. Please watch over us and protect us – if it be Your will Lord. As the psalmist wrote in Psalm 46:1, God is our refuge and strength, a very present help in trouble. So, Lord we again ask for Your will to be done and we give thanks. We ask these things in the name of Jesus, our High Priest… Amen."

Rance thought he heard a muffled "Amen" from Williams as the pilot pushed the throttle and taxied the F-22 trainer to its assigned take off spot. A familiar exhilaration hit Rance in the gut as the sudden G-forces of takeoff pushed him back in his seat. He hadn't been in an F-22 since that fateful day over Northern Germany when he bailed out and almost died.

Rance thought about how significantly that event altered his life. Battered and bleeding to death, he didn't even remember his discovery by a German army unit whose medical officers heroic efforts kept him alive until stable enough to be medevac'd to the Hamburg military hospital. He spent the next month going through numerous surgeries to repair his massive internal injuries. That time of pain and trauma brought on some serious soul searching about his life and its lack of meaning. Before this Rance always thought he had it all; a fulfilling Navy career, beautiful fiancée, loving family, but suddenly because of his near death experience, everything once important now seemed insignificant. He never thought much about God or where a person goes after death but the long forgotten words of a Christian television show Rance viewed as a child kept popping back into his head. Something about a "personal relationship" with Jesus Christ being the only way to salvation and true fulfillment. It made no sense at all. The media depicted Christians as a despised hate group that no one took seriously but something kept pushing him to know more, to find "the truth."

After being sent back to the United States to the Hero's Welcome publicity stunt prepared for him, the hypocrisy of his so called fulfilling existence became overwhelming. He needed to take some time away, to drop out of his present life to continue his search for true meaning. Rance remembered the rainy November day when he spoke to his beautiful fiancée Christine at the local Coffee Haus. With "Hate Me" by Blue October playing from their tables Sensusound system, Rance explained his decision. He managed to tell Christine he didn't think it would be fair for them to marry, dragging her through the embarrassment of the very public multi media circus sure to follow. He couldn't erase horrible memories of the tears, the stunned look in his true love's eyes, the profound hurt that he could sense when she asked what on Earth could possibly make him throw everything away. He couldn't answer because at that point he didn't know the answer himself. He just kept saying, "I'm sorry" as she shook her head, bitterly screamed, "You dirty bastard! I hate you!" and ran crying from the cafe. It was the last time he had ever seen her.

Rance embarked on an interesting but unfulfilling spiritual quest for a few months, studying various Eastern Religions until an anonymous note on his doorstep left cryptic instructions for him to sit on a park bench at a certain time "If he wanted to hear the Truth."

The following day he waited on that bench and met "Pastor Randy" a preacher at an underground house church.

Two days later, at that humble little place of worship Rance's search ended with him becoming a Christian, accepting Jesus Christ as his personal Lord and Savior. The two subsequent arrests, persecution and beatings were a small price to pay in comparison to the priceless gift of Salvation. Soon after that last incarceration his father was diagnosed with cancer, changing everything and leading to the uncertain situation where Rance presently found himself.

Williams spoke through the ships intercom; interrupting the painful and rambling thoughts. "Were approaching Peterson Sir. ETA five minutes."

After a smooth landing, Lieutenant Colonel Williams enthusiastically shook his hand before Rance transferred to the protection of Captain Johnny Rickenbacker, pilot of the X36 shuttle *District of Columbia* scheduled to take him to his next destination. The longhaired, unshaven pilot's interpretation of the military dress code was definitely rather casual since he covered his flabby body in khaki shorts and a stained Led Zeppelin T-shirt.

As they boarded the District of Columbia, Rickenbacker explained the features of the North American X-36 and how aviation experts considered it a direct descendant of the ancient X-15 rocket plane from the mid-20th century. "The main differences are the extended, widened cabin accommodating two crew members, four passengers and some cargo space and the fact that we take off from the ground with the assistance of rocket boosters instead of getting launched from a B-52 like the old X-15. Otherwise, this is still the cheapest, most efficient way to get into space. Not necessarily the safest, but what the hell. You can't have everything."

Rance couldn't help but register surprise that only the two of them were on board. "Do you usually take off without a co-pilot?" he asked.

Rickenbacker rolled his eyes and pointed to the co-pilot seat. "Uh…dude… That would be YOU. Now strap yerself in so we can get this show on the road. Don't worry buddy. This old crate can practically fly herself."

Rance grinned as he adjusted the seating position and tightened his seat straps. "You're quite a character you know that?"

Rickenbacker convulsed in a laughing fit. "Look who's talkin'? I get stuck with a punk ass war hero who's a certified Christian no less. That's rich. Next thing I know yer gonna be askin' me if ya can say yer prayers before we take off!"

Now it was Rance's turn to laugh. "Well actually…"

After Rance finished his prayer for protection the shuttle pilot completed the checklist, taxied to the end of their assigned runway and waited for takeoff approval from the tower. Rance sensed something must be wrong after fifteen minutes passed with no word from the air controller.

Finally Captain Rickenbacker decided he could wait no longer as sitting in a fully fueled X-36 shuttle containing thousands of gallons of highly explosive alcohol and liquid oxygen was comparable to sitting on an armed hydrogen bomb. He sent a signal: "Control this is X-36 asking for takeoff approval, over."

After a few more seconds of silence they finally got a response. "X-36 this is control. We have a …situation here." The voice of the controller seemed high-pitched and cracking under obviously intense stress. "Radicals…

attacking the tower and on runway. Waiting for ground forces to stabilize situation. Stand by for further instructions." The controller kept the mike keyed and they could hear gunshots and yelling in the background. Someone closer screamed out "Please don't kill me. I beg you... don't do..." a gunshot reverberated just before the signal went dead.

Rickenbacker looked out the front glass of the X-36, observing guerrilla militia members on the runway ahead running towards them and the muzzle flashes from their weapons. The pilot shouted out a string of colorful expletives as he triggered the launch sequence controls. "Hang on!" he managed to say as the solid fuel booster rockets erupted in a controlled explosion of millions of pounds of thrust, hurtling them down the runway and immediately incinerating any attackers caught in the blast zone.

It wasn't until they reached an altitude of 100,000 meters and prepared to drop the booster rockets that Rickenbacker could relax enough to glance over and say anything to Rance. "Full diagnostics completed. No sign of damage from small arms fire and all systems on line and functioning properly. Which is a really, really good thing because had we experienced any serious problems we might've been forced to use the emergency crew return system – the only problem is that about half the crews who've used it operationally burned up in re-entry. We were damned lucky."

"I prefer to think of it as a little more than luck my friend," said Rance, looking very composed.

Rickenbacker didn't say anything as he dropped the burned up solid fuel boosters, setting the sequence controls for their primary rocket engine to fire and take them the rest of the way into orbit.

When they were at an altitude of approximately 400,000 meters, the pilot questioned Rance. "I wanted to ask you man, have you ever been in orbit before, I mean not just as a tourist but as a member of the military? I guess what I'm askin' is do you have any idea where the hell yer about to go?"

Rance although very curious about the purpose of the questioning remained outwardly indifferent. "No. Never been in orbit either as a tourist or in the Navy. Singh told me I was going to an orbital station. That's all I know. Now, what do *you* know that you're not telling me?"

Rickenbacker snickered at the question and Rance's apparent ignorance. "Don't worry pal. I'm not going to ruin the surprise. I always like to see the expression on the faces of first timers."

The Captain just smiled when Rance tried to get him to explain himself. "You'll find out soon enough." he said and left it at that.

A short time later Rickenbacker asked Rance if he was able to see anything unusual through the thick front glass of the X-36. Looking forward he began to make out an object, almost completely dark, outlined against the stars. At first Rance speculated that they were approaching their destination, the orbital station. Something didn't seem right however. Although having no reference points in space in order to determine dimensions, the object in front of them seemed huge. Then the X-36 went underneath it, the dark mass above them appearing to go on for what looked like many kilometers. Protuberances jutted out in places, reminding Rance of the twin gun stations he remembered from the USS *Washington*. Dim blue lights emanated from some areas casting an ethereal glow. As Rance observed, he got the distinct impression that the blackness seemed to narrow as they went meaning the ship, if that's what it was, must be triangular in shape. For what felt like an endless period of time, the District of Columbia traveled under the black void until finally they passed it and viewed the brightness of stars once again. The pilot started a slow loop so that they were soon headed directly back at the mysterious, light absorbing apparition. Rance already felt something akin to stunned amazement so it took a few seconds for his thought processes to register what he now gaped at. Along this strange anomalies side, in bright contrast to its shadowy mass were vividly emblazoned huge white letters reflecting the suns unfiltered and burning brightness:

USS HORNET CVS 1

This wasn't any mere "orbital station." The brute, alien majesty of the thing could easily lend plausibility to a mistaken assumption that it might have originated from another galaxy, crafted by another race, were it not for the very familiar human characters inscribed on it. No, only human beings could have done this, an elegant combination of sideshow vulgarity and beauty beyond all comprehension, overflowing with the creative genius and haughtiness needed to conceive of let alone build such a monstrosity.

Suddenly many things became apparent to Rance, everything now made sense. Obviously most of the capital of the once great United States of America had been poured into such a massive project for decades while countless Americans lost their lives due to civil unrest and lack of adequate resources. Clearly, what happened down below on Earth wasn't important to General McLellan when compared to the wealth and talents it must have taken to build this, this spacecraft? Spaceship? Starship? Rance didn't even know the correct terminology for something so wildly outside of his past experience and understanding. Manned orbital travel, in addition to the regular manned moon and mars missions had long been common place, but comparing this "thing" to those still relatively crude hydrogen/oxygen powered space vehicles smacked of comparing the Wright flyer to a modern F-22 fighter.

Without a doubt the creator of this craft intended it for a far greater purpose than some short jaunt in our own solar system. Although feeling disgust at the sickening misuse of the God given prosperity his nation once possessed, Rance still found that he could not take his eyes off of the spellbinding technological achievement that they now quickly approached.

    Rickenbacker, looking over at his astonished companion said simply, "Welcome to Optimus pal."

CHAPTER 4

"DJ Jazzy J here on Armed Forces Comm-Rad 1 bringin' you the greatest hits of all time. You just heard Elvis Presley singing "Suspicious Minds" …one of our Magnificent General's favorite songs of all time and before that the one and only Bowie with "Suffragette City"…now, a record that our Leader listened to as a nine year old way back in 1972…The great Marc Bolan of T-Rex with his huge hit … "Bang A Gong." Comm-Rad 1… your music connection…"

Miss Krantz's grade four students at Linwood Howe Elementary in Culver City California were getting excited. It happened to be the last Friday before Christmas break and Miss Krantz had mercifully agreed to let the students enjoy a Christmas party in the afternoon instead of regular classes. George McLellan volunteered in helping move desks to the edge of the room so they would have an open area for dancing even though most of the boys remained a little self-conscious and shy about asking a girl to dance. Some of the kids had brought their 45 singles (as well as their older sibling's vinyl) and the teacher began playing them on one of the schools old record players. The sound quality wasn't great but it sure beat having normal school stuff like math and science. Some of the kids began to mill around the open area and a few even started dancing, but the majority of the boys found themselves drawn instead to the huge table of snacks sitting near the teacher's desk. At first George just got into the great music, enjoying songs such as T-Rex; "Bang a Gong," Deep Purple with everyone's favorite; "Smoke On The Water," The band Bread with "If" and even "Paranoid" by Black Sabbath (which Miss Krantz almost immediately yanked off the record player, scratching the 45 disc to the dismay of Eddy Wilson, the kid that brought it). Their teacher's musical contributions to the party were "Brandy" by Looking Glass, "You're So Vain" by Carly Simon and "Ben" by Michael Jackson.

Eventually George's attention was drawn to little blonde haired Margie Morton who kept staring at him from across the room. George hated dancing but if it meant he could spend a little time with Margie then he would take the risk of being embarrassed in front of his classmates. George made his way over to her and surprisingly the girl said yes when he shyly asked if she would dance with him. Although a little awkward and nervous, he wasn't noticeably worse than the handful of other boys brave enough to try such a socially risky activity. Afterwards, George sat beside Margie on a desk and built up his nerve to put his arm around her. She looked at him and smiled.

God what a special moment, a memory he would always treasure. Thinking back from the perspective of a worldly, jaded centenarian George McLellan just wished he could return to that innocent time so long ago and maybe do things a little bit differently...

As the X-36 shuttle approached the hulking mass of the USS *Hornet*, Rance began to make out a rectangular shape outlined by glowing blue light. Pointing towards it, he asked Rickenbacker, "Is that what I think it is?"

"You mean a flight deck?" replied the shuttle pilot. "Yer pretty sharp...for a Navy boy. That's exactly what it is. As yer about to find out, the *Hornet* is sort of a bastard cross breed between an aircraft carrier and warship except that she's designed for operations in deep space. Anyway, we're on final approach to land in that very flight deck. Which reminds me - I better call in for landin' approval before some nervous asshole gunner on the *Hornet* decides to shoot first and ask questions later." He arched his eyebrows before smiling. "Hey man, just kiddin'!"

After getting approach approval from the Landing Operations Officer on the *Hornet* and being locked on to the huge vessels automated glide slope beam, Rickenbacker sat back and took his hands off of the control stick. "Look Ma - no hands!"

Even though still somewhat astounded by everything he had just seen, Rance, a born pilot, watched entranced as they were inexorably drawn to the assigned flight deck of the USS *Hornet*. They passed through the blue glow of the airlock and came in for a perfect landing. The protective outer doors closed immediately, which as the shuttle pilot explained, allowed almost instantaneous pressurization of the large flight deck area.

"This is where we say goodbye chum," said Rickenbacker, extending his hand to Rance. "I'm sure you have a welcoming committee waitin' for you out there," he said as the shuttle doors opened with a hum. "Good luck."

Rance shook the pilots hand and smiled "It's been a real pleasure. I pray that God permits us to meet again someday."

Rance said a silent prayer for the salvation of the man's soul as he left the shuttle, noting with some surprised relief the *Hornet* evidently enjoyed a very earth like artificial gravity.

In fact there was a welcoming committee waiting for Rance although it turned out to only consist of one person, a very young Major by the name of William Mitchell who was Rance's assigned aide. Mitchell appeared so youthful it was hard to believe he actually was a Major or had even started shaving yet for that matter.

"It's a great pleasure to meet you sir," said Major Mitchell "but time is somewhat of an issue. We need to get you to your quarters, find a uniform and then get you to the

Bridge as soon as possible. The Leader is anxiously awaiting you in his headquarters office."

Even though exhausted by recent events Rance offered no resistance as the Major hustled him through an almost endless series of monotonous drab military gray halls and elevator tubes to his quarters on H deck, section 3D.

Several new Brigadier General Uniforms hung in the closet waiting for him as he entered his Spartan but comfortable billet. The black attire displaying one small star on the lapel looked like standard Army issue except for the addition of two shoulder bars, which read "SPACE." Rance still found the striking similarity of the recently refashioned US military officers garb to the old German SS uniform somewhat unsettling. After quickly getting dressed and putting on the peaked officer's hat he was ready to meet with General McLellan.

Another meandering, thoroughly confusing journey ensued until finally reaching signs indicating they approached the Main Bridge/Headquarters area.

"Don't worry General Edwards," said Major Mitchell, "It's a little disorientating for everyone at first, but you'll soon get the hang of it."

The Major brought Rance to a reception area where he left the newly promoted General on his own. The other lower ranking crewmembers in the vicinity immediately stood to attention and saluted as he came into the room. He quickly gave them an "at ease" and feeling somewhat uncomfortable as they stared at him, plunked himself into one of the waiting rooms ergo-master chairs. They kept glancing over at him, some even whispering with each other as they gawked. Obviously his reputation had preceded him.

Mercifully, Rance soon found himself ushered into a private briefing room where he waited for his audience with the Great Dictator, General George McLellan. Living

Colour's "Cult of Personality" played softly through the rooms Sensusound system.

A few moments later, the automatic door to the compartment opened and General McLellan stepped in alone, without the typical fawning entourage of aides and flunkies trailing behind. Rance last met the General a little over two years previous during the Hero's Welcome festivities. Even after such a short period of time he had become a little more haggard although still quite fit, trim and amazingly preserved for a man of his advanced years. The movie star good looks had long since faded but the white haired old man was still well groomed and dapper, dressed in a perfectly tailored retro-styled Second World War era U.S. Navy Admiral's uniform.

"Reporting for duty as ordered sir," Rance said, standing to attention and saluting.

The General, a radiant smile on his face, disregarded this formality and warmly grasped Rance's hand.

"It's good to see you again Rance!" said General McLellan in the famous booming "Great Communicator" voice of his. "I wish things had worked out differently the last time we met. I still think the people could have used you as a hero figure following our ah … misfortune in the war, but I do respect your decision to drop out of the public eye even if I did disagree with it at the time." McLellan frowned. "Sometimes a man has to do what he feels is right. As you very well know, I could have forced you but I didn't feel your participation would have been as valuable if it was…uh… compulsory. Anyway that's all behind us now. You probably have a ton of questions-most people do after seeing the *Hornet* for the first time."

McLellan motioned for Rance to take a seat at the conference table. "Normally an aide would be responsible for your orientation, but for someone of your exceptional…value, I personally wanted the honor of explaining the Optimus project and your role here with us."

McLellan took a seat opposite Rance. "Before we start what can become quite a boring technical dissertation however, I wanted to talk about your very interesting family background."

The Great General stared at Rance, almost like he was scanning his face for some subtle characteristic of that interesting family background.

"You know, back when I was planning on using you in the public relations campaign, I had a full ancestry research check done on your lineage going back the last couple of hundred years. As you may have heard in the media, I'm kind of an amateur geneticist and genealogist. I'm absolutely nutty about the topic. I'll share my own pet theory about why I believe some people perform better in highly demanding battle situations like your dog fight in the war. I think it's primarily because you exemplify the genetic supremacy of the melting pot that has produced the Great American People."

He licked the corner of his lips before continuing "You have many different strains of superior blood coursing through your veins, ranging from European and African Royalty, Jewish and even some Sioux Indian. More than most citizens your diverse genetic makeup typifies our great country and the ideal of what I feel is the perfect American."

The General was getting quite excited talking about this subject, but Rance started to become very uncomfortable. This talk of genetic superiority and blood strains echoed of insane Nazi era eugenics and master race pseudo-scientific theories. Perhaps the General found it necessary to delve into his "American Superman" mythology in order to justify the very existence of this abomination he christened the USS *Hornet*.

"Excuse me sir. That's flattering but I have to tell you I feel very strongly background and breeding don't play much of a part in determining success. For me as a

Christian I believe the only thing of any importance is a personal relationship with Jesus Christ."

General McLellan had a sour look on his face like he had just eaten a lemon.

"Oh of course… your…Christian beliefs. As distasteful as that may be, I'm not going to hold it against you son. In fact it may surprise you to learn that I never really had anything against the Christians, it's just that your group's ideas are so…damn extreme."

The General began to lighten up somewhat. "Nothing personal…even some of our greatest past Presidents," he pointed to the picture on the wall behind him, "sometimes called themselves Christians. In fact, in some ways your theology, especially regarding chip implantation is partially responsible for you being on board this ship right now. You see none of the crew on the *Hornet* have chips either, mainly because I didn't want that damn asshole Lanza knowing more than he needed to about Optimus. Who knows? You may even meet some other Christians on board. It really doesn't matter to me at this late stage of project development as long as people continue to do their jobs properly. Now where were we? Ah yes… your family genetics. Now… I want you to listen carefully to what my research department found out. There may be things that even you aren't aware about your heritage."

Rance prepared himself for what might become a rather long monologue from the General as he absently glanced at the other picture on the wall depicting the old, unfortunate USS *Hornet* aircraft carrier sunk by the Japanese in 1942. Even though Rance's mother had told him snippets of his interesting family history, he probably didn't know everything. Maybe this could be a little bit educational after all.

The General grinned like a schoolboy as he started talking. He really did find this topic intriguing.

"One of your forefathers was Lieutenant General Count Friedrich von Eckstaedt-Shoenburg, commander of the German 21st Infantry Division during most of the Second World War. Histories describe him as a very aristocratic Prussian General who although renowned as an able leader and tactician almost got sacked on several occasions for his vehement dislike of der Fuhrer whom he referred to as 'that Bohemian Corporal.' Hitler didn't like the Count either but apparently retained him because of his proven abilities on the increasingly chaotic Eastern Front. He also didn't win any popularity contests with the SS, because like many other members of the German officer class nobility, he had some Jewish blood, in his case a grandmother from the House of Rothschild. Captured by the Russians, he spent five years in a Siberian labor camp even though most allied authorities were adamant that he committed no war crimes. In fact, many Jewish refugees later testified how General von Eckstaedt-Shoenburg used his authority to save their lives by keeping a large number of civilians including women and children attached to his Division as "laborers," thus preventing Eichmann and the SS from deporting them to the death camps. Israel later recognized this act of compassion by granting him the title: "Righteous among the Nations." After being released by the Soviets, he immigrated with his wife and children to the United States to make a fresh start. A man of real…what's the expression…integrity."

Rance of course already knew most of this but still found the noble old General's story captivating. Like his distinguished German ancestor he too tried to always do the right thing even under difficult circumstances.

"One of the other contributors to your gene pool that has always fascinated me is Douglas Baxter, one of the greatest movie legends from the 1930's and 40's. His phenomenal drinking bouts, countless barroom brawls and mythic womanizing made him immortal in the annals of the

Golden Age of Hollywood. Born in South Africa in 1910 from Irish stock, as a young man he became a pretty good amateur boxer. He bummed around the globe until his good looks helped him get a start in theatre by doing a few small roles in third rate London plays. He went on to play bit parts in some British films, and then came an offer for a role in an RKO flick, swiftly leading to him becoming one of the most popular leading men in Hollywood. His movies were good, mainly swashbuckling pirate and costume epics but his off screen exploits were what really made him a household name. Rumored to have slept with thousands of women during his relatively short life, he even got himself involved in an infamous lewd conduct trial before being acquitted of the charges. Along the way he managed to get married several times and produced some legitimate children one of which was your great, great, great grandmother. He died alone and penniless in a Las Vegas hotel room in 1958. I have to admit Rance I'm a confirmed Douglas Baxter fan. I've seen all of his movies."

Rance felt a twinge of embarrassment after coming to the realization that the General knew much more about Douglas Baxter than he did. When his mother had discussed the man she only mentioned they had a movie star from the 20th century in the family tree, but his more "colorful" aspects were perhaps understandably left out of the stories.

The General barely took a pause before continuing on to the next person on his genealogical list.

"I'm not sure how much you know about Moshe Goldman, Rance but here's what my researchers found out about him: He was born in British Palestine in 1922, raised on the farm of his father, a dedicated Zionist and then enlisted in the British Army Jewish Brigade Group in 1944. Moshe joined the Yishuv forces, being seriously wounded while fighting in the War of Independence in 1948. After recovering, he married a beautiful Polish immigrant and

Auschwitz survivor named Dyna Talman who'd also been a soldier in the war. Moshe quickly rose through the ranks of the IDF and commanded a brigade in the Six Day War. He later served as a Security Advisor to Prime Minister Yitzhak Rabin. Moshe and Dyna had two daughters one of which moved to New York City where she eventually met and married the great grandson of the next person on the list; Chief Red Crow."

Chief Red Crow. Out of all his known ancestors, Rance probably knew the least about this one. He looked forward to hearing General McLellan recount the famous warrior's biography.

General McLellan obviously knew the material well. He barely referenced the holo-images as he continued.

"Chief Red Crow is known historically as one of the youngest chiefs of the Great Sioux Nation or Lakota tribe. The Sioux captured his mother at age seven after they massacred her Scottish settler family. Adopted as the daughter of Chief Running Buffalo she became one of the tribe, forgetting her former life and growing into a strong Lakota woman who became the mate of a formidable warrior named Steals Many Horses. They only had one child together, the future chief. Apparently his mother always told her boy that he would become a great man someday as a warrior with very powerful medicine. Around twelve years of age he had a vision of a red crow pecking out and eating the eyes of a yellow haired white man. It was from this dream that he took his adult name. Chief Red Crow became a legend among the Lakota people for his fearless scalping raids against the neighboring tribes such as the Arapahos, but it is for his role in the Battle of The Little Bighorn or Battle of The Greasy Grass as the Native Americans preferred to call it that made him most famous. Some Lakota oral histories even say that Red Crow delivered the fatal wound to Custer. After the Indian Wars, the Chief joined Buffalo Bill Cody's Wild West Show along with the great Sioux holy man Chief Sitting Bull. Apparently the two chiefs would amuse themselves by imaginatively cursing at the white audiences in their native Lakota language. The Wild West Show toured the United States and most of Europe with Chief Red Crow becoming a famous attraction, even celebrated by Royalty for his participation in the re-enactment of the famous battle. For such a ferocious indigenous warrior he later became quite sophisticated, marrying a fiery Italian woman of noble birth that he met in Milan and settling down in San Francisco. He bought a nice home, moved his mother in, raised three kids and lived comfortably and quite happily for the rest of his long life. He passed away peacefully of natural causes in the 1930's. Before his death he quite often did interviews with members of the Bay Area press. He said the one thing he really missed about his former aboriginal life on the plains was the distinctive taste of buffalo jerky or dried meat as he called it". McLellan chuckled. "Another amazing man."

"Thanks for that General McLellan," said Rance, resisting an urge to become prideful after hearing about his remarkable predecessor. "I actually learned a few things about the Chief. Believe it or not I never knew the name of his father or adoptive grandfather."

He needed to move this along so they could get to the important part of the briefing. "Are there any more of my ancestors that you'd like to discuss?"

"There are many more," said McLellan as he referenced the holo-images, "but only two more I will profile in any detail. The first of these is Colonel Jubal Jefferson Shelby III. The Colonel is documented as being a wealthy plantation owner from South Carolina. He fought for the Confederacy, being involved in most of the major engagements during the War Between the States. I'm not sure if you're aware of it but the original General George Brinton McClellan was the commander of the Union Army for a time. In spite of the similarity in our names, as far as I've been able to determine I'm not descended from the man. Good thing too, otherwise you and I would have to settle that whole Civil War thing once and for all!" The General laughed at his little joke before continuing.

"Prior to the Civil War, the married Colonel Shelby enjoyed a physical relationship with a slave girl named Sally who worked for him as a household servant. That coupling produced a son named Thomas. In spite of his flaws, the Colonel was basically a good man who wanted to do the best for his child. He gave Sally her freedom and moved her and the boy north to Pennsylvania. Certain accounts allege he apparently didn't have much of a choice in the matter. Sally Shelby is historically well known in her own right as a fearless crusader for emancipation who according to folk legend became Colonel Shelby's lover and then also demanded that she be treated as his equal. No one in the Old South of that time had ever seen such audaciousness from an African American woman, something very brave but also incredibly dangerous. If anything, Sally probably felt *superior* to Jubal as she told everyone who would listen about her own rich family history. Apparently her grandfather had been an African prince, kidnapped and sold into slavery.

Jubal Shelby set up a fund to support them and made sure Thomas received an education. This event must have deeply affected the Colonel because although he fought for the Confederacy, like General Lee he freed his slaves just prior to the beginning of the war. After surviving several serious wounds during the fighting, including the amputation of an arm, Colonel Shelby became involved in politics during the reconstruction, later on losing a close race for Governor. His illegitimate son Thomas continued his studies and became a lawyer in Philadelphia, a feat made somewhat easier for him because of his light skin that allowed him to "pass" in the racist white society of the time. Absolutely unbelievable! Hollywood couldn't make up stuff like this!" said the General, forgetting that Hollywood as well as much of California for that matter no longer existed, having been destroyed in the Great Earthquake and Tsunami of 2022.

Rance smiled. He had to agree that his family history could be considered to be quite…unusual.

"And finally," said the Leader with a sigh, "last but certainly not least, the closing entry on my list: Prince Henri Victor Charles Louis de Bourbon. Born in Paris in 1925, his father a descendant of the French Royal family, his mother an exiled niece of the last Russian Czar who, although a great, great granddaughter of Queen Victoria was also rumored to have a Mongol Khan as an ancestor. She was a legendary beauty. Anyway, he and his family went into luxurious exile in New York City just before the fall of France to the Germans in 1940 but returned to Paris after the war. In spite of his parent's vigorous objections the Prince became an officer in an elite paratroop unit of the French Army in 1947. He received debilitating wounds during the infamous battle at Dien Bien Phu in 1954 and retired from the Army after being released by the Viet Minh. Prince Henri then became one of the first of the new breed of twentieth century sophisticate: a jet setter. He spent the rest of his life enjoying a sordid existence of alcohol, drugs, parties and women. One of these ladies was the famed English stage actress Cynthia Davis with whom the Prince had a torrid six-month relationship. They almost got married in spite of the fact his family would never have accepted Ms. Davis because they considered her a "commoner." After they broke up, Cynthia gave birth to a daughter, Elisabeth, one of your paternal ancestors. The Prince earned a reputation as an elegant, sophisticated man, a generous patron of the arts and fearless defender of LGBT rights. Unfortunately, he also increasingly became an insatiable alcoholic, a futile attempt to deal with the recurring pain from his war injuries. He met your other hell raising ancestor Douglas Baxter in a Parisian night club in 1957. This chance encounter resulted in a close friendship and legendary week long drinking binge culminating with both of them being arrested by the Gendarmes after they busted up a Lesbian bar, ending up on the losing end of a brawl with some of the patrons. It turned into a huge scandal at the time, even for the French, but sadly was only the beginning of the Prince's long slide into public humiliation. His extravagant yet morally squalid life became standard fodder for the European tabloids. He dated the most glamorous and famous women of his era, as well as enjoying a close but platonic friendship with a famous Greek actress. After seeing the film "The L-Shaped Room" he became smitten with the leading lady after meeting her at a party. Apparently she was one of only a handful of women to resist his considerable charm. The man definitely knew how to live life. Prince Henri died in 1984, bleeding to death in his Paris apartment after falling and cutting his head open while in an intoxicated stupor. He did have good taste in music though. It says here his favorite tune was Burt Bacharach's "I Say A Little Prayer," no doubt because the French Riviera Casinos he frequented probably played the song endlessly."

 The General looked at Rance and smiled. "Now don't expect me to recount the myriad of complicated details of how all of these people and their offspring managed to meet and copulate with each other. I'll let you consult the holo of your family tree to figure that out," he said, tossing over the holo-disk. Rance was slightly disappointed the General didn't profile his Ottoman Sultan ancestor. Was it Mehmed VII or Mehmed VIII? He couldn't remember. Oh well, maybe next time.

 "Now I need a break. As much as I like genealogy, that made me tired and damn hungry. After all I am one hundred freakin' years old you know…" he said with a wink. "Let's retire to my private dining room for a bite before we begin your orientation session."

    Rance politely nodded back assent to his Commander in Chief. The old man, although narcissistic, having crazy theories, sometimes even displaying down right maliciousness, could also be extremely charming and hard to dislike. A bite to eat sounded like a very good idea…

CHAPTER 5

"Wow what a tune! From 1974… "Rikki Don't Lose That Number" by Steely Dan … just before that McCartney and Wings with "Jet." I'm Doctor Luv on your one and only…Comm-Rad 1. Comin' up your gonna be hearin' "This Flight Tonight" from Nazareth…and…sometime in the next half hour …Pilot with their huge hit "Magic" but first… a band that really typifies that classic mid 70's sound. Now, I don't usually drop names, but the General himself once told me that he's got some very vivid memories of this song… Sweet… with … "Barroom Blitz"…on Comm-Rad1!"

George McLellan found himself standing in front of Louie's Place; the local pool hall and pinball arcade located about six blocks from his home in Culver City. Even though his firm but loving parents didn't want him going anywhere near the place he usually managed to sneak over a couple of times per week.

Following a few games of pin ball, standing around trying to look tough and unsuccessfully trying to pick up some of the older girls who hung out at Louie's, he got bored and decided to go out and get some fresh air.

Soon after, two of his friends joined him, Jimmy Madison and Billy Smith. After wasting some time telling half-truths to each other and admiring Louie's silver '74 Cadillac Eldorado parked in front of the pool hall, Billy suddenly became serious. "Hey George," he whispered. "I'll bet ten bucks ya don't have the guts to steal Louie's car."

George glared at Billy. The slightly chubby kid who sort of looked like Donny Osmond wasn't his best friend by any means. When George had hung out with Billy he usually wound up getting into some fairly serious trouble. Like two months ago when Billy invited George to a party at his so called girlfriend's house. Billy swore Karen Bonneville's parents were out of town for the weekend. Of course she wanted the entire school to come to her house for a huge bash on Saturday night. Best of all, her house contained a fully stocked liquor cabinet. To make a long story short, Karen's folks came back home earlier than expected with everyone managing to make their frantic escape except for an already intoxicated George. His livid, fuming mother picked him up, not made any happier by the steady stream of vomit coming from her alcohol poisoned son. George finally came to his senses the next day with a sick realization of the gravity of his error and resulting punishment. He spent the next month grounded from all extracurricular activities with his dad warning him that if there were any more "incidents" he would be shipped off to military school.

"Whaddya talking about ya spazz?" replied George in the commonly used vernacular of that time and place. "Ya wanna scrap with me ya fairy?" he said, trying to slap Billy's head. George was usually, at least to outward appearances the dominant male among his group of friends.

"Shaddup!" said Billy as he defended himself. "I wanna tell ya somethin'."

He drew closer to George and Jimmy and lowered his voice. "I was in Louie's office talkin' to him. The phone rang and when he wasn't lookin' I grabbed the car keys off his desk." Billy held out the garish "TCB" key chain like it was some sacred religious artifact. "Like I said. I bet ya don't have the guts to steal his car." He sensed George's hesitation. "Hey man, maybe you're the *real* fairy."

George spat on the pavement. He needed to look tough even though he could feel his guts rumbling with fear. Louie happened to be one harsh dude, moving to California from New Jersey the previous year. All the kids had heard rumors about his supposed connections to the Gambino crime family. Louie encouraged this belief, entertaining some of them with stories about how he used to be a "wise guy" and a Mafia hit man. Some punk kid daring to steal his prized Eldorado would more than likely really, really piss him off. Still, George couldn't just back down and not steal the car. He would be a joke in school, called a wimp, a pussy and possibly worse. Looking around him he noticed the street in front of Louie's looked deserted, which gave him an idea for a potential way out of this dilemma. If he very carefully borrowed the behemoth pimp-mobile for a quick spin around the block it might just be possible to have the car back before Louie or anyone else even noticed it missing. As he would often do later in his life, George McLellan made an impulsive and flawed decision, something his supporters later mislabelled as one of his greatest traits: decisiveness.

"Let's go ya losers!" he said as he snatched the keys out of Billy's hands and ran towards the driver's side of the Eldo.

As he got into the Caddy, George frantically tried to remember exactly *how* to drive a car. His dad took him out a few times and let him drive the '69 Buick but no one, not even another twelve year old would have ever considered him to be an experienced driver. The key did look similar to the one for the Buick so he inserted it into the ignition, pumping the accelerator twice like his dad taught him. (Luckily he was tall for his age and his feet reached the pedals). The huge 500 cubic inch engine roared to life at the same instant Billy and Jimmy jumped into the cars plush leather pleasure palace interior. He floored the accelerator pedal out of nervousness before dropping the transmission into drive. The front tires of the mammoth automobile spun with an unearthly squeal, leaving a long patch of burning black rubber behind as they accelerated down the street.

Billy kept saying "Holy shit man!" over and over again like a holy mantra but he did have the presence of mind to turn up the 8 track AM/FM stereo when "Barroom Blitz" came on. George tried taking a right turn on Culver Boulevard, turning the wheel much too far and then overcorrected back to the left, somehow avoiding going up onto the sidewalk. The giant mass of the Cadillac reminded George of an ocean liner as he swerved all over the street, barely managing to navigate onto Duquesne Avenue, a much busier thoroughfare.

"Hey man, look at those chicks! Beep the horn!" shouted Billy as he pointed out the driver's side window past George's head at two pubescent girls walking down the street. George looked over at the two young ladies as he beeped the horn. They *were* foxy ladies and looked back at him with more than a casual interest.

He brought his attention back to the road in front of him just in time to see the looming solid mass of a Dodge Monaco police cruiser, not even having time to brake before the crushing impact. They hit so hard George and Billy sitting in the front seat and not wearing seatbelts flew right into the windshield and Jimmy who had been sitting in the backseat, wound up with his head under the dash.

Other than being badly shaken up and having a few cuts, the boys were not badly injured. Not yet anyway. George could only say, "Damn it! Ah shit!" and rub his aching head as he thought about his parents reaction when they found out about what happened. Compared to them he would much rather face the wrath of Louie the so-called mafia hit man…

Following an excellent lunch, Rance Edwards came back to the General's private briefing room with a newfound respect for the Leader. The man proved to be an entertaining, witty dinnertime companion, educating Rance in the finer points of Busby Berkeley musicals, especially the two Warner Brothers classics *"42nd Street"* and *"Gold Diggers of 1933."* The General probably knew more about this obscure subject than any other living person, making Rance wonder why anyone, especially America's all powerful dictator, would be so obsessed about such useless trivia. Even though old movies did not captivate Rance to the same extent as they did the old man, McLellan made the boring topic come alive, describing it with enthusiasm dancing in his eyes.

The fact he cared so passionately about these personal interests did show that his advanced years hadn't yet caused any appreciable adverse intellectual or verbal effects. Oh, the dictator could definitely be defined as eccentric and somewhat corrupted in the unique manner only absolute power can cause, but didn't yet appear to have the dementia common to people his age. Must be some new radical anti-aging treatment thought Rance absently as he sat at the conference table and waited for the next phase of his orientation. The immortal Bob Seger's "Rock and Roll Never Forgets" played from somewhere in the next room.

The General found the correct restricted military holo tech manual and began.

"Boy, what I'm about to say may shock and astound you. It might also influence how you relate to your God and our place in the universe. It's not my intent to shake up your belief system but I do need to give you a general overview before a lot of this technical stuff will make any sense. First of all, I'm not sure whether Christians believe in extraterrestrial life, but I do need you to have an open mind on the subject. So, please tell me your viewpoint on the matter."

Rance carefully thought about his reply. "Sir, the Scriptures don't really mention whether there are other worlds out there with advanced life forms. Because of that I can't really give you a definitive answer. There's one thing

I do know though. I'm one hundred per cent confident that aliens didn't cause the great disappearance of Christians several years back. No matter what lies and propaganda the dictator Lanza spouts off to people, the Bible is quite clear. That event could only have been the great rapture of the Church foretold in the Book of Revelation."

General McLellan rolled his eyes before continuing. "Do you have to measure absolutely everything against that damn ancient book of yours? I just want you to take the figurative blindfold off and at least consider the possibility that alien life is a real phenomenon. And for what it's worth I also know that the Great Disappearance wasn't caused by some huge upsurge in alien abductions. Lanza just wanted to have an excuse that would allow him to consolidate his power base and build up additional military strength. What better reason to form a one-world government than a perceived security threat from outer space?"

He looked thoughtful. "Tell you what. I do have an open mind and will concede that although I don't think your explanation for the disappearance is likely I'll at least admit it's in the realm of possibility. All I ask is that you do the same for what I'm about to tell you. Fair enough?"

Rance agreed to at least listen to his earthly leader's opinions and carefully evaluate anything not directly contradicting God's word.

"Beginning around 1944 a huge number of sightings of unidentified flying objects occurred, most notably the so called Foo Fighters spotted by allied and axis air crews during the Second World War. Shortly after the war ended, classified government files noted another even more massive epidemic of strange craft being reported. You've probably heard of the famous Roswell incident. Well, the truth is it really did happen. The facts are actually much stranger than any bizarre theory some flying saucer nut could ever think up. When the Air Force got to the scene, they found a crashed spacecraft with a crew of four inside, two of which were still alive. One of these creatures died shortly after the crash but the other alien survived for several weeks. They flew the survivor to Washington where it underwent study and interrogation by the brightest minds of the era. Even President Truman came by to ask it a few questions. Most shocking for everyone that came in contact with the creature was the fact that it communicated telepathically. I'll give them credit, the Pentagon officials of the time tried their damndest to wring all the information they could out of 'Andy', which happened to be the cute nickname they gave the ugly little prick." Based on the way he enunciated the word *prick*, McLellan obviously didn't like aliens.

"There was just one little problem with the intense grilling they gave it. Although certainly not their fault, the Army Intelligence types naturally asked questions grounded in a 1947 reality. Because of that a lot of what the alien told them made absolutely no sense, especially when it came to the propulsion system of the spacecraft. The Government had this crashed alien craft with unbelievably advanced technologies. They also had the voluminous transcripts of what 'Andy' told them most of which sounded like a lot of meaningless symbolic nonsense. So what did they do? What else but assemble a team of brilliant scientists and then spend the next fifty years sitting on it and going absolutely nowhere. Well, that isn't totally true. The strange metal of the ship did teach things about alloys they never would have thought of on their own, but as to what made the thing go, well they were in way over their heads and they knew it. This top-secret project continued out at Area 51 for year after year with the ultra-highest level of security protecting it. Even sitting Presidents were only allowed to visit the area *once* shortly after being elected. A couple of them had serious psychological problems afterwards, mainly because of the subsequent CIA/NSA intelligence briefings on the alien's true agenda. You see their ruthless motives happened to be one of the few things that 'Andy' discussed very clearly with absolutely no ambiguity. The alien being explained that their race came from a binary star system called Zeta Reticuli approximately 39 light years from Earth. The reason they are coming to our planet is quite straightforward. Due to millions of years of inbreeding their species has become genetically redundant and they need "new blood" or fresh genetic material to strengthen their dying race. The only place for them to get this "material" is on Earth, from us. For the past century these 'Grays' as the popular media often calls them, embarked upon a program of abducting humans against their will and then conducting brutal breeding experiments. They would attempt to cover their tracks by altering the victims psychologically and inducing a type of artificial amnesia, usually involving a false cover memory. The Grays also injected microscopic tracking chips into the abductees. Actually, the chips now being implanted into people by the World Federation are remarkably similar. Using DNA manipulation they've been able to produce an ungodly strain of alien-human hybrid, which eventually will be used for their own cold, self-seeking benefits. Up until now, the aliens have looked at us like we're livestock, which if you consider the technological gap that once existed between our species, is all we really were. You may have noticed that I don't refer to these beings from Zeta Reticulli by gender and generally call them derogatory names like 'it' or 'creature.' The reason I do that is because these things are nasty little bastards who don't deserve any respect or consideration-after all, they haven't given us any."

    Rance, trying to digest everything he had heard so far, lifted his hand with a question for the General.

"Sir, just one thing. As a Christian I wanted to know if these advanced beings expressed a belief in God or had any form of spirituality."

General McLellan's face displayed a foul looking sneer.

"I knew you were going to ask me that one. Believe me, back in 1947 spirituality logically became one of the topics they discussed in depth with 'Andy' possibly because most people in our country were Christians back then. The viewpoints expressed by the Gray struck the interrogators as somewhat contradictory. On the one hand, their race accepts without question that the universe was created by a higher power, but 'Andy' had a hard time understanding the concept of having a personal relationship with a God, Jesus or any other deity. Apparently they think of 'God" as an abstract concept or power impossible to relate to on any individual level. The classified reports from the forties stated that in spite of all their advanced knowledge, the Zeta Reticullins were almost primitive when it came to spirituality. If you ever meet any of these little buggers Rance, seems to me that they might make a fertile evangelistic opportunity for you Christians." McLellan laughed at the idea.

"Kinda like the Spanish evangelizing the Incas eh? Oh…wait…that didn't turn out so great did it?" he said with devastating sarcasm. "Anyway, let's get back on track. It took a long time but finally by the early 21st century science started to catch up so that a lot of what that little gray dick headed bastard revealed started to make more sense. Radical new concepts espoused by theoretical physicists like Stephen Hawking and Michio Kaku certainly helped. The scientific team working trying to reverse engineer the space craft knew it used some sort of electromagnetic drive system. Took them a while but they slowly started to comprehend some of the complex theories and equations the aliens used. They already had some limited understanding of electromagnetic field theory thanks to the pioneering work of Tesla as well as data from the 'Philadelphia Experiment' in 1943. In that infamous foul up, concentrated energy fields caused the Destroyer Escort USS *Eldridge* to disappear into another dimension and then reappear with devastating consequences for the crew. That helped but what really advanced the science turned out to be an ultra-top-secret government program called the Montauk Project that dealt with freaky things like inter-dimensional travel aided by gifted psychics. There were quite a few horrific deaths because of the cutting edge nature of what they were doing. This led to the project eventually shutting down, but the compiled data became an incredible help to the group studying the Zeta Reticulli spacecraft. The researchers started to realize that they'd been completely wrong in their approach to figuring out how the thing worked. You see, originally they looked at it from a strictly mechanical and aerospace engineering viewpoint when in actual fact the spacecraft's alien designers intended it to be a highly complex symbiotic or if you will, psychotronic organism. Psychotronics, in case you are not familiar with the term is the science of mind machine interfacing. Without mind interface the spacecraft essentially remained a worthless hunk of metal. Finally some genius got the bright idea to place an NSA telepath in the key seating position and the damn flying saucer, to everyone's surprise, came to life. During the early trials they just copied the spacecraft, put an expendable human being with sometimes questionable psychic talents inside and hoped for the best. Of course early prototypes proved to be wildly unpredictable because of the original design specs intended for the much different physiology of the Grays. After a few spectacular failures, but also a few successes, the team gradually gained a more complete understanding of the hyper-drive system and how it can be used for space travel. I'm going to give you a somewhat simplified explanation of this leaving out most of the boring stuff like theoretical quantum physics and Einstein equations."

He paused, taking a deep breath before continuing.

"Try and get your head around this concept: the hyper-drive system involves spatial compression which is basically a warping or wrinkling of our space time continuum, resulting in drastically reduced distances of travel in interplanetary space. So for example, instead of traveling the entire distance to a star let's say five light years away at near light speed, you compress the space between Earth and this star to let's say one twentieth of the normal distance. Voila! Suddenly immensely remote stars are now within our reach so to speak. The USS *Hornet*, as I'm sure you've already guessed, is also powered by a type of hyper drive system, but I'll get to that later. First though I'll discuss the way space can be compressed or warped. A tremendously powerful electrical current flowing in a specific configuration generates an electromagnetic field, which creates in effect a tube, the correct scientific term being a 'working Tipler cylinder.' This forms an artificial, controllable black hole thereby achieving dimensional shifting and the ability to create alterations and manipulation of our own space-time continuum. A human psychic, or more accurately, a psychotronic host is utilized to visualize and stabilize a target destination in a different time/space location on which this vortex is then focused upon. You start your main propulsion system and if everything goes according to plan you should reach your target in a relatively short period of Earth time. The theory sounds fairly simple but the early efforts ran into some problems, including the rather ghastly effects on the psychics or hosts. They found that these people would often experience something similar to a complete psychotic breakdown, actually becoming 'unstuck' in time with their consciousness separated and out of phase from their physical bodies. That would lead to a complete failure of the affected propulsion unit. The way the scientists solved this is again quite complex but in basic terms, they found that some element of a person, something you Christians might call their soul, must remain in synch with their original space time phase while transferring to or from other dimensions. Eventually a method of subliminal messaging was used to keep part of the host grounded in this reality with only a minimal decrease in performance factors. Another even more troubling issue involved the rather unfortunate psychological problems other members of crews sometimes exhibited when exposed to the powerfully volatile electromagnetic fields. Similar to the ill-fated crew of the old USS *Eldridge*, a good percentage of subjects became paranoid and delusional, effects that were unfortunately, permanent. They tried numerous shielding products, finally discovering the rare element Helenium, which dissipated almost all the damaging electromagnetic energy away from the crew areas. Any questions so far?"

Rance managed to suppress a yawn. The subject matter was by no means boring, but he hadn't enjoyed a decent night's sleep in quite a while. In spite of being tired he could sense The Holy Spirit pushing him to do the right thing and ask something he knew would probably get him in very serious trouble. "Actually sir, I do have one question. What possessed you to build the *Hornet,* a project which took huge amounts of resources away from our people in desperate need down on Earth?"

The General's face turned red, his intensity quickly exploding into rage.

"Why you ungrateful little shit! I could have you executed for that!" In an apoplectic rage, McLellan grabbed the holo-discs on the table and flung them across the room, eyes boring into Rance like malevolent laser beams. Obviously it had been quite some time since anyone had dared ask him a hard question.

A large bodyguard in full battle gear burst into the briefing room, laser sight on his M-30 aimed directly at Rance's forehead. "Sir?" he called out to General McLellan, waiting for any little signal to go ahead and eliminate this possible threat to his Leader.

McLellan raised his hand. "It's okay Sergeant. General Edwards here was just sharing his opinions with me. He might be a little bit too honest for his own good but I don't want him shot. You're dismissed."

The bodyguard looked at McLellan like a dog whose master had just taken away a rabbit it was about to rip apart. "Are you absolutely sure Sir?"

The General dismissed the man with a wave, and then sat next to Rance, looking at him with evident curiosity. "You do have some back bone boy even though that question was downright insubordinate. Since you've been out of the military for some time I'm going to cut you a break, but as your commanding officer I need to tell you that future conduct of this manner will not be tolerated. Understood?"

Rance understood perfectly. "Sir, I apologize if I offended you. I respect you as my leader and will follow your orders without hesitation. My conduct and actions must always be guided by and be consistent with my Faith in Jesus Christ but my question was motivated by my beliefs and concern for other people, not legitimate military necessity. Again, you have my apologies."

The General was now calmer, at least to outward appearances. "Rance, Rance. What the hell am I going to do with you? Anyway, as inappropriate as that question may have been I feel you do deserve an answer. After all, I'm the one who brought you to this warship. Sometimes I tend to underestimate what a shock it is for people to see the *Hornet* for the first time. That's probably because it's been such an integral part of my own life for so long. The idea for building the USS *Hornet* first came to me back in the twenties after the countless ecological and natural disasters affecting our country reached a crisis point. After the loss of much of California in the great earthquake, the destruction of New York City and all the weather related disasters, well, during that horrible time I made up my mind that we needed to change our focus and look in a whole new direction for the salvation of the nation. Earth was…still is…dying and the only possible solution for our survival became clear. The Optimus Project started as a simple enough concept. Build a spacecraft so huge and powerful it would serve as a modern day Noah's ark, bringing the best and brightest of the United States of America to another world that we'll colonize and make into a paradise of our own design. There was only one small problem with the plan. We knew of only one habitable earth like planet: Optimus 4 in the Zeta Reticulli system, the very same planet our friends the Grays originate from. That gave us two clear choices. We could either migrate to their home world without the inhabitant's consent or wait until our long-range probes found another suitable, uninhabited planet. Unfortunately, with the geopolitical and ecological situation down below deteriorating as it has we just don't have time to wait. So, of course, I made the difficult decision that we would immediately need to take Optimus 4 with force, subdue the native Grays, use some of the peaceful ones for our own purposes, and then exterminate the rest. After all, these depraved aliens aren't human, no far from it."

Rance looked at the General with incredulity. Even though having just mentioned an unspeakable genocide on a scale heretofore unimagined, the Dictator's voice continued to remain calm, like he was discussing something inane like the *Hornet's* dinner menu rather than the deaths of untold numbers of intelligent beings. Who knew what mind-boggling evil would come out of McLellan's mouth next? Rance was about to find out.

"Operation Blue Book, which I want you to review by the way, is our classified operational plan for conquering and subjugating the natives on the planet. It's a crucial prerequisite to the next step of colonization, since the Grays probably won't look too kindly at many thousands of humans of breeding age showing up on their doorstep." He laughed at that. "Talk about the proverbial unwelcome house guest! Anyway, to be able to accomplish Blue Book properly, we needed to be in a position of power with technology not merely a copy of theirs, but at a level of superiority at least sufficient to give us the clear tactical advantage. We are now at that point. It has taken almost forty years from conception to conclusion but we will soon begin the greatest odyssey mankind has ever embarked upon: Migration to another planet, ensuring the survival of our great nation and race. We embark on our historic journey in one month's time. Let that Damn Antonio Lanza and his Illuminati stooges have what's left of old Earth! We are going to conquer Optimus 4, the New Earth!" McLellan raised his hands in the air, as if he had just finished addressing a crowd and now basked in the resulting adulation and applause.

Rance felt his head spinning. The part of the Generals rant about "subjugating the natives" kept going through his mind. He had a sinking feeling that those three little words were going to be a subject he would be devoting a lot of his prayer time to in the near future…

CHAPTER 6

"This is Captain Dan on Comm-Rad 1, your very own voice of the USS *Hornet*. You just heard "Tear The Roof Off The Sucka" by Parliament. Gotta love that funk! Comin' up in the next ten we've got the Sex Pistols with their classic "Anarchy In The UK" and "Slow Ride" by Foghat but first a song I have had a pile of requests for already today: Thin Lizzy…"The Boys Are Back In Town" …it's goin' out to the 5th Marine Division who at this very moment are busy gettin' ready to kick some Gray ass…"

George McLellan dozed in the back seat of his parent's new 1976 Oldsmobile Regency, trying not to let his annoying little sisters antics bother him. He found it kind of hard to ignore her however considering Joanie sat only two feet away talking non-stop about her best friend's latest hair style. This wouldn't have been too bad except for the fact that her babbling interfered with his ability to hear KXLA the top 40 am station his parents finally agreed to let him listen to (at a moderate volume of course).

They were on a road trip to Billings Montana to see George's paternal Grandfather Joseph Fightin' Joe McLellan. This would be the second summer in a row that his folks dropped George off in Montana to spend time with his hard as nails ex-marine Grampa. It was either that or head off to military school, which became the blunt choice given to him after the shit literally hit the fan following his disastrous experience of driving and then destroying Louie's car. Surprisingly, Louie was quite pleasant (for a former Mafia hit man) when George's dad visited him at the pool hall to make restitution for the ruined Cadillac. Of course his dad made George come along so he could apologize in person for his actions, but Louie just laughed, saying that he "did shit a hell of a lot worse at that age." As it turned out, the pool hall owner only asked for $500 to cover the insurance deductible on the car, an amount his dad immediately wrote a check for. Unfortunately George was still paying off this debt to his dad-with interest. He found the worst thing about the whole episode though not to be his father's anger but his mother crying and tearfully telling George about how disappointed she felt. That really hurt and became the main motivating factor behind why he readily agreed to spend time with his Grampa every summer. For some much needed discipline as his dad put it. The old guy wasn't even half bad, regaling George with lively off color stories about WW2, the big one. He had been a Lieutenant with the United States 5th Marine Division and had fought in all the major battles in the Pacific from Guadalcanal to Iwo Jima. He still showed off the scars to prove it, having taken a Japanese bullet in the arm, then a piece of shell shrapnel in the leg while being evacuated off the beach during that last vicious battle.

 His wife Emma McLellan, the most important thing in his life, had died three years ago leaving Grampa Joe very lonely. Even though the old man never admitted it, George thought he looked forward to these summer visits, keeping the boy busy with fun activities like camping, fishing and plinking at cans or rabbits with his old .22 caliber rifle. They also watched a lot of *Hawaii Five-O* and *Bonanza* reruns, the old man's favorite TV shows. These were welcome diversions as his dad was now so busy as an executive at Hell Cat Aircraft he rarely found time for anything enjoyable anymore, let alone a weekend with his son. George also looked forward to one of the best side benefits of going on the drive to Montana, listening to some really great radio stations on the way. They had barely been on the road an hour and he'd already heard some excellent stuff like "Heart of Gold" by Neil Young, "Show Me the Way" by Frampton, "Fox on the Run" by Sweet and

Chicago "If You Leave Me Now." It was going to be a fun trip. Now if only his little sister would just shut up...

After being dismissed by the General and being ordered back at 07:00 the following morning, Rance Edwards left the briefing room, finding his aide Major Mitchell waiting patiently.

"Hello Sir. I hope everything went well. As General McLellan probably explained to you, normally I'd be responsible for your orientation but you have the rare honor of getting guidance from the great man himself. Because of this I've been ordered not to discuss your role here. I'm to only show you areas of the ship dealing directly with comfort and recreation like the cafeteria or medical center on H Deck. If you have any other questions I need to respectfully defer you to the General who I'm sure will finish your main training by tomorrow. That leaves me to fill in any remaining blanks in your knowledge base. Do you have any urgent requests General Edwards?"

Rance felt so tired there was only one request, urgent or otherwise on his mind. He doubted if he even had the energy to eat a meal.

"I haven't slept in the last three days Major. Once you show me back to my room you're dismissed until 06:30-tomorrow morning. Then you can come back and make sure I get to the Generals briefing room on time. Lead the way."

The journey back to his quarters still confused him, but this time Rance did recognize a few landmarks on the way. The layout of the ship was based on a logical alphabetical and numeric grid emanating outwards from the Bridge/Headquarters area.

After reaching his billet, Rance said his evening prayers before collapsing exhausted onto the comfortable bed. It had been a grueling few days both emotionally and physically, so he fell into a deep sleep quickly, not waking until the chirping sound of his alarm disturbed him at 06:00.

After his morning prayers, Rance enjoyed a cup of strong coffee from the automated dispenser, nearly clearing the cobwebs away by time the Major arrived shortly before 06:30.

"Good morning Sir," said a crisp looking Major Mitchell as he entered Rance's quarters. "I hope you slept well. If you don't mind General, this morning I would like to show you a faster route back to the headquarters area."

Mitchell was a little nervous, perhaps intimidated by his superior officer's reputation. "Basically there are, um two methods of travel throughout the *Hornet*. We usually start by having new people physically walk the route to familiarize them with the layout of the ship, but the preferred method is to take the bullet tube. The bullet tube system is actually the only practical transport system as the *Hornet* is comparable to a city in space. Large numbers of crew are commuting between destinations at all times. The bullet train design is completely fail-safe with literally no possibility of any malfunction, but this ship has been designed with multiple redundancies in every system. If the inconceivable such as a tube system failure did happen during actual battle conditions it is important for every crewmember to have at least a basic understanding of ship layout and how to reach any area by walking there. Later I'll show you the holo of the ship's deck layout, which should help a bit. We also keep a large number of emergency two wheeled ped vehicles placed in strategic locations. Quite important if a person had to travel a number of kilometers in a short period of time."

Rance pointed to the door. "I had a feeling there was probably a faster way to get around such a large ship. One other question ...exactly how big is the *Hornet*?"

"Sorry Sir," said the aide. "As far as exact specifications or any tech questions, my orders are to leave that to Our Glorious Leader. Now if you'd like to follow me…"

Many individuals in uniform crowded the bullet tube station on H deck but Rance and the Major only waited a few minutes before they took seats in a four seat bullet car that accepted voice commands for a destination.

After the Major and two other passengers stated their trip requests, the car pulled away from the station with acceleration comparable to an F-22 fighter.

Thirty five seconds later they disembarked on A Deck at the headquarters station, leaving the car which then sped away to the destination of the two remaining commuters.

It took Rance a few seconds to get his legs again after their ride, making him assume the after effects probably duplicated one of those old fashioned roller coaster rides he once saw described on a PBS holo documentary. While stretching his legs, he noticed a hint of a smile on Major Mitchell's face.

Rance, usually fairly patient, started to feel a hint of anger towards his aide. "And what the heck are you smiling at Major? You find me amusing?"

"I'm sorry Sir. It's just that I'm remembering my first trip in the bullet system. Unlike you I couldn't even walk afterwards. Your history as a fighter pilot probably conditioned you better than most people. I only wanted to let you know it will get easier every time you use the bullet."

Rance didn't say anything to the Major, but he silently asked God for forgiveness and patience in his new military role. He definitely inherited some of his illustrious distant ancestor's fiery dispositions although becoming a Christian had unquestionably improved his temperament. Luckily, it usually took quite a lot to make him lose his temper, but if someone really asked for it-then watch out.

General McLellan, waiting in the briefing room was more formal, accepting Rance's salute with a "Have a seat General Edwards."

Although reserved and business like, the General's mind seemed no less sharp as he began. "Today I want to complete your orientation session. You know the reason for building this warship, now, the details. For instance, you might be wondering about the specifications of the *Hornet*."

Rance didn't show any emotion but he definitely felt some curiosity as to whether mere coincidence led the General to choose this topic to discuss first or if it might be a less than subtle reminder to him of how he remained under surveillance at all times. Probably the latter he thought as McLellan continued.

"The USS *Hornet* is 15,128 meters long from bow to stern, at her widest has a 8,459 meter beam, boasts four main hangar/flight decks and two emergency hangar/flight decks with a total of 5,234 F-72 Sparrow Hawk fighter bombers, 1310 X-52 shuttle craft and 75 Galaxy class heavy lift shuttles. She is powered by an enhanced hyper drive system with an electromagnetic output of approximately 100 quadrillion watts."

He stopped momentarily to let Rance absorb the outrageous but accurate numbers before continuing on.

"One side benefit of the propulsion system is a very earth like gravity on board the ship, although it is slightly heavier than 1G in areas closer to the drive unit and a little less than 1G on the outer areas of the vessel. Most people don't notice any difference. I'm not going to explain exactly how the hyper drive provides energy and gravity or we'd be here all day. I don't even think the experts know for sure and to be honest I couldn't really give a shit-as long as it keeps on working…Top velocity of the *Hornet* is near light speed, roughly 299,000,000 meters per second or if you prefer, a little more than 1,000,000,000 kilometers per hour. Failure of the hyper drive is quite simply not a possibility due to its rock solid simplicity and reliability; however the main propulsion unit does have a nuclear reactor backup system capable of delivering in the region of one half that performance level." McLellan was now beaming as he continued.

"Main armament consists of 35 two trillion watt plasma weapons, 210 five hundred billion watt plasma weapons, 1,009 one hundred billion watt plasma weapons and 2,018 twenty billion watt plasma weapons. In addition, in the unlikely event of main armament power failure the *Hornet* is armed with approximately 5,000 new generation nuclear tipped cruise missiles, 15,000 sidewinder XV nuclear tipped missiles, 30,000 conventional missiles, and about 5,000 fifty caliber gun stations which are designed for use in the airless environment of space. This does not include the large variety of devastating armaments that we designed the F-72's and shuttles to carry. Quite simply she's the most heavily armed warship in the history of the human race, our greatest accomplishment. We didn't just rely exclusively on offensive armaments however. The *Hornet* has an impressive array of defensive systems as well, including a main shield capable of deflecting the force of a 15-megaton nuclear explosion detonated from a distance of 20 meters from the outer skin. Such a strike might shake us up but we'd survive. In the inconceivable event that the vessel does sustain damage, she's designed to automatically seal off any affected areas, preventing fire from spreading. In the case of this system failing which, by the way, is also impossible, there are twenty fire control teams fully trained to fight a fire under battle conditions. The designs of all major systems include at least three or four backup redundancies, to ensure total reliability under all imaginable circumstances." He appeared very smug.

"You may also be curious about the crew numbers. There happens to be four hundred and sixty five thousand, three hundred and twenty seven souls on board. Excuse me, that's actually four hundred and sixty five thousand, three hundred and twenty eight thousand counting you. It's broken down into the following: approximately fifty thousand *Hornet* crewmembers, about three hundred thousand US Marines, US Army and Space Force personnel, with the rest being assorted civilian scientists, specialists and some family members. We made a concerted effort to keep most people on board under age thirty and single with no family attachments. We also tried to keep the ratio between males and females fairly even, for breeding purposes naturally. Those are the people we have on board but the essence our American culture comprises much, much more than just its citizens. To make a proper start on this bizarre alien planet, all of us need inspiring reminders of who we are as a people and where we've come from. With that goal in mind, all surviving museums in the United States were scoured for their most significant art, culture and other pieces that typify our unique values. Vast storage areas on board hold these items until we can safely transfer them to our new home on Optimus 4. These will be tangible examples of the grand significance of the United States of America, especially for the new generations to come with no memories of old Earth. Hell, we even have the "Texas Twister," a complete but partially dismantled B-52 D bomber responsible for dumping a shit load of ordnance on North Vietnam during Operation Linebacker II. To help you understand this better I have something I want to show you. Come with me."

    Rance welcomed the chance to get up out of his chair and go somewhere, anywhere. He still needed to absorb some of the stats General McLellan rattled off. He knew the size of the *Hornet* to be immense, logically also needing a large crew but really had no idea of the enormity, not just of the ship he now found himself in but also of the ego and driving force of the American Dictator who first envisioned and then built it. Unlike General George McLellan however, Rance felt no pride at this, likely the human race's most monumental achievement. He knew even the greatest triumph of mere mortals paled in insignificance next to what his Lord and Savior Jesus Christ had done: coming to Earth and redeeming the entire human race by dying on the cross for our sins. Rance followed McLellan out of the briefing room and into the Generals personal elevator system.

Soon after, he stood in an enormous warehouse area situated more or less directly below the General's headquarters and Bridge section of the USS *Hornet*. A fan of twentieth century boxing, Rance spotted priceless autographed photos of some of the greatest fighters of that era visible inside a display case. Many hundreds, possibly thousands of other display cases filled the vast space.

As McLellan went on to explain, this storage depot held "the lifeblood" of the nation, most of the historically noteworthy assets of the formerly wealthy American people.

"There are so many riches in this room I could literally spend years showing them all to you. There is only one however that I personally really treasure above all others, something that played a key role in the history of our nation a little over a century ago. This is what I wanted to show you."

The General walked over to a large object completely covered by a large white canvas cover. As he pulled on the cloth the true nature of the thing hidden underneath became apparent. It was an extremely ancient vehicle; dark blue paint gleaming in the artificial lights of the cargo area. It struck him at once as something strange and yet somehow familiar.

It took Rance a few seconds to recall where he had seen this automobile before. When he finally remembered the holo documentary he watched in school showing this very car that now somehow sat in front of him, his jaw dropped unconsciously in amazement.

General George Brinton McLellan became very pleased when he saw the observable reaction this museum piece put on Rance's scarred face.

"You do recognize it! Excellent!" he said with something approaching boyish glee in his voice.

"Yes you are correct. It is the automobile known as the SS-100-X, the 1961 Lincoln Continental Presidential Limousine that carried John F. Kennedy on that fateful day in 1963. One of the first things I did after I achieved power involved rescuing this once proud symbol of our country from obscurity and neglect. Even some historians aren't aware the original body panels and seats were stripped from the car shortly after the assassination in order to cover up the truth about what really happened, but that's a whole other topic of discussion. The missing parts and bloodstained upholstery were found in a CIA storage area in Langley. The car then received a complete restoration to make it exactly the way it appeared at that historic moment. I later had the priceless artifact installed in a special climate controlled room in one of my Presidential Palaces. Sometimes if I couldn't sleep at night I would go out and just sit in the thing, exactly where President Kennedy had been caught in the deadly crossfire. I could almost hear, feel and even smell those events happening, something I found strangely calming. After the Optimus project became a reality, I suddenly realized how the true destiny of the SS-100 remained to be fulfilled. I knew that once we conquered Optimus 4 I would ride in this automobile during our triumphant victory parade over the vanquished Grays."

General McLellan then jumped into the back of the convertible Presidential Limousine, something he did easily enough considering some men half his age couldn't display such physical prowess. His presence triggered the cars updated sound system, which started playing historically appropriate music, the haunting vocals of Del Shannon's "Runaway" echoing in the vast storage space.

To Rance the song sounded like a funeral dirge, November 22, 1963 and President Kennedy's assassination signifying the beginning of his nation's long humiliating decline, a path leading to this moment of absurdity. Peaked cap sitting at a jaunty angle, America's Dictator, himself only an infant on that disastrous day a century ago began to wave at the imaginary people (or possibly Grays) along the make-believe parade route. The General seemed unaware of anyone else being there with him, enjoying the fantasy he had created, the sounds of Danny and the Juniors "Rock and Roll is Here to Stay" adding to the illusion. Finally Rance called out softly and interrupted the old man's fantasy.

"Oh yes, we must be going. I have a few more things to discuss before you are ready for active duty. Come along." said the General as he carefully stepped out of the car, showing a lot less exuberance than just a few minutes earlier. The strains of "Little Darlin" by the Diamonds cut out abruptly when the death car no longer sensed McLellan's presence.

A few minutes later they stood in the K Deck #2 hangar and flight deck, an area nearly identical to the K Deck #1 hangar and flight deck where Rance arrived on the X-36 shuttle. The main difference between the two involved the frenetic activity going on here at hangar #2. Large numbers of flight crew personnel swarmed like disturbed ants around several sleek looking fighter craft the likes of which Rance had never seen before. Obviously not expecting the Great General himself to be making an unannounced visit to the flight deck, a comedy of errors ensued as men and women fell all over each other as they came to attention and saluted.

"At ease! All of you!" called out McLellan, obviously well accustomed to speaking to large groups of people and captivating them with his soothing voice.

"I wanted to take this opportunity to thank you valuable crew members for all of your hard work and dedication in preparing the *Hornet* as well as her fighters for our looming departure date. You have been given impossible deadlines but you achieved your goals in spite of sometimes overwhelming adversity. People like you exemplify our great country and that's the reason Operation Optimus will succeed – I salute each and every one of you!"

The smattering of applause started with just a few of the crew members, growing until everyone present started clapping. Some even yelled out things like "Long live the General!" and "We love The Leader!"

Rance stared in amazement. It wasn't so much what the General said but more the way he said it that mesmerized his audience. His cult of personality even went beyond some of the great orators and communicators of history like Reagan, Kennedy and Churchill. In some ways he was comparable to the greatest dictator of all time, Antonio Lanza.

General McLellan soon ordered everyone off the flight deck, giving Rance a clearer view of that sleek killer craft. He walked closer to one of them, clearly making out the following small script under the cockpit area of the ship:

USS HORNET F-72 SPARROW HAWK
PROUDLY BUILT BY
THE BLMD GROUP
Boeing Lockheed Martin Douglas

Somewhat smaller than the familiar F-22 Rance knew so well, the all-white F-72 presented sleeker, cleaner lines reminiscent of an ancient 1950's delta wing fighter like the

F-102 Delta Dagger or the Canadian CF-105 Avro Arrow. The standard US military star and bar roundels marked the wings and side of the fuselage, but in addition UNITED STATES SPACE FORCE script adorned its side behind the cockpit. Conveniently, the bubble glass was in the up position, allowing easy access to the cockpit. Rance took full advantage of this, quickly climbing the access ramp and seating himself at the unfamiliar controls.

General McLellan smiled at him saying, "Rance you remind me of a kid in a freakin' candy store. That, my boy, as you've probably already figured out is the F-72 Sparrow Hawk fighter-bomber, specifically designed to kick the living shit out of those dirty little gray scumbags and quickly gain us air/space superiority. Soon you'll be going through the *Hornet's* fighter orientation training course...before you know it you'll be fully qualified to fly and land one of these beauties. Should be a breeze for a former Navy man like you. Now, get your ass down here so we can get back to my office and finish your briefing."

Rance didn't want to leave the futuristic fighter craft. What he really found intriguing weren't the similarities in controls and instrumentation to the old F-22 he once flew but the many other things that looked completely foreign and strange. Actually alien could better describe the feeling Rance got while sitting in the cockpit. Learning to fly it would undoubtedly be an awesome experience, he thought while waiting for General McLellan to begin the conclusion of the basic orientation. The General consulted the holo screen with the privacy on, thus preventing Rance from seeing the 3-D images being displayed.

"Before we get started discussing your role on the USS *Hornet*, I wanted to get back to the Montauk Project that I mentioned earlier. One of the other areas of experimentation that they worked on besides psychotronics was dabbling in psychological warfare techniques. You see, they hooked up enormously talented telepaths to the laughable supercomputers of the time, converting their thought waves to a digital format which could be subliminally attached to conventional radio signals and broadcast to an unsuspecting populace. As crude as these efforts were they did have some effect on people. For instance, if the psychic concentrated on citizens buying brand X laundry detergent, sales of that product went up noticeably in the broadcast area. More dramatically, if the telepath visualized citizens murdering each other, the homicide rate went up significantly. You get my point. Anyway, like a lot of other people, you've probably wondered about the method behind the madness of my ordering Comm-Rad1 to broadcast the ancient music it does. Besides the fact that I like it and have some fond memories of that era, there is also a significant Psych Ops factor. For the last three years subliminal messages have been attached to the signals. These varied between geographical areas depending on needs of course, ranging from 'BE VIOLENT' to 'BE PEACEFUL.' Believe me my boy, as bad as Detroit looked during your extraction, it most certainly would have been a hell of a lot worse if we hadn't been beaming powerful non-violent signals to the area. Of course, once you were safely out of the city we could go back to broadcasting the destructive signals designed to eliminate the trouble makers bottled up in the now useless Dead City of Detroit."

    The old man had a distorted smile on his face as he said this, giving Rance a disgusted, nauseated feeling. The charming, witty dinner companion was gone, replaced now by the heartless and ruthless dictator.

    "Based on our success in mood altering methods with humans, in essence what we've now done is design the ultimate Psychological Warfare Unit, something calculated to give those alien mothers the worst case of depression you can imagine. We'll start broadcasting powerful signals to Zeta Reticuli as soon as we're within range. After all we aren't relying on any surprise factor in our war strategy, so we'll keep blasting them until we reach orbit around Optimus 4. Using the hyper drive of the *Hornet*, we can start hitting the bastards with radio signals of a strength previously unimagined. I am talking trillions of watts in power, something that will probably kill a large number of the Grays in the immediate vicinity of the targeted zone even without involving any form of radio receiver. They will actually feel the music before their internal organs and brains turn to mush. Can you imagine that? Just think of it: Long after the deaths of Robert Plant and Jimmy Page their songs live on and will be used to fry the brain cells of not just another generation but of an entire alien race! What a wonderful tribute to the acid rock sound of Led Zeppelin! I used to be quite a fan you know..." the General appeared misty eyed as he continued "the thing is, even the aliens that don't die because of the signal force will be adversely affected by the choice of music being played.

 We did a little testing on some Grays we managed to capture while they attempted to abduct some of their helpless human breeding research subjects. Imagine their surprise when they turned into the laboratory rats instead of the other way around? The clinical assessments involved all known forms of human music and the effects these different compositions had on the aliens. Well guess what. Turns out the Grays really loved classical and opera, with a special affinity for Mozart, Strauss or any of the great Italian tenors. What they hate, I mean really hate, is late twentieth century popular music, the stuff I grew up on. It's literally emotionally toxic to the warped little bastards, something we observed after subjecting 'em to month after month of the shit at different wattages. This directly impacts your role here on the *Hornet*; Psych Ops functioning well from the beginning will mean a lot less work for you and the fighter squadrons later in the campaign."

As an astute observer of people, The General must have detected Rance's thinly veiled revulsion. "I may seem like a mean son of a bitch to you Rance but you have to believe me: the fight our race is about to engage in is going to be the most brutal one humans have ever been a part of, a fight not only for territory but also for survival of our very species. Which brings me to your role on this ship. I wanted you and only you for the position of Fighter Operations Tactical Advisor on the *Hornet*. I know our fighter pilots will listen to the famous Rance Edwards teaching them strategy and tactics but most importantly, they will also respect you because of your stellar war record. You see I've been watching you for some time, those arrests by the authorities, your dad's cancer, I knew all about it. I wanted to get you on board sooner but knew that someone of your misguided faith and integrity wouldn't have agreed until after your father died. Now that he's gone, there's no reason not to fulfill your destiny as the True American Hero teaching others how to do their part in our war of survival against the aliens!"

Rance stood up, the anger coursing through his body making it difficult for him to talk. "You mean to say that you knew about my father's illness, that you could've saved him if you hadn't wanted me aboard this, fuc…" even in anger he caught himself from reverting to his old speech patterns…"this damned ship?"

General McLellan didn't have to give an answer, just stood there silently smirking at him.

If Rance hadn't been a believer in Jesus Christ the General would have died at that very instant. In fact he could clearly visualize squeezing the elderly man's neck and choking the life right out of him. Rance needed to take a deep breath and remind himself of the scripture Romans 12:19 which reads "Vengeance is mine; I will repay, sayeth the Lord." It wasn't up to him to obtain retribution against this clearly malevolent, quite possibly insane man, but as Luke 6:28

commanded instead, to pray for McLellan, something he would have to do later, but not at this moment. Right now Rance could only leave the briefing room without delay, before his first impulse won out and he murdered the Dictator.

Chapter 7

"Yo. Lieutenant Fevah talkin.' Aight that was "Saturday Night" from da Bay City Rollers an before that you heard "Float On" by the Floaters an some Fugees, "Killing Me Softly." Hope you peoples ready fo some kick ass tunes... cause you is hooked up to Comm-Rad 1 yo voice of da USS *Hornet*. Now Ise gittin some shit from da 1st Infantry Division, They's sayin' we only bin givin' recognition to da Marines an told me if it don't stop someone's gonna come down heah an bust a cap in mah ass. Since we don't want dat to be happinin' now, dis next one is dedicated to all you pimps, playas, hos and money makas of da Big Red One, seasly do, we all hopin' you kill lots uh dose gray muthas. So heah you go... The Spinners from 1977 with some pimpin' Deetroit soul vibes ... "Rubber Band Man"..."

George decided he better try and do something constructive with what remained of his Saturday afternoon instead of sitting around flipping through the latest issue of Mad magazine, watching TV in his room and listening to Gerry Rafferty singing "Baker Street" for at least the hundredth time that day.

He eventually came up with the idea of walking down to the Orbit Roller Boogie Disco on Lincoln Avenue. Not the best skater in the world, George still liked the Orbit because it happened to be a cool place to hang out and to meet chicks. Although technically a disco, the music they played on Saturday afternoons tended to also include some pop and rock for the high school crowd. Maybe they would even play a song from that hot new girl group The Runaways. "Mama Weer All Crazee Now" would be good. George started out on the five-block walk, his Sure Grip roller skates hanging around his neck. He wished he could drive his car, a blue and brown primer 1967 Chevelle Malibu parked temptingly in the driveway almost audibly calling out "Drive me! Drive me!" But…no. George had learned his lesson about driving when he wasn't supposed to. His parents finally gave in to his pleading and let him buy the sharp looking two door hardtop with his earnings as a bag boy at Busby's Grocers on the condition he solemnly promise that he not drive it until after some much needed drivers training when he turned sixteen, nearly a full year away.

Oh, well. George had some other more pressing things on his mind anyway, mainly a certain girl he had met at Joey Erickson's party last night. He couldn't explain why she still stuck in his thoughts despite the head splitting after effects of drinking too much straight Vodka at the bash. George first saw the girl across Joey's crowded living room when their eyes met, and sparks flew. Julie was her first name (he just realized something…she never did give her last name). The next thing he knew he found himself sitting on an old couch in the less crowded basement with Julie talking about every silly thing that came into their heads. Even though her pretty features and Farrah Fawcett styled brunette hair made her very attractive, George felt his feelings for her going much deeper than a mere physical attraction. He just felt so…comfortable with her. They wound up necking a little bit, something that George found to be very enjoyable in spite of the fact it made his thumping heart feel like it might be going into some fatal irregular rhythm. After all, he wasn't some experienced ladies' man even if he bragged about kissing at least three girls before, okay, make that two.

Julie seemed to know what she was doing but very primly pulled his hand away when he started reaching for areas he probably shouldn't have. She ended the evening by asking for his phone number, giving him a very long kiss and locking eyes with him for what felt like a full minute before she went back upstairs to talk with her girlfriends, about him no doubt. Even though the room was spinning due to a combination of the booze and Julie, he didn't say no when another kid in the basement lit up a joint and offered him a toke.

As George entered the Orbit, he suddenly realized he felt an odd mixture of anticipation and apprehension at the thought of possibly running into this girl again. What if she happened to be here? What would he say to her? What if she acted differently towards him today? What ifs kept running through his brain as he started bootin' it on the roller boogie rinks polished surface? George enjoyed getting into the music, imagining the free feeling of being on ice, pretending to be some great NHL hockey player like Boston's Bobby Orr. He visualized flying through the air in dramatic fashion after scoring the winning goal in game seven of the Stanley Cup Final (in overtime of course) at least until the illusion shattered when his ineptness on skates became evident every time he bumped into someone or fell. Even with his bad knees George's favorite sports hero Bobby Orr remained about a million times better at skating.

He suffered through the typical disco standards like "Stayin' Alive" by the Bee Gees and "If I Can't Have You" by Yvonne Elliman, not to mention the usual ABBA hook filled harmonies. Great thing was they also put on stuff not considered typical for a disco environment probably because Eddy the DJ possessed a somewhat eclectic taste in music. He played tracks like "My Way" by Sid Vicious, "Ebony Eyes" by Bob Welch, Billy Joel's "My Life" and Boz Skaggs with his big hit the "Lido Shuffle."

Eddy then kept the roller boogie party rockin' with "Just What I Needed" by The Cars, "Still the Same" by Bob Seger, a live version of "Carry on Wayward Son" by Kansas and the wild Wilson sisters of Heart wailing "Barracuda." George even heard (for reasons only the DJ could explain), "Don't Give Up On Us Baby," by David Soul and Al Stewart's "Year Of The Cat."

He didn't see Julie anywhere but met up with a few acquaintances, discussing the previous night's party and where tonight's big events were rumored to be happening. This soon became tiresome however, so George started to walk back home, planning on a relatively quiet evening, maybe inviting a couple friends over to listen to some old records and watch a little TV.

As he neared his home, George could see quite a few cars parked on the normally very quiet street. He soon realized they all belonged to family members, recognizing his Uncle Paul's Ford, Gramma Jeans old Plymouth and Auntie Gina's Cadillac. That's funny, he thought. There wasn't any family event planned for tonight-at least not that he knew of. As he walked in the front door his Uncle Paul waited for him with a look that made it abundantly clear something was very, very, wrong. He would always remember his Uncle sitting him down and telling him the bad news, how his dad's private company jet crashed earlier in the day on a flight to Houston, killing him instantly. He didn't suffer; he could recall his father's brother saying as if such a meaningless consolation mattered at all to a fifteen-year-old boy whose life had just been altered – forever.

That evening and the days to follow were like some hellish nightmare, his grief stricken mother breaking his heart with her tears. He knew that nothing he could do would be able to relieve her pain. George later looked back to that experience as the one defining moment that made him grow up, changed him from a spoiled boy into a great man of character and resolve. He swore that whatever he did with the rest of his life, one thing was sure; he would do something important someday to make his mother as well as his father's memory proud...

After leaving the Generals presence, Rance walked back to his quarters giving him some much needed time to calm down and gather his thoughts. His aide, Major Mitchell was nowhere to be seen, probably because the orientation session finished up so much earlier than expected. Rance didn't mind. Considering the mood he found himself in after finding out about McLellan's true motives, he didn't really feel like being around anyone anyway.

He started to feel more focused by the time he made it back to his little living space. Since becoming a Christian Rance had experienced several "bad days" and found out the hard way that prayer and studying the Word of God became even more important during these times of turmoil. After praying for guidance, Rance began reading the old book style bible he managed to smuggle on board. He found the hands on feel comfortably reassuring compared to the many illegal underground digital and holographic Bibles now available on the Supernet. He found Romans 8:18-28 especially useful in helping him deal with the Dictator not supplying medical care for his father, indirectly causing his death. This scripture teaches: "We know that all things work together for good to those who love God, to those who are called according to his purpose." Knowing and believing that God is in control of all things, even his father's loss, it became clear what Rance needed to do: forgive the old man and pray for him. After all he had the assurance in the Word that he would be meeting his Christian dad again. The General's status as a doomed unbeliever and also his leader provided Rance with two clear reasons for immediately getting on his knees before Father God and praying for the man.

"Dear Father in Heaven," Rance began, "I humbly approach you and ask your forgiveness for my anger at my earthly leader General McLellan. I ask for your Holy Spirit to guide his leadership and watch over him and everyone else on the journey we are about to undertake. If it be your will Lord I ask for your presence to touch his heart and move him to accept Jesus as his personal Lord and Savior. I ask you these things in the name of Jesus Christ whose name is exalted above all others. Amen."

As always, Rance felt calmed and reassured after studying the Word and praying. Although he still sometimes contemplated the emptiness of life's earthly accomplishments, he now felt most thankful for the gift of eternal salvation Jesus Christ gave him and all undeserving sinners.

In spite of this peace, Rance still had a lot to absorb and think about. Before being brought to the *Hornet*, his life consisted of just two things: serving in the overwhelmed Detroit hospital and preparing for the imminent return of Jesus Christ as foretold in Revelation 1:7. Even though no one except God the Father knew the exact moment of the Judgment, current world events made it clear time now grew very short. Thankfully the Lord would soon be returning to set up Gods Kingdom, establishing a Paradise on Earth during the one thousand year millennial period. He found it easy enough to accept that, because after all the scriptures predicted Jesus Christ's physical return, but God's Holy Word mentioned nothing about the amazing things he'd seen and heard since arriving on board the USS *Hornet*. Rance needed to pray for understanding when it came to the Generals twisted scheme to embark on an expedition of conquest to another planet in a distant star system. Where did such an outlandish thing fit into God's plan? To find some answers, Rance turned back to the Bible. He spent the rest of that day and evening studying and meditating on Scripture, finding nothing that would either support or contradict the mission they were undertaking. Genesis 1:1 does say that "In the beginning God created the heavens and the earth," Genesis 1:16 going on to say "He also made the stars." Since God created the universe, Rance reasoned, logically he also made any alien life that may exist on the planets revolving around those distant stars. Only God knew what the outcome of their journey and resulting war would be, but Rance knew one thing for sure, the Creator wanted him on board the *Hornet* for a reason. Like all believers in whatever situation they found themselves, he had one assignment that remained a clear duty. The Great Commission commanded him to preach fearlessly the Good News of Jesus Christ and His priceless gift of eternal life.

After saying his evening prayers and before drifting off to sleep, Rance resolved that he would soon make contact with any other Christians on board the ship and organize some organized worship services, either with or without the consent of the General.

Major Mitchell arrived at Rance's quarters punctually at 06:30, outlining the jam-packed learning day he had planned. "After we have a quick breakfast, I thought we'd start with Main Engineering, the 'guts' of the ship if you will, but of course all of this is at your discretion Sir…Sir?"

Rance allowed his mind to wander back to what he considered his main role on board ship, the job of saving souls, and found himself uncharacteristically daydreaming as the Major outlined their day. He still had a secular job to do however, and as Ephesians 6:5 stated Christians needed to be obedient to those who are considered their masters. Colossians 3:23 also made it clear that whatever work your involved in, do it heartily, as to the Lord and not to men. It was about time he got his act together so he could become what God clearly wanted him to be, the finest Fighter Operations Tactical Advisor his unique set of experience and skills allowed him to be. Those pilot's lives depended on him being at his very best. "Yes Major that'll be fine. I trust your judgment about what areas of the ship you want to show me first. After today's touring is finished, I also need to hear any ideas you have regarding the fighter pilot training curriculum we need to develop."

Major Mitchell was taken aback by his superior officer's request for his input, probably unused to being taken too seriously as an officer at his young age. "Yes Sir! Actually I do have several strategies I've been working on and would welcome the opportunity to have you look at them. I just wanted to tell you again General Edwards, how much I look forward to working with you!"

The young man although sincere and probably bursting with raw potential reminded Rance of an adoring puppy ready to jump all over his master. Hopefully though, he wasn't too full of the type of childish gung ho like enthusiasm that could get him and others killed in action. Rance knew that if Mitchell showed too much immaturity it would then be up to him as his commander to try and develop the boy into a seasoned officer. "Don't mention it Major. Just get me to the cafeteria. I'm starved!"

Major Mitchell brought Rance to the Orbitz Recreation Area, a vast mall like district of the ship comprising the better part of two decks.

After finishing breakfast at the 'Cosmic Food Plaza' the two officers took a short walk through a section of exclusive shops reserved for higher ranking officers, with Rance trying hard not to look like some proverbial country bumpkin visiting the big city for the first time. That 1930's Irving Berlin standard "Puttin' on the Ritz" emanated from somewhere, very appropriate for this area still dealing in good old fashioned American dollars instead of Lanza's world credits. Stores like Neiman Marcus sold the latest fashions from Dolce & Gabbana, Armani, Gucci and Christian Louboutin. Every luxury and extravagance must have been available in these boutiques and once again the disparity between what he had seen in burning Detroit compared to the wealth of the *Hornet* made him want to vomit the meal still digesting in his gut. He had a feeling that he would be more comfortable doing his shopping in the lower class enlisted ranks department stores.

They boarded the bullet and soon after arrived at the engineering/engine room department of the ship contained in the very aft section of the USS *Hornet*.

Before starting the tour of the 'heart' of the warship, Major Mitchell took Rance to an anteroom containing the protective gear they would have to don before going into the engine room. "These suits contain a microscopic layer of Helenium," explained the Major. "Anyone entering this area has to wear them for protection against the harmful levels of electromagnetic energy that's present. If we went in there without shielding we might survive physically but would most likely wind up with an irreversible form of paranoid delusional psychosis. Very unpleasant."

After putting on the loosely fitting garments resembling a cross between a space suit and an old radiation protective outfit, Rance followed Mitchell into the inner sanctum of stolen alien technology. "You may notice a feeling of dizziness or light-headedness Sir," said Mitchell as he stopped and looked back at Rance. "If you feel like you're going to pass out or start experiencing delusions please let me know. Harmful effects are rare but do occasionally happen."

Rance didn't say anything, just motioned for the aide to start with the tour. So far he felt okay, the most noticeable annoyance being an invasive hum penetrating his brain and causing the hairs on the back of his neck to stand on end.

After going through a heavily guarded security checkpoint, the Major led him into a control room containing seating stations for about a dozen technicians with one person in a seat on a higher vantage point somewhat above and behind the others. Major Mitchell pointed out this person as being the Control Room Supervisor, who acknowledged their presence by giving a barely perceptible nod. Rance couldn't help but notice that in addition to the thirteen engineering crewmembers, the room contained two security troops who appeared to be very businesslike, their plasma weapons aimed directly at the two newcomers. They personified the phrase shoot first and ask questions later thought Rance as he glared right back at them. Rance feared no mere man, knowing only God deserved such respect.

    The Major explained that the angled windows of the control room gave a clear view of the Main Propulsion Unit Grids, comprising an area at least as large as a full city block and probably ten stories high. The area appeared to have some sort of a black asphalt surface with various white and yellow lines painted on in strange designs, resembling a form of alien looking hieroglyphics. In actual fact as Mitchell pointed out, these were engineering markings in the Gray's native language. He didn't explain (probably because he didn't really know) why markings in English wouldn't have sufficed just as well. Off to a distance of one to two hundred meters sat three large cylindrical objects arranged in a triangular configuration lit up with brilliant arcs of electricity zapping between them at random intervals. The strong smell of ozone hung in the air along with something much harder to place, an oppressive feeling like a murky fog all around them. Ghost hunters from another era would most likely have termed it "that haunted house atmosphere."

    As Rance bent over to look at the propulsion unit in order to get a view closer to the technician's vantage point, something else grabbed his attention. There was a man suspended in mid-air approximately three meters directly in front of the control room windows. He appeared unconscious; wearing only stained white boxer shorts with numerous tubes and hoses violating his near emaciated body. The man's nails obviously had not been trimmed in quite some time and his unkempt hair blew around in a cushion of air, evidently explaining what force kept him floating in front of them. "That Sir is the host," said Major Mitchell when he noticed Rance staring at the poor wretch.

"It allows the psychotronic hyper drive apparatus to function according to design parameters. The host is also used to target our destination once we are underway. If you have any questions I am sure these technical experts would be happy to answer them," he pointed towards the control room personnel.

"I have one question," said Rance, barely able to restrain his rage, "why is that man being subjected to the harmful effects of the electromagnetic energy without any protective gear?"

Major Mitchell and some of the control room technicians exchanged nervous glances. Apparently the thought of having any concern for the host's safety never occurred to them, at least not outside of a strictly academic engineering standpoint.

"Why, Sir," said Mitchell. "I thought the General explained the...ah... expendable nature of the psychotronic subjects that we use. Some even last up to a few weeks as host, but we literally have thousands of them ready to ensure... uninterrupted service. Situated slightly lower than this depleted and almost drained host you will see another fresh subject that is ready to take its place. Battery would perhaps be the best analogy for their function here."

Sure enough as Rance leaned over the control panel to look through the glass another man became visible, identical to the first except for shorter hair and closely trimmed nails hovering on a cushion of air.

He had seen enough. "Major Mitchell," he barked out. "Follow me." He stormed out with the perplexed Major following close behind. As he pulled off the protective gear Rance realized it was high time he and his aide had a little talk. Finding an unused office in the anteroom he told his aide to sit down. Mitchell looked a little scared as Rance, while still standing, began to speak. "Major, I'm sure you know I'm a Christian, right?" The young man nodded as Rance continued. "I don't expect you to share my faith, though I would be overjoyed at the prospect of sharing my beliefs with you sometime soon if you'd like. However, since I'm a Believer in Jesus Christ, there are a few things you need to know about me. Firstly, I believe that life, yes even the life of a so called host, is a sacred gift from the Creator and should never be taken lightly or snuffed out. The callous disregard for the sanctity of human life I just witnessed in there angers me beyond belief and is an attitude that I as a Christian can't be part of. I have two choices when I'm faced with something so blatantly contrary to my Faith. Number one, I can go back into that room, take one of those guard's plasma weapons and destroy the control booth as well as the hyper drive. That action would of course result in many deaths and probably only slightly delay Our Great Leader from fulfilling his sick ambition. My second choice, and the one I've decided to follow, is to try and work within the system as a Christian. With your assistance I want to develop the very best Fighter Pilot Tactics program possible, however I'll never bend or change my Christian ethics and beliefs. What you also need to know is that the path I'm choosing is the tough one, making the right choice usually is, but my decision will also impact you significantly. You're a bright young man; the fact that you're already a Major is proof enough of that. It doesn't take a genius to figure out that if you continue serving as my aide any chance you have to make Colonel any time soon is shot all to heck. I *intend* on rocking this boat. That is why if you want out I'll sign your transfer papers immediately with no hard feelings. All I ask is that if you're leaving my service, you let me know right now so I have time to start searching for a suitable replacement."

 Major Mitchell looked like a six year old who just had his feelings hurt but Rance could also see the intensity in his eyes showing a resolve and maturity out of place with the youthful face. "Sir, I meant what I said before. I consider it a real honor to serve as your aide. The fact that you are a Christian doesn't change your war record or reputation as an officer and a gentleman. I apologize if my explanation regarding the hosts seemed rather callous. I'm not excusing my attitude Sir, in fact I know my own parents would've been ashamed of my conduct were they still alive, it's just that everyone on this ship is encouraged to think of those people as something less than human. I guess I started feeling that way too in spite of knowing deep down inside it was wrong. All I can tell you is this: if you still want me as your assistant I'm in - for the long term. And I don't give a damn about being promoted!"

Rance smiled. The kid did have some character after all. "I'm glad we've gotten that out of the way. I'll let you continue on with the tour of the ship. Just promise me one thing. If you're going to show me anything else that's going to upset my Christian sensibilities please warn me first because those people in the control room don't know how close they came to dying today." The semi grin still on his face made the young Major think the comment a joke but Rance didn't have the heart to tell him the truth-he had damn near decided on taking the first more violent course of action. As they left the room, Rance silently asked the Lord for forgiveness. He had almost taken the drastic and irreversible step of trying to correct things on his own instead of leaving it all in God's very capable hands.

The next part of the ship on Major Mitchell's itinerary proved to be the immense Environmental Sciences department on M Deck. The aroma assailing Rance's nostrils as they got out of the bullet compartment made it clear that in addition to all its other treasures, the *Hornet* also carried live animals.

The Major introduced him to the Head of the Department, Dr. Hugo Speer who because of his thick German accent and high intensity level immediately evoked in Rance some memories of an old classic film he had once seen. The obviously eccentric man wore classic wayfarer style eyeglasses.

"It's goot to meet you my boy." said the Doctor of Environmental Studies as he grabbed onto Rance, eagerly launching into an explanation of his sector. "Velcome to mine vorld. Actually, I should be saying zee future vorld of everyone on board zis vessel. You see ve have been busy zese last few years locating, cataloging and storing every known surviving piece of flora and fauna on zat dying eco system of ours down below. Not an easy task I might add, especially lately vith all zee shit happening all around us."

Surprisingly in spite of the thick, guttural German inflection in the man's speech, the word 'shit' came out crystal clear. "As you can see on zose animal enclosure levels ve have several dozen examples of each sex of zee larger quadrupeds used for human consumption. Zee females of each species vill be implanted with fertilized ova once ve reach our destination, enabling us to rapidly jump-start a breeding program to establish a good genetic cross section of each species. Ven zat is done ve can start supplying stock for food production. It's not just zee species zats ve eats however. Ve are also bringing along examples of most land mammals as vell as a good cross section of major sea dvelling life, even zough apparently zis planet ve are colonizing has more of a desert environment. Vonce getting zere ve may be able to terra form portions of zis new vorld to become more earth like; somethings ve cannot really assess till arriving at our destination. Zere may also be issues of compatibility between native life forms and our own earth species. Since even on a spaceship as gigantic as zeese ve still can't bring zee numbers of each life form ve vould like, in many cases ve are storing and reanimating certain varieties such as many plants, fungi and some mammals."

Rance and Major Mitchell, having great difficulty in not cracking a smile at the doctor's hilarious rapid fire vocalizations, were saved by Speer needing to go personally supervise a junior biologist. Apparently assisting with preparing a holo tech disk on "the breeding habits of the Snowy Owl" was something pressing enough to require the personal attention of the Head of the Department.

Although Rance found this to be a remarkable part of the ship, they had to get on with the tour as time was getting short. The two of them needed to at least get started today working on more important matters such as the Fighter School curriculum.

Stepping off of the bullet, Rance's aide explained why this unspectacular looking little department with signage reading Child Psychology/Pilot Project 1 could be important enough to merit a stop. "This is a special program that the General has given his blessing to although I don't believe he's ever actually been down here. Basically five or six years ago some bright child psychologist in the Department of Orphanages came up with the idea of raising early intervention orphans, babies put into care shortly after birth, in highly specialized settings. The goal of this experiment is to try and provide the ideal conditions for a child from birth to adult hood in order to produce the Superior American. This includes surrogate parents, limited contact with outsiders and extremely supportive learning structures. I believe this first batch of children is about five years of age by now. They won't let us actually go in and see the kids of course, but I thought it might be interesting if we were to speak to the Director of the project, Dr. Janice Vandenburg. She's a very interesting lady."

Rance followed the Major into a reception area where they stood for a few moments while waiting for Dr. Vandenburg to see them. The timeless sounds of "Don't Go Breaking My Heart" by Elton John and Kiki Dee emanated from the reception desk.

Unexpectedly, as if from a drug induced vision, Rance heard familiar laughter, a distinctive voice once very important and meaning a great deal to him. Turning towards the source of this soothing and comfortable sound, he found himself face to face with his former fiancée Lieutenant Commander Christine St. James, walking into the room with another female officer. He saw the beautiful face, the striking eyes and lovely mouth suddenly turn from happy and carefree to mean and hard when she finally comprehended who stood in front of her. His one-time lover looked like she had just seen a ghost and in some ways perhaps she had, an apparition from her former life, a happy time that he had thrown away. Immediately she turned around and was gone, leaving Rance shaken and needing to get away and be alone. Making an excuse about not feeling well he found the nearest washroom, telling the Major to wait outside while he sat in one of the stalls silently mourning her loss, unleashing a long forgotten pain that was still raw, deep and fresh like it happened just yesterday.

CHAPTER 8

"Hello Troops! How the hells it goin' out there? Hope you're settlin' down with a few joints, a couple beers and a good friend-if ya all know what I mean. I've got some absolutely fantabulous tunes for ya today… that was Harlequin, "You are the Light" and Collective Soul with "Run." Comin' up your gonna hear Joe Jackson with his big hit "Is She Really Going Out With Him" and XTC's classic "Making Plans For Nigel" but first a song that became legendary way back in 1979. You're askin' what's this dude talkin' about? Well I'll give ya a hint: LA band, summer of '79…you guessed it– what else but The Knack with "My Sharona" on Comm-Rad 1 the music source of the USS *Hornet*…

   It was the summer of '79. George's mother had reluctantly, after shedding a few tears agreed to let him take his Chevelle on a road trip with two of his friends, Jimmy Madison and Gerry Ferrel. After specifying a veritable encyclopedic array of conditional rules for him to follow, he and his two friends started out on the trip along the Pacific Coast Highway to the Bay area where they were going to stay the weekend at his Auntie June's house in Oakland. Not that newly licensed George planned on spending an overly ample amount of time hanging out with his family anyway.
   No, the real reason for the road trip if truth were told was to check out the (according to legend) exotic variety of Northern California girls. That being said, however, George had done a whole heck of a lot of growing up since the death of his father the year before. He didn't spend undue amounts of time hanging out with his friends; usually ensuring his homework came first. Consequently his grades improved dramatically. In addition, George rarely used drugs or drank excessively anymore, something his still

grieving mother was especially thankful for. He still remained driven by the strong resolve he felt immediately after his dad died. The desire to try and make life a little easier for his mother, alone now except for him, his little sister and a few close extended family members consumed him. Thankfully Hell Cat Aircraft had given his mom a very generous pay out, after all, negligence on the part of the company-employed pilot of the private jet caused her husband's death. So money was not a problem, but his mother's emotional health definitely continued to be a concern, with George quite often hearing her sobbing during the middle of the night. She didn't even watch her favorite soap, *"The Edge of Night"* anymore. George didn't even know if he himself had properly grieved for his dad. Sometimes he would think about the man wondering why he couldn't remember his face clearly anymore. He had cried when first hearing the news but then needed to bottle up those emotions in order to be strong for his mother and sister. The death of her father hit his sister Joanie really hard but she seemed to be coping with it by literally burying herself in an endless array of school related activities. Every so often he gave Joanie a hug, just to reassure her she had a big brother who still cared. Other than those brief moments however, he didn't really see his sister a whole bunch.

    George also started giving his future a lot of thought. Although sure he would be going to college he didn't know for certain what career choice to follow afterwards, although he had some semi formed ideas. His Grampa's tales of his exploits as a Marine during World War 2, killing Japs, and raising hell in various bars and whorehouses throughout the Pacific made a very real impression on his young, suggestible mind. Those stories and watching John Wayne in a late night showing of *"The Green Berets"* almost made him decide on a military career, but he still wasn't sure. He also found himself drawn to the simple black and white, no nonsense realities of engineering, a safe if not wholly satisfying choice.

Something in the back of his mind, he imagined it to be his dead fathers voice, told him that his decision about what path to take had greater importance and cosmic significance than it did for other kids his age. He got the feeling deciding on engineering would be a great tragedy. The voice told him true greatness awaited him if he chose a military career.

George occasionally asked himself a hypothetical question: what would have happened if Julius Caesar decided on being an engineer and building roads in the provinces instead of being one of history's greatest conquerors? The simple answer was Rome probably wouldn't have had so many roads to build without a man like Caesar conquering those provinces in the first place. On the other hand, engineering would be so damn…easy.

Oh well… he still had some time to decide about his future, but right now he and his friends were going to have one freakin' wild weekend! Depending of course on the availability and quality of the female companionship they managed to find and charm.

Right now though, a long drive lay ahead of them before getting anywhere near Oakland and George looked forward to the tunes they were going to hear on the AM/FM/eight track custom sound system he had just installed in his blue Chevy. After leaving Carmel, the boys were listening to KFRC a pretty good top 40 station out of San Francisco, playing "Gold" by John Stewart for at least the third time in the last hour. His friends Jimmy and Gerry were also getting pretty excited finally realizing that George's mother wouldn't be able to sabotage this long anticipated trip after all. Jimmy, sitting in the front passenger seat cranked the volume as "What a Fool Believes" by the Doobie Brothers came on the radio, followed by one of George's favorite songs "Cruel to be Kind" by Nick Lowe.

George couldn't wipe the smile off his face as the miles slipped away beneath the wheels of the old Chevelle while somewhere in the far off future an old debauched man listened to Cheap Trick and dreamed of his youth…

After a few minutes sitting alone in the washroom stall and grieving the past, Rance pulled himself together. He went to the Lord in prayer whereupon the Holy Spirit reminded him of the scripture Isaiah 40:29; He gives strength to the weary and increases the power of the weak.

Even though obviously still somewhat preoccupied with the brief, yet traumatic encounter with his former fiancée Christine St. James, he knew he had a duty to try and give Dr. Vandenburg his full attention as she explained her child rearing pilot project. Major Mitchell had characterized Dr. Vandenburg as a very interesting lady but after meeting her Rance felt he might have understated the facts. The good Doctor, probably in her mid-forties, looking like some Dickens era schoolmistress, also exuded an air of quiet, old world elegance. Most experts considered her to be the preeminent expert in the field of child psychology in the United States, maybe even the entire world.

"Thank you for honoring us with your presence General Edwards," she said. "We aren't used to that many high ranking officers visiting our locale. Except for your aide the Major here taking us under his wing so to speak, we almost feel as if we are a backwater, there are so many other projects well deserving of attention on board this vessel. Thankfully, our Glorious Leader General McLellan thought us justified in receiving some modest space and funding."

The way Dr. Vandenburg emphasized 'Glorious Leader' she reminded Rance of a gung ho Political Officer he once knew on board the USS *Washington* whose loyalty had gotten him nothing but an early, watery grave at the bottom of the North Sea.

"We like to think that we are well deserving of the meager support we do get. I want to bring your attention to the displays in this area General," she said, pointing at several holographic monitors showing some of the innocent and unknowing six-year-old subjects of the experiment. "As you can see by the activities that are being displayed, we have organized a rigid, orderly setting for these subjects to grow and thrive in. I based my original premise on a quite simple notion. I looked back in American History to find the one era that, although far from perfect produced the most stable, well-rounded individuals of all time. Of course I am talking about the Baby Boom generation, from 1946 until around 1964, specifically those raised in traditional two parent, upper middle class families in the 1950's. What we have done is to place these orphans into a simulated 1958 World, complete with characteristic housing from that time period on a tree lined street, apparently loving parents, a school as well as the archetypal recreational activities for the time. Of course we had no difficulty getting orphans for the program, plentiful as they've now become. No, the real challenge was getting the surrogate parents willing to give up many years of their lives to act in what is essentially a make believe existence. General McLellan solved that little dilemma for us by offering certain suitable political prisoners a simple choice: participate in the pilot or die. Most, but not all chose the former option. Encouragingly, we have started to see evidence that some of the surrogate couples are starting to become genuinely affectionate to each other and also to their adopted children, something that promises long term sustainability and success of this program. In order to be successful here the objective is to shift our American society back to the elements that led to successful child rearing and productive citizenship in our distant past. Travelling to a new planet presents the opportunity to establish a true American utopia without any negative historical baggage. Do you have any questions General?"

With all of the strange things he'd seen recently, Rance almost imagined himself in some bizarre alternate dimension. What was the name of the popular old television show his great grandparents spoke of? Was it *The Twilight Zone*?

Ah well...looked like it was up to him to ask the tough questions on this ship. "Dr. Vandenburg I...uh applaud your efforts to raise these orphans with a measure of stability and care even if there are some...deceptive elements to their surroundings. However, I do have an important question. Since one of the hallmarks of the 1950's era, please correct me if I'm wrong, would have been most people's very strong belief in an all-powerful Creator, is there any type of Faith based instruction for these children?"

The doctor coughed and sputtered before answering. "Of course not! We teach them to always honor and follow President Eisenhower, the Great Leader of their simulated era, not some pagan idol!" she said, venom spiking her words. She glanced at Major Mitchell with a betrayed expression before continuing. "General Edwards, your rank may carry some weight on this vessel, considering that it is a warship, but I refuse to follow your primitive superstitious belief systems. Of course I am a humanistic atheist as all intellectuals and scientists must *always* be. I believe that only through mankind's own efforts is it possible to achieve anything close to perfection. Now if you will please excuse me I have work to do. Good day." She walked back to the displays, leaving Rance alone with an apologetic Major Mitchell.

"I'm sorry Sir," he said under his breath. "I didn't know she felt so strongly about Christians."

Rance wasn't upset. After all, the Bible predicted how believers would be persecuted and mistreated in the Last

Days. "Don't worry about it Major. Why don't you show me our offices so we can get started on doing what they're actually paying us for?"

Soon they were in their workplace, a small sign outside the entrance stating:

Fighter Operations Tactical Officer
Brigadier General Rance Edwards

The space comprised three large offices, a conference room boasting the latest in holographic learning aids capable of comfortably accommodating approximately one hundred pilots and a small reception area. Unfortunately no receptionist was included. "That's me I guess," said the Major when Rance pointed that glaring vacancy out to him. Their offices were located conveniently close to the fighter pilot ready room and hangar on K-Deck.

The rest of that first day in their little administrative center they devoted mainly to getting "on line" with the Supernet database of the *Hornet* and learning how the interactive learning systems functioned.

When Rance checked his mailbox, he found two messages waiting; one the standard log on welcome but the other communication revealed itself to be anything but typical. It was a very brief text message from Christine asking to meet him after work at the cafeteria near his quarters on H Deck, saying simply "We need to talk." At first Rance wasn't so sure that would be a good idea, not looking forward to more of those long submerged emotions coming to the surface again.

After leaving work for the day and going back to his berth and praying about the situation however, he realized meeting with her and resolving some of these issues would be necessary no matter how uncomfortable it might be. If they were going to coexist on a ship even as large as this one then they both needed to have some type of closure regarding their former relationship. Rance still felt some foreboding in his heart as he entered the cafeteria and at once recognized Christine's lovely face, knowing every familiar little laugh line and feature. Even now, after all that had happened, just looking at her stirred up those same old feelings, the feelings of love, of caring, of belonging... of wanting her. She had a unique beauty, with a touch of Eastern European ancestry being evident in her features. The combination of delicate full lips, high cheekbones, brown eyes sparkling with flecks of green and yellow, along with her long brown blonde chunked hair cut in the latest style, resulted in one very stunning woman. Not to mention the hourglass figure with the luscious full breasts, one of the things in addition to her lively intelligence that had attracted him to her that first day they met.

But all that happened a long time ago... he now noticed that she wasn't sitting alone. A man sat across from her, somehow all too familiar even though Rance knew he had never met him. Rance then recalled seeing this man's face just yesterday in an old movie on the *Hornet's* Entertainment system, solving the mystery of why the features looked so recognizable. He could have been a twin to a long dead actor from the film *"Logan's Run,"* another one of General McLellan's favorite movies. Not that the guy's appearance could be called anything but a trivial detail anyway. All that really mattered was the obvious fact that Christine seemed to have a connection with the man and he with her, a familiarity that Rance recognized instantly as meaning they were lovers. What the hell did he expect? He couldn't have asked her to wait for him for God only knew how long until he found what he needed to find: the gift of Salvation. Besides, he broke up with her. Even so, it hurt. Every pore in his body screamed out the injustice of it all and how Christine must still love him, in spite of everything.

Not anymore he told himself as somehow, only through a concerted force of will he managed to approach their booth. As if in a stupor he heard Christine introduce him to her husband, Colonel Rick Santchez, one of the *Hornet's* shuttle pilots. He shook Rick's hand, hearing him say, "You two probably have a lot to talk about. Go ahead. I'll see you a little later honey," the look they gave each other as he left spoke volumes. The simple fact he could be that at ease giving his partner this chance to clear up some unpleasant "baggage" from her past also said a lot about the man. He had confidence and class, Rance could grant him that much.

Santchez left, leaving them alone. For a few seconds he just stared at his former lover knowing how much more painful this reunion could become but unwilling to look away, almost like a moth that is drawn towards the flame.

Finally she broke the ice. "It's good to see you again Rance. I see you're a General now. Congratulations." she said, no hint of emotion showing in her eyes. "As you can see, I received an upgrade too…they made me a Colonel when I transferred over to the Space Branch, but coming here wasn't even about the promotion. I actually enjoy what I'm doing now, assisting Doctor Vandenburg with her project and best of all, I finally get to use that child psychology degree. What about you?" She came across as distant, making Rance feel like she didn't really care what response he gave, but just wanted to get through these formalities before the real guts of this caustic little meeting could begin.

"I'm Director of Fighter Operations, Tactical Training, but that doesn't matter… Christine, there are some things I need to tell you. First of all I need to apologize. I'm so, so sorry for what I did to you, did to us, I know it doesn't make any diff…"

Christine cut in. "How dare you!" she blurted out, most of the people in the cafeteria turning towards them as her voice grew louder. "You bastard! You think an apology is going to do any good now? I love…I mean… loved you damn it! And you threw it all away! And for what? Did you find whatever in hell it was that you were looking for Rance? Was it worth it?" She turned her face away, looking at the ceiling and sobbing.

"Christine, this may not be the best time for me to tell you this, but I wanted you to know I did find what I was looking for…His name was Jesus Christ."

Christine managed to suppress her crying in order to respond to that comment. Sarcasm tainted her laugh. "You've got to be kidding me! Your telling me that you destroyed what we had so you could become some…some…brain addled Christian?" She had to look away, biting her lip to stop from starting to sob again before she could continue. "You know what? I don't care. It's actually a good thing all this… shit happened. I never would have met Rick if you hadn't gone crazy like you did, and I'll tell you something else…he makes me very happy. I love him Rance."

Rance closed his eyes, saying a small prayer in his head and focusing on getting through this difficult reunion. Later on though he knew what she had just said would cut him to the core. Rance knew he still loved her, always would love her. "I uh…I'm happy for you Christine. My Christian Faith makes me happy too, happier than I've ever been in my entire life. I'm actually at peace for the first time. I now know what my true purpose is…at last." His voice was starting to crack. "Sometime…hopefully sometime soon I would really like to explain this precious gift of Salvation and how you can have it too."

"Don't start preaching to me!" said Christine, her icy tone making it very clear to Rance this was neither the right time or place to further discuss his beliefs. There were some other things that needed to be said though.

"Christine, you need to know I wish things could've turned out differently, but of course that's all just talk... it's too late for any of that now. One thing I do know is that we have to put all this behind us. Even though this is a big ship there's still a good chance we may run into each other once in a while, and because of that I think we should at least be on speaking terms. I'm willing to give it a try ...if you are. Whaddya say?"

Christine started to say something, and then thought better of it. "That's fine. Look, I think we've said everything that we needed to." she said, standing up and extending her hand. "Good luck Rance. Have a nice life."

Rance took her hand, feeling (or was it just his imagination?) the familiar electricity between them when they touched. "Goodbye Christine. It was nice to see you again." The strange formality of the words suddenly hit him.

Then she left, leaving Rance alone with his thoughts. At that very moment in one of life's little ironies their favorite song "You and I" by Eddie Rabbitt & Crystal Gayle came on the cafeterias sound system as if to rub salt in his wounded heart. It would be extremely difficult and awkward to see Christine with her new husband, even briefly. Rance pushed that unpleasant possibility out of his head as he left the cafeteria. He needed to get some shuteye, something Rance knew could be very elusive tonight. Regardless, he had to try as tomorrow promised to be a very busy day.

After a fidgety night, Rance arrived at the office at around 04:30, planning to get an early start on the day's tasks. He had already identified several priorities he needed to fast track in order to get a proper fighter pilot curriculum organized. The first thing on the agenda might also become the most challenging: getting certified on the F-72 Sparrow Hawk and getting in some flight hours. He needed the ability to not only fly it but also know every little nuance of the craft. Fighter pilots would never listen to some "desk jockey" even a one-time war hero if he didn't know the F-72 at least as well as they did, preferably better. Rance immersed himself into the holographic flight manuals, becoming more and more amazed the further he explored. This fighter allowed a pilot to actually merge himself with the machine, or more correctly, the machine became an extension of the pilot and his thoughts. Each F-72 sported its own little modified version of the *Hornet's* hyper drive system. Although the F-72 used conventional looking controls, more for operator familiarity than any other reason, it also utilized the pilots mind to enhance flight performance. Quite simply, previously impossible maneuvers now became a reality, the speed of thought being the only limiting factor to where or how you wanted the ship to go. The thing could almost turn right angle corners at hundreds of thousands of kilometers per hour even when operated in atmospheric conditions close to a planet's surface, G force shielding preventing that once restrictive factor on performance from having any impact. Inside the little cockpit compartment, the pilot remained slightly out of phase to their normal physical environment, being literally in a different dimension while controlling the fighter. This permitted the outside of the fighter to perform stunning maneuvers without negatively affecting the operator inside it. Flying the thing looked easy in the manuals but as Rance quickly found out in the simulator program – it wasn't. You had a stick just like the old F-22, but then you used visualization techniques to picture it going faster, turning at impossible angles and stopping with absolutely no deceleration time at all. Obviously it would take Rance some time to get the hang of a flying method so radically unconventional. He had crashed his simulated F-72 several times by the time Major Mitchell came in to the office promptly at exactly 06:30.

"Good Morning General," he said. "I see your getting an early start today. After we spoke yesterday about my ideas regarding the training curriculum I took the liberty of putting together a few simulations for you to consider. If you would like I…"

Without warning the "General Quarters" alarm klaxon, so familiar to Rance from his years on the USS *Washington* started ringing out which cut off the mellow background music, "Rock with You" by Michael Jackson. A voice came on the audio system announcing "Battle stations-this is not a drill!" making it clear to everyone on board the USS *Hornet* how something, somewhere must be profoundly amiss. Rance and Major Mitchell proceeded to their assigned area of responsibility; the Main Battle Bridge, their role being to give fighter related tactical advice to Command Officers.

As they stepped onto the Bridge, General McLellan could be seen consulting with General Wilbur Pattinson, the slovenly, graying and overweight nominal commander of the ship and several other high-ranking officers. The other fifty or sixty assorted officers, tactical advisors and technicians all had their eyes riveted on the huge holographic display dancing in vivid colors high above the huge room. The strikingly lifelike image showed a triangular shaped object Rance assumed to be another unknown spacecraft. According to the distance, altitude and speed counters on the display, this "bogey" rapidly approached the *Hornet*, being only two hundred kilometers away at roughly the same orbit.

One of the harried technicians yelled out "Communication just received from the bogey sir. They say the name of their vessel is the World Federation Warship *Charles de Gaulle* and that they are"… the man paused as if making sure he had heard the message correctly, "…demanding our immediate surrender…"

CHAPTER 9

"Hi folks… You're listening to Captain Dan here on Comm-Rad 1 your voice of the USS *Hornet*. That of course was The Human League, "Don't You Want Me?" You also just heard two of my personal favorites, Depeche Mode with "Just Can't Get Enough" and the Ramones doin' "Rock N Roll High School." Comin' up we've got some Automatic 7 acing their version of The Psychedelic Furs "Pretty in Pink" but this next one I'm dedicating to Generals McLellan and Pattinson plus all the other capable high-ranking Officers we have on board. Sometimes junior people, like me for instance, we don't always appreciate just how good our leadership is until things really hit the fan, at times like now. So in respect to all those great men and women, here's my salute to all of you …Ozzy Osbourne from 1981 with "Crazy Train"…enjoy…"

    The last summer night of 1981 arrived quickly for George McLellan, so quickly in fact that recently he had started to develop some troubling second thoughts about the path he would be embarking on Monday morning. George almost wished he had settled on some "easy" career choice but oh no, he had to decide on a military career, applying to the prestigious United States Military Academy at West Point. The letter of recommendation from his local Congressman had been no problem as his father had been friends with the man. It still came as something of a surprise when he had been accepted to the famous school that once trained his Civil War era namesake George Brinton McClellan in addition to the man's adversary Robert E. Lee. It shouldn't have come as a shocker though, not with all the effort George put in during the last two years preparing for that acceptance letter. From the onetime screw up, dope smoking, car wrecking kid he evolved into a responsible, hardworking young man. His academic achievements made his widowed mother proud, only narrowly losing first place in his entire Senior Class to a very nerdy girl by the name of Cathy Olson with the scholastic advantage of not participating in any social activities. As an Officer Candidate, he took all the necessary college prep courses, civics training and second language classes, becoming quite fluent in Spanish. While George's intellect showed dramatic improvement, his physical transformation was probably even more remarkable.

    Knowing the rumors about how tough West Point could be, he enthusiastically embarked on a rigid self-imposed fitness program, now running at least two miles most mornings with a lot of push up and sit ups thrown in for good measure. He took and easily passed West Point's rigorous physical aptitude test administered by the high school football coach, Jimmy Jackson. Partly because Coach Jackson kept encouraging him, during senior year George tried out for and got a spot on the football team. Although not good enough to be starting quarterback, he remained a pretty good backup and got his big chance during an important outing when the star Jake Wilson pulled his hamstring. While definitely not an NFL quality or even college level performance, he managed to avoid getting sacked and threw enough yards to get his team positioned for a rushing touchdown in the dying seconds that won them the game. This suddenly made him the big man on campus. Even though fairly popular before the big game, George also couldn't have been considered the most admired guy either. The plans and preparations for his future Army career meant he just didn't have the time or the inclination to do all the silly little teenage rituals that would have allowed his status to move from the merely "cool" to the "super stud level." In fact he once heard some unknown voice call out "army boy" as he walked down the hall. Not that surprising as it was hard not to notice his shorter military cut hairstyle. But with his previously tenuous position on the football team now solidly cemented, the highly evolved high school pecking order considered him a "jock," with all the cool guys wanting to hang out with him. The hot girls, well they wanted to hang out with him too, just in a very different way. George finished his last year at school basking in that aura of triumph and now here he was on the last night of the summer before catching a plane for West Point first thing Monday morning.

Time just passed too damned fast he thought looking over at his two best friends sharing the Chevelles vinyl upholstered cabin with him, Jimmy Madison and Gerry Ferrel. Last week George had split up with his most recent girlfriend, the slightly crazy Teresa Sacco, who totally flipped out when he ended their one-month long relationship. His poor Chevelle still bore the scratches she inflicted on it later that same night. George ended their thing, not because he didn't like her, but because he knew deep down it would have been impossible to keep it on the rails with him going to West Point and her to UCLA.

Oh well, he thought, listening to "Any Way You Want it" by Journey. It's not like they were planning on getting married anyway. George considered high school dating to be nothing more than an amusing learning experience. Because of his dark movie star good looks he had the good fortune to have enjoyed more than his share of these "educational" experiences. Jimmy and Gerry, well they weren't quite as, how would you put it… knowledgeable in that area of study, which explained why they happened to be hanging out with him on this all-important last night of the summer. Since his two friends had much more difficulty in attracting girls, George sympathetically agreed to take them along in his Blue Chevy and go cruising for chicks. He still considered the two losers to be his best friends after all, so he wanted to make this pivotal evening fun for them as well as for himself. Of course they'd listen to some cool tunes, continuing to wear out the Alice Cooper 8 track listening to the song "Clones (Were All)." He needed to remember everything about this moment for the rest of his life. After all, West Point meant saying goodbye to his present world and accepting his destiny, a career transforming him from a mere high school boy, into a man… no something more than just a mere man… something much more…yes people would soon be looking up to him as …an officer, a gentleman and a great leader…

    The holo-image of the World Federation warship *Charles de Gaulle* changed to one displaying the vessels commander delivering a communiqué on behalf of World Leader Antonio Lanza. The lean, dark face of Captain Julio Vincente Mantano wavered like a mirage before finally stabilizing with the old national, now World anthem "La Marseillaise" playing faintly in the background. Rance recognized Mantano as the idolized so-called "great hero of the Euro-American War," the former Euro fighter pilot responsible for launching the small nuclear missile that destroyed his old ship, the USS *Washington*. Had Rance not been a Christian he could never have forgiven this man for killing his shipmates. His Spanish accent remained noticeable. "Dictator General George McLellan and the crew of the rogue warship USS *Hornet*: World Leader Lanza respectfully orders the immediate surrender of your vessel to the rightful ownership of the World Federation. Section 67, subsection H of the articles of the World Constitution states that any property, technology, and wealth of any kind, real or imagined at the time a nation joins the alliance becomes the property of the Empire, more specifically becoming a personal possession of the Exalted New Caesar Antonio Lanza. We assure you that all crewmembers other than the subversive criminals, Generals

George McLellan and Wilbur Pattinson will be treated humanely as non-combatants to be released after a brief re-education session and chip implantation. We make it clear to you however that disobeying these instructions will be taken as a sign of non-compliance, an event that would unfortunately result in the destruction of the USS *Hornet*. You have one minute to respond to this demand."

The image disappeared, leaving all the now shaken crewmembers (other than Rance who's solid faith in God helped him to remain calm in all circumstances) on the Bridge suddenly looking to General McLellan and the rest of the Staff Officers for instructions.

To his credit, the Great General did not disappoint, if anything firmly in his element dealing with this crisis. "Communications Department!" he yelled out. "I want a one word text response sent to those damned Europeans. The word is the following: 'NUTS!' Some of you amateur historians may recognize it as the same reply General Anthony McAuliffe gave to the Germans at Bastogne during the Battle of the Bulge. Send it now!"

"Yes Sir!" replied the Communications Officer.

"I want to know dimensions, armament; I want to know everything there is to know about that freakin' Euro trash ship! Dammit, how much time do we have? You people…" He said pointing at several of the Bridge crew who seemed frozen, "Don't just stand around waiting for orders, get your asses in gear! I want a full tactical report now!" The Generals authoritative voice immediately had dozens of officers and technicians literally jumping. The Commander in Chief received his report within less than a minute.

Several officers in turn yelled out data. "Enemy vessel is approximately 4200 meters in length - Propulsion unknown but minor subspace wrinkling could indicate hyper drive capabilities - May have plasma or nuclear armament - at present velocity vessel will intercept us in twelve minutes, thirty four seconds."

"Damn!" snarled the General as he shook his head. "That has got to be the most sorry ass tactical report I have ever heard in my life. In other words we know dick all. How in hell did that damned Lanza keep something this big a secret from us? Looks like the bastard was planning on double-crossing me the whole time…shit! …Never mind… all hands prepare for immediate enemy attack." McLellan moved like a dervish, going from station to station personally overseeing their defensive preparations.

"Make sure the main shielding is at full strength, it is? Good. Prepare main plasma weapons for guidance control targeting; tell secondary plasma crews and fifties they can fire at will at targets. Shoot at anything that moves out there in case the enemy has already launched missiles. I want twenty 10 megaton cruise missiles launched at target now with another twenty on standby ready for launch!"

During this whole time Rance and Major Mitchell could only watch these events unfold frustrated and helpless from the sidelines since fighter operations did not seem to be a part of the Generals defensive plan. Rance started to say something to Major Mitchell when without warning time slowed down as some powerful force shot him high up in the air above the Bridge. He noticed with an odd sense of detachment how everyone else in the room including the General also remained suspended. He floated there for longer than would have been possible were they still under the dominion of Earth's gravity, then abruptly found himself hurtling the other way, falling a good ten meters back onto the metal flooring of the Bridge with a hard thump. Breaking the shocked silence, someone yelled out "Must have been a nuke!" As Rance jumped to his feet, he felt miraculously uninjured but judging by the moans and screams around him others weren't as fortunate. Major Mitchell, also unhurt, joined him in searching for the senior officers and technicians who needed assistance. Most of the higher-ranking leaders came through the explosion unscathed, with General George McLellan loudly bellowing rapid fire commands, making it crystal clear he also remained healthy and firmly in charge.

"I need damage reports! Everyone get back to your workstations!" He dragged one man by the collar back to his seat, literally hoisting him up, saying "It's just a broken arm damn you! I need some tactical information! Get me that damage report people!" Many of the most essential crewmembers had now made it back to their stations and within less than a minute managed to compile the information that rapidly flowed to the Bridge into a somewhat coherent status report for the General.

"Damage and tactical reports ready Sir!" called out an African American Major as he activated the main holo array, instantly projecting several essential displays for the benefit of the Officers on the Battle Bridge. One multicolor image visualized strength and impact area of the nuclear explosion that had hit them, another showed speed and location of the enemy vessel with the last displaying the results of the *Hornets* defensive actions thus far. Major Gooding interpreted the data being shown.

"A twenty megaton thermonuclear discharge hit us on our port side approximately two thousand meters amidships. Main shield contained the worst of the blast damages although it appears the strength of the detonation pushed our energy shielding into the side of the *Hornet*, causing a sudden, devastating decompression of the affected area. That area unfortunately happened to include the port side emergency hangar. This event resulted in the loss of fifty two F-72 fighters and at least thirty support technicians. In addition, fifteen deaths have been reported throughout the ship as well as several hundred relatively serious injuries and probably thousands of less seriously wounded suffering from broken bones and soft tissue injuries. Enemy vessel is now approximately four minutes distant from us at its present velocity. Our offensive capability is undamaged. The twenty cruise missiles we launched prior to the blast apparently have been…neutralized. It is now inadvisable to launch the remaining twenty missiles on standby due to the close proximity of the enemy as we would also sustain undesirable blast effects. All main plasma weapons on board the *Hornet* are about to engage our opponent as the vessel is now within range, secondary plasma and fifty caliber gun crews continue to be on orders to shoot appropriate targets at will. No data at this time on how the enemy missile got through our defensive screening. That is the report, Sir!"

 The Major finished his anxious but concise description with a flourish, waiting for further instructions. The General and every other senior officer voiced no further orders for him however as all they could now do was helplessly wait and watch the holographs dancing above them to see how their impressive array of weapons did against their attacker. Rance knew there happened to be one very important thing he personally could do: pray for their safety in the coming battle, reciting the very appropriate words of the 23rd Psalm in a low voice. Even though the prayer carried audibly in the eerie silence on the Bridge, no one offered any complaints. Suddenly the view of the *Charles de Gaulle* lit up with a blinding light as every main plasma weapon on board the USS *Hornet* powered up and sent their dazzling beams containing quadrillions of watts of pure energy hurtling towards the European vessel. Even with visual brightness dampers on the image became hard to make out, but by squinting hard, Rance observed how the enormous force of the plasma blasts had been stopped cold by some form of shielding emanating from the enemy ship. A fascinating conflict between the incalculable strength of the *Hornet's* weapons and powerful defensive shield of the rapidly approaching *Charles de Gaulle* then ensued, the victor of such a titanic struggle uncertain.

Rance subconsciously speculated that perhaps this is what the epic clash in Heaven between Michael the Arch Angel and Satan written about in Revelation 12:7may have been like.

For a few seconds the immensely powerful plasma weapons bearing down on their adversaries ship seemed to be making a little progress, almost touching it, then in turn the shielding would push back their attacking beams, at times nearly overwhelming them. Finally, slowly but inexorably the *Hornet's* energy beams appeared to be winning the terrific contest, consistently pushing their challengers defensive shielding towards the approaching craft, plasma finally actually coming in direct contact with it.

What happened next only took a millisecond. In that tiny fraction of time a blinding blast lit up the Bridge, luridly displaying the instantaneous end of the World Federation Starship *Charles de Gaulle* and the thousands of human beings unfortunate enough to have been on board. The holographic display only showed empty space with the few twinkling stars now very hard to see in the suddenly black void. Rance prayed for the souls of all those lost, both friend and foe, giving thanks that the Lord chose to show them favor during this short but costly battle in space. General Pattinson gave an exaggerated salute to his Commander in Chief General McLellan, starting a round of clapping which rapidly turned into several loud hurrahs for the old man. Rance, although also thankful for the Generals leadership did not take part in this fawning adulation, preferring to remain focused on the one who in fact deserved thanks in all circumstances: Jesus Christ.

General McLellan soon raised his hand and put a stop to the applause and cheering. "Thank you…everyone, but this isn't over… not yet. We still have a helluva lot of work to do. That shithead Lanza won't take kindly to us destroying his pride and joy…oh no, not one little bit. Unfortunately that gives us no other choice but to begin our voyage somewhat sooner than we had originally planned. Too bad…there were still a few more vital cargo loads of essentials remaining to be delivered… but we remain at real risk sitting here in Earth orbit. The Europeans could attack us with shuttles or even hit us with ICBM's from Earth for that matter. We have to leave…NOW. I want conventional rocket thrusters to power us to the outer edge of the solar system where we will remain, somewhat more secure until our battle damage can be repaired – then it's off to Zeta Reticulli!"

That led to another frenzy of activity on the Bridge as officers and technicians readied the *Hornet* for her short voyage to the farthest limit of the Sun's planets. Amazingly, they finished preparing the warship for departure within twenty-five minutes; all crewmembers remaining on battle stations as the count down for conventional rocket thruster launch ensued. "Four, Three, Two, main ignition of primary rocket boosters," intoned the calm controllers voice as the engines ignited, sending a barely perceptible shudder throughout the colossal mass of the USS *Hornet*. These conventional rockets weren't really intended for propelling the warship on such a long journey, but as the General and his High Command Staff Officers explained they couldn't risk using the hyper drive system until a full inspection of the damaged areas of the ship could be conducted and repairs completed. Slowly, the view of Earth that filled the holographic imaging became smaller and fainter until eventually it looked like nothing more than a bright blue star. Rance suddenly become conscious of the brutal fact he would never see his home world again, not the only one on the Bridge to shed a tear at such a gut wrenching realization.

It would take the USS *Hornet* approximately fifteen days to reach their destination near the farthest orbit of the dwarf planet Pluto. While traveling to the remotest edge of

Sol's orbiting planets could not be a guarantee of safety from further European attacks, common sense indicated it would be unlikely that the World Federation had been able to manufacture two marvels like the *Charles de Gaulle*, just as the United States couldn't have mustered enough resources to build another *Hornet*.

Once the ship had traveled a few hours away from Earth, McLellan rescinded the general quarters order and to a small extent the tremendous tension level began to ease on board ship. Rance and Major Mitchell left the Bridge, dismissed with strict orders to be on call and return at a moment's notice if necessary.

After returning to the office and discovering with relief none of their equipment sustained any serious damage, Rance sent the Major home to his quarters. It was doubtful they would be able to focus on the fighter pilot training program after such an eventful day. That didn't stop Rance from staying to devote some more time on the F-72 simulator. He kept working at it until early in the morning hours, and while not exactly super proficient, he thought he might be good enough to actually pilot the real thing someday soon without getting himself killed.

After heading back to his quarters and saying a brief prayer before hitting his bed, it felt like he had just fallen asleep before the annoying birdlike chirping of his alarm woke him at 06:00. The morning cup of strong coffee barely took the edge off his fatigue by the time he made the return trip to work, starting the day's tasks by checking his mail messages. Lieutenant Dennis Crowder sent one of the e-mails. He mentioned he was a fellow Christian and asked if it would be possible to meet with Rance sometime soon to discuss setting up organized worship services aboard the *Hornet*. Rance thanked the Lord for answering one of his prayers; having just this morning submitted the request for other believers to be brought into his life. In replying to the message, he suggested the Lieutenant meet him at 19:00

hours at the office for a brief visit and planning session. Hopefully he wasn't one of the General's spies.

Another pleasant surprise occurred when Major Mitchell arrived. The young man had something preoccupying him of an importance far beyond the day's work. He was uncharacteristically nervous. "General, I've been giving a lot of thought to what you told me the other day, you know, saying that you'd be willing to share your beliefs with me, your Christianity I mean."

Rance gave him a calm reassuring smile. "I'd love to talk to you about it Major, but if you don't mind me asking, what made you want to hear about my faith?"
Mitchell became thoughtful, and then answered. "My parents Sir, they were going to a little church in our hometown, before the great disappearance. I refused to go, wouldn't listen when they tried to tell me about Jesus Christ and being "born again." I thought Mom and Dad were just going through some weird phase and then, well they disappeared along with a lot of other people I knew. Still being fairly young, I bought the explanation about the alien abductions, actually it became the main reason I joined Optimus, to get even, maybe even rescue them. Now I'm not so sure. That's why I wanted to talk to you, especially after yesterday, I mean almost dying kinda makes you think. You know what I mean?"

"Major," said Rance, "your parents are believers in Jesus Christ and they were snatched away to be with the Lord in the Rapture of the Church, not abducted by alien beings. You don't have to worry about them because they are now in the safest place imaginable and are very, very happy. Yes, your mother and father are now with Jesus Christ waiting until the moment they'll return to earth at the end of the Great Tribulation, a time that is soon approaching. The Bible, which is God's Holy Word, tells us that all of mankind, including the two of us, have been condemned as imperfect sinners. Sin is something that estranges us from God and should lawfully mean we are doomed to an eternity in Hell. However, Jesus Christ, God in human form came to earth and paid our sin-debt by dying on the cross. Because of this," Rance hesitated slightly before using the young man's first name "…William, there is the blessed assurance that if you acknowledge you are a sinner, believe Jesus Christ died on the cross for your sins and accept Him into your heart then you too can have eternal life and see your parents again. If you believe what I have just said is true then repeat after me: Lord I admit I am a sinner. I know you died on the Cross for my sins and I ask you to come into my heart." Major Mitchell said the prayer and then as if some great emotional burden had just been lifted from his heart began weeping uncontrollably. Rance grasped the young major in a rough embrace, not caring how unprofessional or unseemly it may have looked to an outsider.

Some tears also clouded his eyes as he said. "It's that simple…congratulations William! You are now my brother in Christ, which reminds me. Tonight at 19:00 hours I am expecting a fellow Christian by the name of Lieutenant Dennis Crowder to be here for a meeting. Why not have a little worship service and praise the Lord for all of His blessings but especially for your new life in Christ!"

After starting out on such a highlight, the rest of the workday could be nothing but pale in comparison, however, they actually made some good progress. Using the holo-displays as an aid, Rance and Major Mitchell did some performance comparisons of the F-72 versus the latest model of the Gray's flying disks. Latest model was probably somewhat of a misnomer as evidence suggested that the Gray's, being an ancient race, made few if any changes to their technologies once they seemingly perfected them. Rance hated to think about the techniques NSA interrogators used in gathering some of their latest intelligence from the aliens but the reports said that the present Zeta Reticullan craft had been in use for at least the past millennium and possibly longer. They were instinctual followers of that old motto "if it aint broke, don't fix it." The General could take credit for being right about the USA now having the edge over the aliens technologically, the holographs indicating the general superiority of the F-72 Sparrow Hawk over the Grays ships.

    Rance found something rather troubling about the displays though. The holos indicated the alien craft had remarkably consistent performance characteristics while the F-72's flight data was all over the map so to speak, ranging from only slightly better than the alien disk to vastly superior depending on who was flying it. The Earth built ship seemed to be more reliant on the uncertain variable of the human operator and their ability to grasp and excel at visualization, picturing their ship doing some of those wild, impossible maneuvers. Like any human talent some people were just better at it than others. Hopefully repetitive practice would be something that could consistently improve all the pilots. Rance knew the fighter pilot's training program needed quick development. They had to take advantage of the brief window of opportunity that made fighter operations possible while the inactive USS *Hornet* received repairs to the battle damage she received from the World Federation ship. The big variable of course would be exactly how long they would have for training, something no one knew for sure until they stopped at the edge of the solar system for a full inspection. If repairs were completed quickly, well, Rance hoped he would be able to talk the General into delaying the departure for Zeta Reticulli until one hundred percent confident all pilots had reached adequate proficiency in the F-72. If the General insisted on embarking immediately before they were combat ready…well, Rance prayed such a scenario would not be the case.

The rest of the day passed quickly and before they knew it suppertime had arrived. Rance and the Major each had a quick burger and fries at the cafeteria before heading back to the office to wait for Lieutenant Crowder. The slightly overweight, dark bearded and balding young man, obviously excited to meet some other Christians rushed through the door fifteen minutes early, saluting and then warmly greeting Rance and Major Mitchell. Rance wasn't the first person to get the impression Crowder would have made an ideal "Friar Tuck" in some theatrical presentation of Robin Hood had his army uniform been replaced with a monk's habit and a mug of ale. The man was obviously sincere and Rance instinctively knew that he was not one of the General's informers. Lieutenant Dennis Crowder explained how he recently became one of the legendary Seabees. His role was to build towns, bridges and roads once the war against the Grays ended and the next step became colonization and reconstruction of Optimus 4. Once hearing the good news about Major Mitchell receiving Christ that very day, Crowder also gave thanks to the Lord. Since being assigned to the USS *Hornet* three months before, he thought he might have been the lone Christian on board. Naturally Crowder became overjoyed when the ships rumor mill announced another believer, the famous war hero General Rance Edwards would be arriving on board. But now he discovered the Lord had blessed him with not just one but two new brothers in Christ, and double the reason to praise God, which he enthusiastically proceeded to do, first in prayer and then by singing an old fashioned hymn, "I Saw the Light," originally sung by Hank Williams Sr. Neither Rance nor Mitchell knew the hymn but even so they tried to sing along, finding the ancient words profound and its melody actually quite pleasant.

After conducting a short period of reading scripture, prayer and meditating on the glory of God, they decided to schedule a regular Sunday morning worship service and Wednesday evening scripture reading, both to take place in their office conference room. They also made the decision to publicly announce the services on one of the *Hornet* e-message boards; something that Rance knew would immediately be brought to General McLellan's attention. It didn't matter. As Christians, the three men would all be willing to make the supreme sacrifice-if that's what it took. As always, they could achieve nothing by worrying, combating their pointless Satanic inspired fears by leaving everything in the hands of their all-powerful Creator God...

CHAPTER 10

"Hey Guys! You're hangin' out with Lieutenant Gina Jensen on Comm-Rad 1, the fave of all you US Army Rangers! Hope you enjoyed that one…Split Enz with "I Got You" Before that you heard A Flock of Seagulls with their monster hit, "I Ran" and "Whip It" from whom else but those new traditionalists of Devo. Up next though is a very special delight, especially for our Glorious Leader. This one goes way back to the year 1983 when General McLellan and his forces invaded the communist stronghold of Grenada…I know how much you like this song Grandfather General…"When I'm With You" by Sheriff…on Comm-Rad 1…"

The date happened to be October 25, 1983 and for third year, second class West Point Cadet George McLellan, all hell just broke loose. George hadn't yet decided if it could be considered his good fortune, or instead gross misfortune, of being attached to a US Army Ranger unit for an advanced airborne training course on this fateful day. While with the Rangers, he nominally held a rank of Cadet Sergeant but for all intents and purposes filled the role of a typical Platoon Sergeant. George felt confident enough being a Sergeant to the enlisted men while they did their practice jumps at low altitude, but this Grenada thing promised to be a real war situation. If he didn't do his job properly men could die and it would be entirely his fault. Normally cadets wouldn't have even been considered for a role in actual combat but his Platoon Lieutenant Jeff Jorgenson and the Company Commander, Captain Ron Monroe were impressed by how well he'd done in the training program thus far. They recognized some real leadership potential in him and besides, there just happened to be a vacancy for a Sergeant in Jorgensen's platoon.

George knew they were risking their careers if he screwed up when the shooting started. In fact if anything at all went wrong, the shit would really fly. Because of such a crushing responsibility, he needed to get his act together, subduing the waves of nervousness by focusing on getting the men following him ready for their imminent jump from the C130 Hercules aircraft. Even though the veteran Rangers often referred to George (out of his earshot) as the "damn punk" they all recognized in this kid a strong charismatic confidence, demanding their reluctant respect.

    Lieutenant Jorgenson told George how this mission; christened "Operation Urgent Fury" involved the invasion of the island of Grenada by US Marines and Army Rangers. Captain Monroe's Ranger Company had been assigned the task of seizing the unfinished runway at Point Salines, going up against second-rate Grenadian troops but more dangerously, also some Cuban Army regulars attached as advisers. Because of the very real risk of heavy ground fire on approach, the Hercules aircraft carrying them would only be flying at approximately eight hundred feet at the time of the drop. As they came in low, sure enough up from the ground came the telltale tracers from small arms fire, one round clipping George's boot heel as he jumped. The chute barely had enough time to open and break his fall before he landed-hard.

    Once on the deck, he got the men of his platoon together, directing their fire towards an area at the edge of the runway where the majority of the enemy were located. Shortly after hitting the tarmac, an enemy bullet had struck Lieutenant Jorgenson in the face, killing him instantly. Two other members of the Platoon were hit during the initial drop, quickly followed by three more getting seriously wounded, including the tough but popular old Vietnam vet Sergeant John Skelly. Cut off from Captain Monroe, without orders due to faulty radio communications, the Platoon remained pinned down in an open and untenable situation. Facing certain death in the face of heavy hostile fire, Platoon Sergeant McLellan ordered the movement of his men, including the wounded to the cover of a Caterpillar Tractor parked on the runway. George himself carried one of the injured Rangers to safety. From this position he kept the men under his command directing steady streams of fire at the enemy strong points until Captain Monroe could call in air support. An AC130 Specter gunship soon silenced all enemy resistance and by early afternoon Point Salines airfield had been secured. West Point Cadet, Platoon Sergeant George McLellan received a commendation on his file for "bravery while under enemy fire" that day, but most importantly for him, he proved to himself and the whole world that he had what it took to be tough in combat…to be a hero…

Brigadier General Rance Edwards and his Aide Major Mitchell made amazing progress on the Fighter Pilot Training curriculum. They had almost finished by the time the USS *Hornet* approached the solar systems outer limits to stop for inspection and repairs. The young Major proved to be an able assistant to Rance, coming up with some truly innovative training ideas for a man with no actual combat flying experience. Instinctively he somehow knew a few basic truths about fighter tactics, realizing that regardless of how sophisticated the aircraft (or spacecraft in this case) became and no matter who you were fighting (whether human or alien) a lot of the air combat strategies going way back to the early twentieth century still applied. Mitchell found a holo-manual on old Second World War fighter pilot formations Rance then used as a valuable reference source when they started developing a program for the *Hornet's* pilots. Even more importantly, after some initial friction, Rance found out he enjoyed working with the young man, especially now since they shared the same Christian faith. The only mildly annoying thing about

Mitchell had to be his eccentric taste in music, especially at this time of year. Rance noted with some relief that today was December 25th, Earth date. Even though the Christmas holiday was now nothing more than a pagan Winter Solstice Festival, the Major insisted on playing his "festive music" on the office holo-comm continuously for a week leading up to Christmas day. He especially liked "Christmas in Hollis" by RUN-D.M.C. Rance allowed this irritant because Mitchell insisted it somehow made him more efficient at work. Apparently his family also had the bizarre custom of playing old Christmas hymns sung by an ancient twentieth century Italian tenor called Mario Lanza (apparently no relation to the Antichrist). At least the songs mentioned Jesus Christ. Some of the other selections he favored were a great deal worse, including one prehistoric tune called "Run Run Rudolph" by a long dead singer named Chuck Berry. After hearing it for at least the twentieth time this week he found himself unable to stop from subconsciously singing the lyrics, a hypnotic effect no doubt caused by some early attempt at subliminal influencing. Even so, Rance considered it all a small price to pay to keep such a valuable aide happy and completing his duties.

General Wilbur Pattinson's gruff voice came over the *Hornet's* audio system announcing they had at last reached their destination and were coming to a complete stop for inspection and repair crews to begin their critical work. Rance now took his first opportunity to try flying the F-72, having already received clearance from the Bridge to take one of the new fighters on a test flight. He also booked Major Mitchell for some flight time alternating with his own so both of them could quickly become proficient operating the futuristic craft. Formation flying would come later. The Major actually held a slight advantage on Rance, having flown the F-72 twice while the *Hornet* still remained in Earth orbit. After proceeding to K Deck

Hangar #2, Rance sat in his assigned F-72, having noticed with satisfaction that the very considerate and thoughtful flight crews had added the following script on the side of the fuselage:

Brig. Gen. Rance Edwards
"Chief"

In addition to remembering his famous handle of Chief, they even thought to paint the tail section of Rance's fighter with a stylized Rising Sun Japanese flag, exactly like his old F-22. Rance always felt the symbol to be a fitting tribute to another of his heroic forefathers, Commander Toyoaki Takizawa. The Imperial Japanese Navy pilot participated in the attack on Pearl Harbor and later helped sink the old USS *Hornet* in the Second World War. Takizawa died on board the ill-fated super battleship Yamato after he volunteered to fly the ships catapult fighter on a Kamikaze mission in operation Ten-Go. The Yamato was destroyed by American carrier based bombers long before reaching her objective.

As the crews checked his fighter for the final time before the hangar deck became depressurized, he went through his checklist again. After the green ready light indicated all crewmembers had safely vacated the area, a whoosh sound announced that the outer armored doors of the flight deck were now opened up to the cold vacuum of space. He mentally completed the takeoff procedures: Main engine power, roger. Boosters on, roger. Mental link green, roger. Rance then requested takeoff clearance from the Landing Signals Officer or "Air Boss" as pilots preferred to call him. That part of the process at least remained the same as it had on his old aircraft carrier the USS *Washington*.

"DOG 12 requesting take off clearance," said Rance through the internal comm-link.

"Roger. Takeoff approved," said the professional, crystal clear voice of the Air Boss.

Rance glanced to his left at the control area window, seeing the faces of several officers looking out on the flight deck. No doubt General McLellan would be among them, not wanting to miss the famous Rance Edwards embarking on his first flight in an F-72. Better not crash then, thought Rance as he gave the thumbs up signal, which gave the go ahead for the catapult to launch his fighter out into the black coldness of space. Whump! Rance felt rather than heard the catapult propelling his fighter far out and away from the *Hornet* before the main conventional rocket thrusters took over and he found himself on the ride of his life. Even after all of the simulation time he put in learning how to fly this wonder, the experience of actually physically doing it exhilarated him more than he thought it would. After trying some routine maneuvers using the hydrogen/oxygen rocket motor and stick only, Rance began to feel comfortable controlling his fighter. Now as ready as he would ever be, it was time to attempt flying with the aid of the hyper drive aided by visualization techniques. After trying it out on the simulator, Rance was starting to get the hang of the mental picturing needed, finding that the best analogy he could think of for training purposes would be to remember when you were a youngster in school daydreaming about how you'd like to be somewhere else. The familiar feeling of being somewhat inattentive to your present physical environment yet being focused on another place mentally seemed to be the best description of the psychological state a person needed to be in when utilizing the hyper drive. You remained relaxed and fully aware of everything going on around you, but a part of your mind stayed separate. It was necessary to basically imagine your ship doing things it had no business doing, at least not in our boring old universe. He started by picturing the F-72 turning at a near right angle, faster than should ever be possible and turn it did, appearing to ignore the laws of physics. The adrenaline pumped through his veins, a physical response similar to what a twentieth century race car driver may have experienced after pushing their primitive vehicle way beyond its normal limits while still retaining control. It felt like that except probably a thousand times, no, make that a million times better. Rance then visualized the craft going faster, faster, faster; soon hurtling at a speed the instruments indicated approached the velocity of light itself, and then…STOP! Almost instantaneously he found himself sitting at a total standstill, the twinkling stars in the blackness of deep space being his only companion. The *Hornet* of course was long gone. "Dear Lord!" said Rance half in prayer, realizing that the F-72 had rocketed at near light speed for approximately ten seconds, traveling millions of kilometers away from the safety of the mother ship and making him at that moment quite literally the loneliest human being in the cosmos. That fact would have unnerved many less stable, non-Christian individuals but Rance knew he had nothing to worry about. The designers of the F-72 put many safeguards into their creation to prevent a pilot from roaming immense distances without also being able to make it back to the USS *Hornet*. A holographic display automatically popped up in front of Rance showing him the distance and location of his home ship and how to get there. All he needed to do was simply imagine being in that spot, something done easily enough those many times in a simulator but which became slightly unsettling when the immense distances involved meant even a tiny error would result in missing the *Hornet* by many thousands of kilometers. Only one way to find out for sure thought Rance as he grabbed the stick, looking at the target holograph, visualizing his F-72 going to the place focused firmly in his mind's eye, traveling faster and faster until a matter of mere seconds later he found himself starting to slow as he approached the beautiful sight of home...the *Hornet*. Stopping approximately five kilometers away from the colossal vessel, he absorbed the immensity of General McLellan's pet project, mankind's blasphemous tribute to the ultimately flawed and doomed theology of humanism. Rance knew from his Bible reading the dire consequences resulting from the first attempt to build such a shrine to the concept of human achievement without need for God: The Tower of Babel.

Sitting there silently, Rance gave thanks to the Lord for getting him back safely to this haven in space and also asked for the Creators hand to guide their coming mission, whatever the outcome may be, win or lose. He activated his voice comm, asking the Air Boss for landing approval, knowing he probably had done enough flying for one day. Time for the Major to also get in some flight hours, he thought as the *Hornet's* automated glide beam grabbed onto his fighter, drawing it unerringly towards that glowing blue rectangular shape and bringing it in for a perfect landing on the flight deck. When the outer doors closed, Rance opened his canopy, still absorbing how much of a wonder this fighter really could be once his pilots were properly trained. Rance briefly acknowledged Major Mitchell who waited patiently to begin his training flight.

Still absorbed by his own experience and how what he learned could be incorporated into the training course, Rance didn't notice the familiar voluptuous figure of Christine St. James standing in the hangar maintenance area until he bumped right into her. Their eyes locked for what seemed like an eternity before Christine spoke.

"I'm sorry Rance. You probably didn't expect to see me here, it's just, well I heard about your flight in the F-72 and I guess I wanted to make sure you made it back okay. It *is* experimental. What can I say? ...Old habits die hard."

Rance honestly didn't know what to say in response. He sort of expected an officer, maybe even the General to meet him for a debrief session but no one waited here except

Christine. Indeed, old habits do die hard…very hard. He remembered when they were both on the USS *Washington* how she would wait for him in the fighter pilots ready room, greeting him with tears of relief when he came back from a mission…except… the last time when things changed…irrevocably. In one way he thanked God he had been shot down and she was sent stateside for compassionate reasons. Two days later the *Washington* had been nuked with the loss of all hands. But…that felt like a century ago. Right now he had to say something and not just stand here with his mouth open like a dimwit. "Thanks Christine. I really appreciate that."

Christine's beautiful face held an odd, unreadable expression that completely baffled him. "Anyway," she said, "I'm sorry about the other day. You didn't deserve all of that anger. Yes, probably some of it, but not all. I guess I just needed to see you again to make things right. I really want us to try meeting again, hopefully to put some closure on our…um…former relationship. You okay with that Rance?"

In spite of her now being a married woman, the wife of Colonel Rick Santchez, Rance wanted to…needed to see her again, desperately, with every ounce of his being. "Yes Christine I'd like to talk with you again. Hopefully we can get this all sorted. The cafeteria okay, tonight at twenty one hundred hours?"

"Nine sounds good, but if you don't mind I would prefer someplace a little more private. I'm afraid our conversation last time raised a few eyebrows among the other patrons in the cafeteria. Sorry." She smiled sheepishly. "Would your quarters be all right?"

As a Christian Rance knew having her for a visit alone in his quarters could be interpreted as improper. She immediately recognized what was going through his mind. He obviously wasn't very good at hiding his thoughts, at least not from her.

"Don't worry Rance. I'm not planning on doing anything…scandalous. And besides, Rick will know exactly where I am. I wouldn't dream of seeing you without him first agreeing to it. He's my husband after all and I do respect him…okay?"

Rance, although having some misgivings about seeing her alone, agreed. "Tonight at twenty one hundred hours. I'm in the directory," he said, before leaving her standing there alone. He had to get out of the awkwardness of the situation, anywhere away from her. Rance tried to kid himself their meeting would provide resolution, but how could being alone with a married woman he still loved ever be considered a good idea?

Rance pushed all this personal stuff out of his head after going back to the office and incorporated some of what he learned on the test flight into the pilots training. Major Mitchell also benefited from a successful test flight of the F-72, his outing focused mainly on performing stunning, impossible maneuvers like extreme right angle turns at near light speed. They compared the holo-displays of both flights, putting a lot more data into their pilot orientation package. Rance realized a lot of blanks still needed filling in regarding what they still didn't know about the F-72's flight characteristics. In some very important areas, the flight manuals prepared by the BLMD test pilots looked very sparse for an approved operational spacecraft. Maybe the fighter had been rushed into production. Knowing the Generals infamous impatience, that probably was the case. He just hoped BMLD hadn't missed any bugs in the F-72, as finding and fixing possible flaws in the craft during actual combat conditions would be unfortunate to say the least.

During the flight comparisons Major Mitchell shared something else with Rance, something not recorded on the flight data. He did a flyby of the battle-damaged region of the *Hornet*. Disturbingly, Mitchell noted how the doors on the affected emergency flight deck and hangar appeared to be stuck in the half way open position. If the repair crews couldn't fix the doors, the *Hornet* would lose one of her six flight decks, possibly creating serious problems in the coming campaign. Rance didn't have time to worry about it though. Extremely capable people already knew all about it and at were this very moment giving their absolute best effort in having the ship ready for departure as soon as possible meaning he'd better get the training program ready to roll… and quickly.

The remainder of the day passed productively until Rance found himself back at his billet shortly before twenty one hundred hours. Christine showed up at his room only a few minutes later.

"Sorry I'm late," she said. Rance stared at her perhaps a little too long, her beauty having its familiar drug like influence on him. She looked good; wearing a low cut glittery top and a short skirt showing off her gorgeous legs, made even more stunning by killer five-inch heels.

"Have a seat. Anything to drink?" he asked, turning on the holo for some low volume background music, recognizing the old Irving Berlin tune "Cheek to Cheek."

"No thank you Rance… I think we should get started." She looked very petite in his large armchair. "I'm afraid Rick didn't think my coming here was a very good idea but I told him this is something I had to do…that he would just have to trust me." She locked eyes with him, Rance again finding it enormously difficult to look away. "Look Christine," he said, "I hate to agree with Rick, but he may be right. This might not be the best place for us to sit down and talk. Maybe we should go to the cafeteria after all."

Christine's eyes began to well up with tears. "Why Rance? Are you afraid to be alone with me, afraid of what might happen?"

Oh my God, thought Rance. He didn't say anything but he knew the situation could easily get out of hand. How he wanted to take her in his arms, to kiss her, to…No! Lord give me strength!

"Yes, actually I am. This is very inappropriate. You need to leave now. If you still want to talk, we can go to a more public area but…"

"Damn you Rance!" she said, her voice breaking. "How blind are you? Don't you see that I still love you, that I never stopped loving you? I know the whole thing is crazy, me being married to Rick; you with your Christian obsession but I can't help it… my feelings for you never went away. I love you. I always will love you and I want you. I want you right now. Right here."

Rance took a moment before answering. He said a small silent prayer, knowing what he said next would either lead to a condition of moral and spiritual ruin or to the highroad of doing the right thing, something his Christian faith always demanded.

"Christine, you know I still love you, but nothing can happen between us. You're a married woman. As a Christian I've found Salvation in Jesus Christ. Once you become a believer, to knowingly wallow in sin or immorality is just…incomprehensible." Rance found himself getting choked up as he spoke of his faith. "Jesus Christ has given me something beyond value; yes even more precious than my love for you. I can't do anything that might jeopardize my eternal soul, my relationship with my Lord. I'm sorry Christine."

Christine didn't make a sound, just sat silently on the chair, absorbing his words. Then suddenly it was like the floodgates of a dam had burst. "Rance… forgive…me!" she said in between bouts of tears. Oh God I'm so pathetic… I'm so unhappy! I…I don't love him Rance. Rick is a nice guy but he can't ever replace you…what am I going to do…without you?"

Christine completely broke down as Rance knelt and tenderly embraced his former lover, letting her vent before she became calm enough to speak. "Rance... tell me about your Jesus. Tell me how I can have what you have...I need that peace...I need... Jesus Christ." Then, right there in Rance's small billet, Christine St. James accepted Jesus Christ as her Lord and Savior, an experience that caused another bout of emotions, this time from joy not sadness. After they'd both shed many tears in celebration, Christine left to go back to her husband leaving Rance alone, grieving the loss of his one true love but celebrating another soul having been won for Jesus.

Rance and his aide had just started their work the following morning when a terse announcement came over the audio system requesting all senior officers needing to assemble at Bridge Conference Room #2.

Since "senior officer" meant those with a rank of Brigadier General and higher, Rance left the Major behind to continue working while he made his way to the specified meeting place. The conference room, more like a university lecture hall, held most of the ship's top brass by the time he got there. A few stragglers topped off the assembly of probably well over five hundred officers. Looking around, Rance could see several people he recognized from the academy who now held the rank of General, rapid promotion of "suitable" young men and women clearly being very widespread in McLellan's New Space Force.

A few minutes later Generals Pattinson and McLellan took to the podium along with a thirty something two star Major General with the name of Jeb Longstreet. General Pattinson made the introductions, explaining General Longstreet was the officer in charge of the *Hornet's* inspection and repair efforts. A holographic display popped up above the assembled officers as Longstreet started to give details of the warships colorful representation. He had a noticeable Atlanta accent.

"Thank you Generals McClellan and Pattinson for the gracious introduction. I'll get right to the point. Our inspection teams found most of the *Hornet's* damage could quite easily be repaired. The majority of that repair work has already been carried out. That is the good news. Here is the...bad news." General Longstreet focused the imaging on the affected emergency hangar and flight deck. "As you can see from these images, the outer blast doors of this area were pushed in by the blast, completely jamming them and leaving an approximately twenty meter opening. Although we can seal this breach with reinforced liquid alloy patches, our flight launch and recovery capabilities in this area will be permanently lost. Our work to finish repairs will take another two, possibly three weeks. I'll now turn the floor over to my distinguished superiors...Thank you."

Rance now had a rough estimate of how much time he had to get the *Hornet's* pilots ready for combat if the General didn't give him an extension. He knew two or three weeks would not be enough.

General Pattinson began to speak. "In spite of losing this flight deck, we still have four full hangars and one remaining emergency hangar, more than enough to vanquish our enemy in our coming war to liberate Optimus Four. We need to honor our Glorious Leader for having the foresight to build a redundancy of flight decks on the *Hornet*. Long live the General!" he said as he gave one of his ridiculous looking embellished salutes, starting yet another wave of unabashed Leader worship. Before Rance became a Christian he would have called the assembled group of Officers, particularly Pattinson as the worst group of ass kissers he'd ever seen. As a believer in Christ however, he needed to pray for his superiors, hoping the over confidence regarding their seeming abundance of flight decks didn't get proven wrong when they actually faced the aliens in battle. In spite of his prayer, Rance had a gut feeling, borne of his intense combat experience that before all was said and done, the upper brass might wish they hadn't lost such an apparently insignificant little emergency hangar…

CHAPTER 11

"Hello everyone, this is Major Schlossberg filling in for the incomparable Captain Dan. The poor guys got a bad case of the flu...what can I say... people do get sick right? I just hope he doesn't have Super Avian Three. Anyway, while he's away I'll do my very best to give you folks your all time most wanted music. You just heard some great Eighties tunes, Simple Minds with "Don't You Forget About Me," "Your Love" performed by The Outfield and my personal favorite, "Red Red Wine" from UB40. Now I just had a couple of requests come in, one for "Obsession" by Animation and New Order with "Blue Monday" so I'll try and get those on sometime in the next ten. Up next though is a song that I hear just got added to the play list for General McLellan's victory celebration on Optimus Four..."King For A Day"...The Thompson Twins... on your voice of the *Hornet*...Comm-Rad 1..."

Captain George McLellan drove his black Pontiac Trans Am up to the guard post entrance of Fort Campbell Kentucky. "Kickstart My Heart" by Motley Crue blared from his stereo. Although plain and nondescript compared to the stainless steel bodied DeLorean DMC-12 he dreamed of getting, the Pontiac looked like an exact duplicate for the *Knight Rider* car and still drew stares. The guards, who knew him well, waved him through. The assholes should know him well enough; George thought as he floored the cars accelerator and roared past them. After all he had been driving through that gate every day now for the last three years, ever since getting posted to 1st Brigade of the "Screaming Eagles," the famed 101st Airborne Division. Actually George would have preferred the convenience of living on base but his beautiful yet haughty wife Catherine insisted they own a house in a moderately upscale neighborhood in nearby Clarksville Tennessee. Except for the financial help from George's mom and Catherine's wealthy business man father, there would have been no way they could have afforded the mortgage and car payments, at least not on his present army wages. George and Cathy, as he preferred to call her, had an explosive and volatile relationship, usually fighting like cats and dogs, quickly followed by making up and making love, that physical compatibility being about the only thing still keeping them together. Because of this, their marriage was declining rapidly even though they had only just celebrated their third wedding anniversary. Thankfully, there weren't any kids yet, George having insisted on waiting until his military career became a little more secure.

Lately though, thought George there seemed to be more combat going on in his home than he could likely hope to see anytime soon in the Army. The extremely dramatic scenes between them now reached a new level of intensity, with George, while not physically aggressive to his wife, becoming an expert at delivering the cutting verbal insult. Last night's fracas resulted in the neighbors calling the cops after Cathy threw a heavy vase, which (thankfully for him) missed George and shattered their large picture window. With all of the breaking glass and screaming, the poor buggers next door thought they better call the police before someone got hurt. That actually could have been a distinct possibility without some intervention.

After the officers had left, George and Cathy found themselves in the predictable but enjoyable next stage of their destructive cycle, mad passionate lovemaking. He still thought back to that part of the night's events with some fondness. George did know they would have to divorce soon or later before they caused some real damage, maybe even killed each other, but what a ride they had enjoyed along the way! He wouldn't have been too traumatized if Cathy hit him with the divorce papers first anyway. There happened to be a cute little brunette civilian administrative assistant by the name of Samantha Lee on base who had been giving him the eye. Sam, as she preferred to be called lit up every time he found some excuse to drop by the office with some paperwork. No, George thought, he wouldn't mind getting to know Sam, getting to know her a whole lot better. Wasn't life one whole hell of a lot of fun?

    Rance had been kept waiting by General McLellan's snobbish flunky of an adjutant Colonel Ellison for the last forty five minutes. He urgently needed to see the General in order to convince the leader that he needed more time to fully train his fighter squadrons in tactics. Rance knew that the two or three weeks while the *Hornet* underwent repairs would not be enough. The snooty way Ellison treated him when he came in for this unscheduled appointment made Rance think he might have to wait quite a while longer. Apparently in spite of his "superior American melting pot" genetics, he no longer held the General's favor. Surprisingly however, only a few minutes later, Ellison ushered Rance into the General's private briefing room to await an audience at the great man's convenience.

    Ten minutes later McLellan came into the room, Rance immediately standing to attention and saluting. "Have a seat Rance," said McLellan as he himself sat down in one of the overstuffed conference room chairs. "I hear you had a successful test flight of the Sparrow Hawk fighter." He smiled. "I told you she'd knock your socks off...didn't I?"

    Rance wanted to get the formalities over with. "Yes Sir. The F-72 is an unbelievable piece of technology. I think that given the right training for our pilots we could have the clear advantage over the enemy, but..."

    McLellan interrupted him, an ornery expression clouding his aged face. "What the hell do you mean *could* give us the clear advantage? The pilots have already received their basic flight training, now it's up to you to smooth off the rough edges before we get to Optimus. Now if you don't think you're up to the challenge, well, I'll get somebody else."

Rance knew his integrity, not to mention many lives, depended on standing his ground against his elderly Commander in Chief. The man had gotten his own way most of his life… but Rance wasn't at all like the General's typical yes men. "Sir, I am more than up to the task. However you need to be aware that only having two or three weeks to fully train the squadrons in tactics is not enough. These pilots have a basic knowledge of how to fly the F–72, but they also need to practice actual formation flying, not just with holo simulator programs. If we don't prepare them properly now it doesn't bode well for the later success of our mission. I estimate it'll take a minimum of about eight weeks of intensive flying to get our squadrons ready. I need that extra time General!"

McLellan had no intention of changing his internal timetable. He waved his hands in the air and shook his head. "Rance that's complete bullshit! Like I said, these pilots already know how to fly their ships. Now I'm going to make this very clear to you so we don't have any more misunderstandings. You have two, maybe three weeks while repairs are underway to do the hands on training with your crews. After that we jumpstart the hyper drive and launch the ship on our journey to Optimus, a trip that is estimated to take about one month. During that time you can do all the damned holographic simulations you want, more than adequate enough in my opinion. Is that clear General Edwards?"

Rance knew there could be no reasoning with this man, realizing with a grim certainty their whole mission had probably been negatively impacted by this one, stupid, bull headed decision. "Yes Sir! That is clear Sir! Am I dismissed Sir?" Rance's justified anger for the sake of his fighter crews was impossible to hide as he stood waiting for the General to release him.

The General softened somewhat. "Rance, try to understand something…I've been waiting twenty years to reach this point, eating, sleeping and breathing this project. I can't wait any longer. I have complete confidence in you, in all of the pilots that when the time comes you'll all do your jobs to the best of your abilities. That famous American fighting spirit can easily take care of the rest. Those weakling Grays won't know what the hell hit 'em. You're dismissed…now get your ass out of here and get back to work!"

Rance immediately went to plan B. If they only had as little as two weeks, then he needed to implement some of the most intensive training in the history of the United States military. This required twenty four hour training, operating in three eight hour shifts, something Rance knew would leave him with very little time for sleep, but so be it. He had a responsibility to his fighter squadrons, to the United States of America and of course to his God to do his absolute best in preparing these young men and women for combat. After all, they would be the ones putting their lives on the line when the shooting started.

When he got back to the office Rance informed Major Mitchell of the exhaustive upcoming schedule, then paged the top BLMD test pilot to meet with him. Colonel Gary Nguyen showed up only a few minutes later. Colonel Nguyen literally wrote the book on the F-72 Sparrow Hawk, having been involved with the project from the very beginning. Even though only a civilian pilot, The General had wanted Nguyen to join the *Hornet* crew so badly he drafted the man into the Space Force as a full eagle Colonel. His flying skills were legendary, most aviation experts rightly considering him to be the best pilot in the world. In addition, he also had a Doctorate in Artificial Intelligence Technology from MIT. Nguyen, a small man of obvious Vietnamese descent sported the latest twenty something fad looks, star facial tattoos and funky green spiked hair. After coming in the office he gave Rance an awkward salute, his newness to the Military glaringly obvious. "It's a pleasure to finally meet you Sir. After the war, I watched that amazing documentary on PBS that profiled your combat experiences, something that gave me a great respect for your flying ability. Your story really inspired me. This is kind of embarrassing but…ah…could I get your autograph Sir?" said Nguyen graciously.

"Actually I wanted to ask for *your* autograph," said Rance only half-jokingly, knowing of the young pilot's exceptional talent. He signed a piece of letterhead for Nguyen, who looked at the signature with noticeable excitement. Signing autographs or doing anything that drew attention away from his Savior and Lord always made Rance extremely uncomfortable.

"The reason I called you here Colonel is to review the fighter school curriculum. I need you to help in its implementation by being one of my instructors; after all, no one knows more about the Sparrow Hawk than you do. I have to get this started ASAP since we only have two, maybe three weeks to complete the necessary formation flying with all of the pilots." Rance could see Nguyen visibly wince at the impossible deadline. "I know it's nowhere near enough time but I'm afraid we don't have any choice in the matter. So this is how I think we can get the most bang for our buck in that very short period: we'll have three continuous eight hour training courses with you, Major Mitchell and myself acting as instructors. The first two hours of the course will involve holographic teaching with the last six hours being actual practice time in the F-72. I anticipate that all fighter pilots can complete the basic phase one course in approximately fifteen days. If any more time becomes available to us we can then start putting more gifted pilots from each squadron through the more advanced phase two program, something I'm still working on. So that's that. Any questions?" Colonel Nguyen didn't have any questions but Rance knew he probably had a lot of concerns, though he kept those to himself. They did a run through of the course and reviewed two hours of holo-displays.

The three of them then occupied the rest of their day with some practice formation flying in their F-72s. Rance found formations easy to master in the fighter, all of the advanced proximity accident avoidance systems making it nearly impossible to crash into Nguyen's or Mitchell's fighters in spite of putting his spacecraft through some pretty vigorous maneuvers.

Following some reviewing and fine-tuning of the holographic format Rance thought they would be ready to start training the next morning.

They scheduled the 1st Fighter Squadron at 08:00. The men and women of the 1st or "Fighting Furies" as they preferred to be called had all assembled on time and waited for Rance to begin their brief but valuable educational session.

"Good morning and welcome to the USS *Hornet's* fighter orientation course." Rance began slowly, the fighter pilot training milieu being a completely new experience for him. "I'm General Rance Edwards and these are my colleagues Major Mitchell and Colonel Nguyen." He pointed to the men standing beside him at the front of the room. "The first part of this course takes approximately two hours and involves some holo instruction. As you can see, you each have your own workstation in front of you. At this time I want you all to activate your holo post. You should all see the basic four-fighter formation being displayed. Does everyone have that? …Good. After we complete the first phase on the simulators, we'll proceed down to the flight deck and let you all try out what you've just learned."

There were a few muffled cheers at the prospect of some good old-fashioned hands on training. "Okay let's get started. That basic staggered V, four spacecraft configuration you're seeing is called the "finger four" formation. Some of you may have even seen it before. It dates all the way back to the Second World War. As you can see, the flight is split into two 2-plane elements. The first element is led by the flight leader and covered by their wingman. The element two-segment leader is covered by his or her wingman. Each two-fighter element fights as a unit, engaging the enemy together, and also covering each other. Your stations have been programmed to let you fly your assigned flight positions. Try taking the controls on your simulator. Just get used to flying the basic arrangement. Everyone doing okay? Great. All right... next step will involve you trying to make a slow navigational turn while in the finger four. The best way to accomplish that is by executing a tactical turn. You all know what a TAC turn is right?" Someone yelled out the standard Academy basic training explanation.

"You got it... Instead of trying to maintain the exact entry formation, the TAC turn is basically creating and retaining a mirror image for exiting the turn. How's everybody doin'? Okay...one of the most basic tactical maneuvers in this formation is what's called the Bracket. Fairly self-explanatory given the name. You bracket the alien ship between you and your wingman and force him to make the first of two critical decisions, whether to run or engage. If he runs you've got him, if he attacks then he has to decide on whom to engage. Whoever the alien decides to fight is called the engaged fighter; the other one is the free fighter. The free fighter's job is simple: pour as much weapon fire into that alien ship as possible. Fights over. Okay... Now I want you all to take the controls. You can see on your simulator display that we have introduced an enemy-flying disc so you can get some target practice. See if you can shoot him down. I'll give you all a few minutes to give it a try."

Rance watched all of his students while they focused intently on taking out the simulated Gray ship. Judging by some of the curses coming from the class, they weren't all achieving success. "Now keep in mind that if you're the engaged fighter you need to keep moving in such a way that you prevent the enemy from making a lead turn. A variation on this is the famous thatch weave maneuver. Basically, it involves the engaged fighter completing a series of turns, thus giving the free fighter multiple deflection shots. We'll talk more about that later. How did everyone do? Not so good? That's okay; we'll be doing some more practicing shortly. First though I want to talk a bit about some other basic variations of the bracket. Take a look at your holo. That one is called the half split, showing the maneuvers you will need to complete when the enemy attacks the turning fighter and alternatively when the enemy attacks the extending fighter. Try some of those for a while before we get to the next on my list, the sandwich."

Rance could tell these pilots would give their absolute best effort during real combat, but they first needed to get a grasp on some of these fundamentals. Weapons technology had been so advanced for the last half century that formation flying and tactics almost became relegated to the trash bin, but Rance knew the coming campaign would very likely involve dogfights on a scale not seen since the Second World War. Just like in that ancient conflict, the aerial combat promised to be both intense and deadly. Holographic simulations were all well and good but most importantly they needed to try it out in the real thing, flying the F-72 in mock combat. The two hours of classroom instruction passed quickly, with all squadron members then assembling on the flight deck to take their Sparrow Hawk fighters out for some war games. Rance, Major Mitchell and Colonel Nguyen would be the mock "aliens" while elements of the "Fighting Furies" split into units comprising four fighter craft each would attempt to intercept and shoot them down with harmless light lasers. A "hit" showed on the target fighter's holo-display, immediately taking them out of the game. The first round could be considered nothing but an absolute disaster for the student pilots. Not only were they unable to intercept the targets, the hunted soon became the hunters with Rance, Nguyen and Mitchell shooting down most of the pilots of the 1st Squadron. The second round, while still far from a stellar performance for the students went a little better with Captain Minnie Martell actually being able to "shoot down" Major Mitchell. The third and last round turned into a near draw with the Fighting Furies being unable to shoot down any of the instructors but Rance, Mitchell and Nguyen each downing only one student. The eight-hour session went better than Rance had expected but by no stretch of the imagination did he feel overly confident about the squadron's chances when the shooting really started. No time to worry about it now, he thought as his F-72 came in for a perfect landing on the flight deck.

    The next day would be an exhausting one with three 8-hour training sessions being scheduled. Even though Mitchell and Nguyen were instructing the next two classes, Rance knew he needed to oversee them and would probably be getting little if any sleep for the next two weeks. After a short but solid three-hour catnap, Rance taught the first session the next morning for the 2nd Squadron. The classroom session went well but their practical flying didn't go quite as smoothly as it did the previous day since only Rance flew as a simulated target. He told Major Mitchell and Colonel Nguyen to only put in their normal eight hour days for the simple reason that he didn't want them getting burnt out from exhaustion, something that would negatively impact their teaching abilities. Rance didn't stop to think about how going days without any real sleep could affect him. Training these squadrons was his job and had to be carried out, sleep or no sleep. He'd have no alternative but to survive on a diet of prayer supplemented by some very strong coffee. "Jolt drugs" such as amphetamines remained out of the question both from an ethical and safety standpoint. Duty would be enough of a motivating stimulant. After all, he knew there'd be more than enough time for sleep once the voyage to Optimus 4 began. If on the other hand he didn't train these men and women adequately, he wouldn't be able to sleep peacefully ever again, or even live with his conscience for that matter.

    The first few days of the rigorous training regime clicked along nicely. Major Mitchell and Colonel Nguyen both showed a flair for teaching although in dramatically different ways. Mitchell was gifted with the human touch, being able to connect with the student pilots even though still a young man with absolutely no combat experience. Rance observed the Major taking his role as instructor very seriously; also recognizing how doing a good job literally meant the difference between life and death for the brave pilots of the USS *Hornet*.

    Colonel Nguyen, well, his approach could only be described as… different. While not very personable with students his thoroughness went far beyond the call of duty. Having written the book on the F-72s flight characteristics (even though not as comprehensively as he would have liked due to time constraints), the man still remained the undisputed expert on the craft. Because of this knowledge base Rance sensed an urgency influencing his teaching technique, like he wanted to cram every possible bit of knowledge and data into the limited amount of classroom instruction. With Rance teaching one session a day, plus monitoring the other two classes and trying to pull duty as a target during the practice sessions, it wasn't too long before he teetered on the edge of complete mental and physical exhaustion. Those little catnaps he managed to fit in his busy schedule just weren't cutting it. Somehow however, he forced himself to carry on, if anything praying harder than ever for strength during this trial. He had no business whining when comparing his situation to the ordeal that his Savior, Jesus Christ suffered while on the cross.

After eight or nine days of this grueling schedule, Rance caught his second wind. He wasn't just going through the motions but actually streamlining and maximizing the content for his students. From all reports the efforts to seal off the *Hornet's* damaged flight deck went better than expected with completion targeted in six or seven days. Rance, although feeling disappointed that this upcoming date spelled the end to his planned phase two training sessions, knew God Almighty remained in control of everything. Their departure, the training, the war with the Grays, Christine, all of it was in His hands.

At the end of training day fourteen, Rance received a communication from General Wilbur Pattinson advising him to wrap up all flight operations the following day by 12:00 hours. Rance thanked the Lord that only one squadron remained untrained, something they could easily complete tomorrow by starting early. Rance had done his duty, preparing all of those pilots and crews to the best of his human ability. He just prayed to God it would be enough...

CHAPTER 12

"Hi folks! Well it's me Captain Dan and I'm back and ready to play the all-time greats from our nations wonderful past! That was Sinead O'Connor with "Nothing Compares2U" and of course before Sinead you heard Whitesnake with "Here I Go Again" along with House of Pain, "Jump Around." Comin' up next I've got one of the greatest hits from the year 1991, back when Our Glorious Leader General McLellan almost singlehandedly defeated the Iraqi Army during the first Gulf War...hope this one brings back some memories for you Magnificent Sir...EMF ..."Unbelievable"...on Comm-Rad1..."

Captain George McLellan was having the time of his life on February 23rd 1991, only thirty-six hours since the start of Operation Desert Saber, the Gulf War ground offensive. His Company, part of the 101st Airborne Division made swift and stunning progress during that brief span of time, driving well ahead of all the other coalition forces. Only encountering very light resistance thus far probably played the largest part in this early success. Their Division had been given the objective to drive deep into the largely undefended southern Iraqi desert, part of the ambitious and sweeping "left hook" which would then turn eastward and launch a flanking attack against the Republican Guard. George's platoons progressed so rapidly they left the rest of his battalion far behind. In fact he wouldn't know it until much later, but right at that moment his Company had advanced deeper into Iraq than any other allied unit with the possible exception of two small recon patrols. Even George, his reputation for brashness already earning him the nickname "Custer" from the other Company Commanders, thought he better halt their advance and have a little conference with the Lieutenants in his platoon. After pulling their Humvees into a loose protective circle, Captain McLellan spread out his map on the hood of the command vehicle. He showed his Lieutenants McCain, O'Neil, Vanzetti and Green their exact location or more precisely, his best guess at their exact location. Their damned handheld GPS receiver stopped working a few hours ago. That wouldn't normally be a big concern to most even moderately competent leaders, but being excited about the advance and hoping for enemy action meant George sort of, well, disregarded the importance of maintaining their exact positioning on the maps. Not that he would ever admit even a hint of incompetence to anyone though.

    As McLellan gave his men a longwinded lecture on how he knew exactly where they were, Vanzetti interrupted him with an impertinent "What the hell? Did you hear that Sir?" The noise of approaching vehicles soon became clear to all of them. It sounded like heavy motorized traffic; probably tanks, clearly coming from the Iraqi direction of the front. McLellan ordered his Company to roll, sending half his force on a long circuitous route westward to hopefully outflank the enemy and hit them from behind while he led his other two platoons against the approaching Iraqi's.

    A matter of minutes later a force comprising two Soviet built Iraqi T-72 tanks accompanied by several troop transports came over the lip of a large sand dune. George noticed with concern that the Russian made tanks looked like late model versions, boasting the heavy "Dolly Parton" armor on the front of the turret. He could also see the tanks turrets traversing in order to get his Humvees in the crosshairs of their massive 125mm main gun. Captain McLellan ordered his men manning the Humvees .50 calibre guns to open up on the trucks while telling the drivers to make a fast and wide right flanking maneuver, with the objective of getting a clear shot at the T-72's more vulnerable side tracks. The Humvees veered back and forth through the sand dunes, eventually working George McLellan's two-platoon strength force into the best position for their Humvee mounted TOW weapon to hit the tanks. The TOW or tube launched optically tracked wire guided weapon launched its missile, hitting the side of the nearest T-72. The tank immediately did a jack in the box, blowing the turret as the ammunition cooked off. The other tank and bullet riddled troop transports immediately stopped, the frightened Iraqi troops and tank crew putting their hands on top of their heads and offering surrender. Soon after, the other part of his company rejoined them, surprised to find the battle already over. As his men searched the prisoners George reached Battalion on the radio and waited for instructions. His actions resulted in the capture of three troop transports, fifty-three Iraqi prisoners and one completely undamaged T-72 tank. Not until later when Lieutenant Colonel Jenkins debriefed him did he realize (sort of) how his brave but reckless actions might have gotten most of his men killed. All he needed to do was to call in air support, give an approximate location and have an A10 safely take out the tanks but of course he never even thought of taking the easy way out. He merely saw a problem and overcame it, knowing by force of will, he and his men would win the battle.

    Since everything somehow miraculously worked out okay, George got promoted to Major and received the Silver Star. With the upper brass however, this action in the Gulf War forever marked him as a loose cannon, the resulting glass ceiling probably limiting his career ambitions to the rank of Colonel or maybe if he was very lucky, Brigadier General. Major George McLellan returned to the States, to his moderately happy life with second wife Marie. (He never did get Samantha the administrative assistant past the level of being anything more than just a casual lover). Even though George could feel the chill wind on his once promising military career he still felt very confident, knowing somehow, someday the dream of reaching the upper echelons of command, the mythical rank of Five Star General would be his. He would do whatever it took…one way…or another…

Rance, Major Mitchell and all other Bridge Officers received a summons to be present at the historic moment when the Hyper Drive would be activated, launching them on their journey to Optimus 4 in the Zeta Reticulli system. At least two hundred officers jammed the Bridge waiting for General McLellan to say a few words before giving the order to "engage." The general "worked the room" by going around and saying a few words to everyone including a very brief awkward moment with Rance and Major Mitchell.

General McLellan then took the Commander in Chief's plush seat to give the order. "I've wanted to say this for the last eighty years…Engage!" he said, dramatically raising and then dropping his arm. The holo-display of the stars sparkling above them wavered as a slight shudder went through the *Hornet*, the Hyper Drive immediately taking them to near light speed with high pitched humming indicating everything worked according to its "design parameters." General McLellan basked in the reflected glow of his glory, all the high-ranking members of the Dictator's entourage congratulating him at this moment of great triumph.

Then without warning it became apparent something must be wrong. Very, very wrong. The humming of the Hyper Drive abruptly stopped and technicians started calling for an explanation from Main Engineering as to why the USS *Hornet* suddenly became the Universe's largest glider, coasting along at a very respectable rate, but coasting just the same. General George Brinton McLellan started behaving like the capricious child he had been nearly a century ago, shouting expletives that would make an outlaw biker blush.

He then started roaring like some injured animal, mere cursing no longer adequate to express his monumental rage. He jumped out of his seat, rushing towards the nearest male technician who he viciously backhanded. Then the General started kicking and spitting at anyone within range, not considering the possibility his outburst probably interfered with the ability of these poor people to give him the answers to why his vaunted "Hyper Drive" failed in such a humiliating manner. Finally after his century old frame ran out of energy because of the violent tirade, he could only sit in his command seat muttering the F word over and over again.

After a few minutes the image of the officer in charge of Main Engineering, General Bill Williams displayed on the huge Bridge holo-display. Realizing what a perilous position this embarrassment had put him in, he did some humiliating grovelling in an attempt to save his life. The sweat could be seen visibly pouring off his gaunt face, already appearing like a death mask.

"Glorious Leader, on behalf of everyone in Engineering I offer our most humble apologies for this…this malfunction. It appears that we experienced a host failure at the very moment of critical stress…this happened to be a fresh host with no indications of weakness. Apparently it must have been defective, probably from an undiagnosed cardiac condition. A new host has been installed and is awaiting your orders for activation. Again, Most Gracious, Merciful General I ask for forgiveness. Please…"

General McLellan cut off the Engineering Departments transmission with a dismissive wave. Drained from his outburst, General McLellan could only utter, "Start the damn thing" to the now traumatized and silent Bridge Crew. Rance, standing fairly close, could also hear the General issue General Williams's execution orders to

General Polgard, the feared head of his Security Force. No one humiliated the Great General McLellan publicly and survived, even if the screw up wasn't the poor man's fault.

This time the Hyper Drive functioned properly, accelerating the USS *Hornet* to near light velocity according to telemetry indicators integrated into the holo-display. Rance didn't realize exactly how tired he must have been until the start of their journey finally signaled the possibility of getting some uninterrupted sleep. The events of the last month had left him functioning on adrenaline, now swiftly diminishing. Knowing he would not be needed for a time, his overly stressed and drained body began to shut down. He just needed to focus on getting back to his quarters with maybe a little help from Major Mitchell.

Just when the glorious prospect of much-needed sleep looked temptingly within reach, fate yanked it away, like a hyena snatching a piece of carrion from a starving buzzard. Proceeding to leave the Bridge, he experienced the misfortune of bumping into General of the Fighters James Cross. Up until this time, the pompous, incompetent General chose to let Rance proceed with his Training School Program without any interference. Now, at the worst possible moment, the buffoon ordered that Rance immediately proceed to his luxurious Headquarters Office Suite and deliver a verbal report on the outcome of the Pilot Training Program. He dismissed Rance's incoherent protest about needing sleep with a "Come now my good man. You will have more than enough time for sleep before we reach our destination. The time for a debriefing is now while it's still fresh in your mind. Five minutes. I will be waiting."

If Rance had not been a Christian he may have been tempted to use his Wing Chun Kung Fu skills on this idiot of a man, regardless of the consequences. Now all he could manage was a slight nod, before telling Major Mitchell to guide him to the office of his supposed superior.

A few minutes later Rance stood in front of the desk of his somewhat flabby boss. The shiny metalwork on the man's gaudy customized uniform glittered in the bright halogen lights, "Creep" by Radiohead setting an appropriate musical backdrop. His chubby, rosy cheeks glowed as he flashed his famous smile with the eyes sparkling in accompaniment. The media often referred to him as "Uncle Jimmy" but many people had gone to prison or to their deaths after coming in contact with this seemingly affable man. Although no expert on art, Rance recognized a Goya, a Turner and a Rembrandt hanging on the wall behind Cross, who made a hobby of "borrowing" priceless masterpieces.

"I've been looking forward to speaking with you Rance," said the flashy, decadent officer, third in the Chain of Command on the USS *Hornet*. How he had achieved that level of responsibility in spite of gross ineptitude could only be attributed to his impeccable record of worshipful adulation to General McLellan.

"Here...have a drink." He poured a shot of expensive Scotch. Rance declined the alcohol, explaining he didn't drink strong liquor because of his Christian faith. This made the man's eyes sparkle even more. "You know," said General Cross, stretching back in his comfortable chair, "ever since the war I've been following your life story. I could never figure out why you threw away such a promising career. You had the world by the balls. All you needed to do was go through that hero worship routine for a little while and you could have had your pick of assignments, of women, of everything. Instead, you became a Christian," he paused, in thought "...hmm...very, very interesting." The eyes gave a hint of the evil and rot lying just below the surface of this clownish oaf. "Anyway, I've kept tabs on your training program for the pilots. I must say it's very good. Completely unnecessary, but very good all the same. I know you disagree with that." A cloud came over his features.

"Oh yes, I'm fully aware of your conversation with the General, requesting more time for the training. I probably could have talked the Old Man into it…had I agreed with you. Which of course I don't. I personally made sure the pilots received all the training they'd ever need against those second rate alien bastards, but McLellan insisted on giving you a role here so I had no choice but to agree and allow your training regime. It gave the pilots something to keep themselves occupied so I guess it did serve some minor purpose. No, the real reason I called you here is to make one thing exceedingly clear: Your job on this ship is finished. We have no further need for any of your backwards ideas on fighter tactics. As our Glorious General says, all we need to do is hit 'em hard. That's it. Oh. And one other thing. If you ever get in my way or try and curry the General's favor, I will have you killed." His malevolent glare made Rance realize it was no idle threat.

"I know McLellan is in love with your so-called superior American melting pot DNA, but I swear to you I will get you. Just stay the hell out of my way! You got that?"

Rance didn't say anything. This sick man deserved immediate death, not only for his outrageous comments but also for all of the good young pilots who were going to lose their lives if his ineffectual leadership continued during a time of war. Rance now understood that as a Christian he could never take the law into his own hands, no matter how worthy someone might be of needing justice. He said as little as possible, not even looking at this inept excuse for an officer. "Yes Sir. I understand perfectly." Hearing the iciness in Rance's voice, The "Uncle Jimmy" persona came back.

"Look Rance, I don't hate you. You have to understand something though. It's taken me a long time to get where I am and I don't want anyone messing up my comfortable little world. Why don't you just relax, enjoy the ride, and maybe screw that girl of yours...what's her name? Christine? Am I right?"

Now it was Rance's turn to make a threat. "Look at me," he said, voice and gaze deadly serious. "If you ever mention Christine St. James in such a manner again, I'll be forced to do something we'll both be sorry for. Do you understand me?"

"Uncle Jimmy" looked like a chastised child. "I didn't mean anything by that Rance. Just trying to make conversation, that's all. Obviously I hit a nerve. I guess now we both understand each other. Anyway...you're dismissed."

The underlying threat remained in the eyes however, like some cowardly jackal, prepared to wait and bide his time for revenge until his prey happened to be at their lowest, weakest point. Rance left the office, not telling Major Mitchell what transpired during the brief meeting, although the aide knew it couldn't have been pleasant judging by his boss's mood.

Rance really didn't care anymore however, focusing only on the bullet journey back to his quarters where he collapsed on his bed following a brief prayer, enjoying the first real sleep since coming on board the USS *Hornet*. He slept for a solid forty eight hours, the constant hum of the Hyper Drive putting him into an even deeper state of unconsciousness. During his slumber, the *Hornet* traveled immense distances, clawing towards their destination and inevitable conflict at a rate close to 290,000,000 meters per second.

When Rance finally woke up on Saturday afternoon, he could only think of one thing. He needed to clear out the cobwebs and focus on getting ready for the Sunday morning worship service. Even with his military training role now made redundant he could at least assist other crewmembers with spiritual matters before the *Hornet* reached her destination. He decided to prepare a short discussion on purity, both of the spirit and of the flesh. Rance really didn't know if the little Church gathering in his office conference room would attract anyone other than Major Mitchell, Lieutenant Crowder and himself. He hoped others might come to the service either out of genuine interest or curiosity; after all it remained listed on all of the *Hornet's* message sites. He prayed about the sermon before working on it, asking the Lord for wisdom and discernment. By early Sunday morning Rance felt he had developed something that his fellow Christians and also non-believers might be able to gain inspirational strength from.

He arrived at the conference room early, praying again that God would somehow work a miracle and bring sinners to the service. Major Mitchell and Lieutenant Crowder both greeted him warmly. The three of them decided to start singing the old hymns "What a Friend We Have in Jesus" and then "Standing on the Promises." Even though the ancient songs of praise technically remained on the list of banned "subversive materials," Major Mitchell didn't have any problem downloading them from the *Hornet's* Supernet database.

Before they finished the last hymn, Rance could see two people outlined through the frosted glass approaching the office. The door opened and there in front of them stood Christine St. James, holding hands with her husband Colonel Rick Santchez. He immediately jumped to his feet, extending his hand to Rick who graciously accepted the handshake, in spite of the emotional hold Rance still had on his wife.

Christine was very happy. "Rance you won't believe what happened. That night after I accepted the Lord as my savior, I went back home and told Rick. I told him everything, even the reason why I went to your quarters. I needed to repent. Anyway, even though Rick was understandably upset with me, he still asked some questions about Jesus. I tried to explain as best as I could how everyone has a spot in their heart that can only be filled by one thing: Jesus Christ." Christine's eyes lit up as she continued. "He kept asking me things about Christianity and although I don't really know that much, I did know the Sinners Prayer. All that really matters is that two days ago, Rick accepted Jesus as his personal Lord and Savior!"

Rance gave the man a hug, welcoming his new brother in Christ to their little Church group. The simple fact their God could transform such a complicated interpersonal situation into something good capable of saving lost souls, pointed to His all-powerful magnificence. Rance started his little Church presentation, reciting the Lord's Prayer and then launching right into the oration.

"Glory be to God!" exclaimed Rance. "I would like to talk to you today about cleanliness. Cleanliness of the spirit and the flesh." He fumbled through his old-fashioned book style Bible. "The apostle Paul tells us in 2 Corinthians 7:1 that we need to cleanse ourselves from all filthiness of the flesh and spirit. Sometimes it may seem to those around us that we're living an upstanding and clean life but deep inside in our spirit we could be fostering an attitude that displeases our Lord. It's human nature to ignore sins of the spirit because we think they're hidden. We ignore them until that hidden sin finally leads to outward behavior no one can ignore. The Bible is full of examples of people who held onto that inner sinful attitude, whether it is the sin of pride or lust or anything else that draws us away from God. If any of us harbor any of these inner sins we must repent! Pride and lust have been compared to hidden stones over which many people stumble. We must always rely on our God completely and never think that we can do things on our own. That road only leads to humiliation and failure. So ask yourselves friends…"

The door to the conference room opened. There in the doorway stood a young female NCO looking like a deer caught in the beam of auto headlights. Rance walked over to greet her. "Welcome to our humble little Church! I'm Rance Edwards. And your name is…?" The tall willowy girl couldn't have been much over the age of twenty one. She was a very attractive brunette. "Calloway, Corporal Heather Calloway. It's nice to meet you all."

Rance introduced the rest of the group before he continued on with his sermon. "As Christians, it's important to remember that we are held to a higher moral standard than non-believers still under the influence of the satanically inspired Great Lie. What is the Great Lie, you ask? It is simply the belief that man is God, that as God, he will never die. Sin and depravity are mere illusions, nothing more than passing blemishes. This philosophy seeks to blot out the reality of consequences for our actions. As you know planet Earth is currently controlled by this deluding influence fostered by the Antichrist and False Prophet. Adam and Eve were created with immense intellects and clear consciences, without the taint of sin. Satan tempted them with the Great Lie and mankind has paid the price ever since. We can learn the following lesson from this: If our two perfect ancestors fell victim to this false theology how can we be so confident that we will not fall prey to the enemies lures, to the Devil's temptations?" Rance paused to give the next point emphasis.

"My friends, we have only one guarantee, to rely totally and completely on our Lord and Savior, Jesus Christ. It is important for us as believers to maintain purity both of the flesh and of the spirit so we can minister to the lost souls on this ship. Our lives need to be free of hypocrisy. The only way to achieve this is to always put our trust in Jesus! Praise the Lord!"

They concluded the service by singing "In the Garden" and "O Sacred Head, Now Wounded" followed by a brief prayer of thanksgiving.

Afterwards, while old recordings of the Brooklyn Tabernacle Choir played in the background, they all did their best to make young Heather Calloway comfortable hoping she would continue to attend Worship Services. All in all, thought Rance, it had been a very good day.

The next few weeks were a blur of Church and bible study sessions through which the ever-present humming of the Hyper Drive acted like some annoying type of background music. Two of the new Church attendees, Corporal Heather Calloway as well as a young sallow, dark haired Marine, PFC Edward Furlong, accepted Jesus Christ as their Lord and Savior. Five or six others attended occasionally, curious, but not yet ready to give their hearts to the Lord. The *Hornet* continued her tremendous pace, pushing rapidly towards their destination, the alien star named Zeta Reticulli. America's top engineers and scientists had done their job well. Other than a few already unstable individuals being adversely affected by the electromagnetic energy of the Hyper Drive, including two Marines who went on killing sprees with their M-30s, everything worked perfectly. The artificial black hole created by the Hyper Drive drastically compressed the space between earth and Zeta Reticulli, shortening a journey that would normally take approximately thirty-seven years at near light speed into a short jaunt of about thirty-one days. Rance hated to think about how many hosts had been "drained" in order for them to achieve their goal but after traveling thirty days, the USS *Hornet* began to slow on the last leg of her journey to the two increasingly bright binary stars around which orbited their destination and final destiny: Optimus 4…

CHAPTER 13

"Hey folks! You've connected with Comm-Rad 1, bringing you non-stop invasion coverage! I'm Lieutenant Colonel Troy Wilson and you just heard some good ol' Guns N Roses, November Rain." Before that we enjoyed everyone's favorite from the Proclaimers, "I'm Gonna Be 500 Miles," "Hey Jealousy" by the Gin Blossoms and of course "Mr. Jones" from the Counting Crows. I've been deluged with a lot of requests for "What Is Love" from Haddaway and "Friday I'm In Love" by The Cure so I'll try and get those out to ya in the next while but first a special treat for all you Grays listenin' down there on Optimus. A little taste of Earth music for you little fairies…Nirvana…"Smells Like Teen Spirit"…Comm-Rad 1…your voice of the grand invasion…"

George McLellan read the divorce papers with a shocked expression pasted across his face. If he'd taken a moment to give it any serious thought however, he might have realized how his long-suffering second wife Marie put up with a hell of a lot before she finally decided to give him the boot. After all, not many wives would be patient enough to allow his endless one-night stands and affairs with various female trollops and tramps. The final straw that really finished off their marriage happened two weeks before when Marie listened in on a phone conversation he was having with that silly little airhead Shannon McGuire, his latest mistress. Even though he instinctively knew the divorce couldn't be avoided, it still hurt like a bugger. He did love Marie in his own strange way. Following the exposure of his most recent liaison, he tried explaining to her that these other women meant nothing to him, how they were just playthings, but of course she didn't listen. Marie tearfully packed up some clothes and moved back in with her parents. And now these damned divorce papers had just been dumped on him…Oh well, no sense crying over spilt milk. He decided not to contest the divorce. She could have the house, the almost new '93 Buick, everything. He didn't care. At least there weren't any kids to worry about. It wasn't like they didn't try but it just didn't happen, which from his present viewpoint could only be considered a good thing. Marie never understood how all these trashy women acted as a mere distraction, helping him forget the present tattered state of his military career.

Even though he recently received a promotion to Lieutenant Colonel, mainly due to his excellent administrative skills, the new divisional commander General Rogers made no secret of the fact George's command aspirations in the 101st Airborne could go no higher than maybe full eagle Colonel. Well screw him thought George. Screw our asshole President for that matter. In fact, screw all of the bastards who kept him from achieving his true destiny.

Lately George had started getting these… ideas concerning his future. These ideas, visions if you will were so wildly crazy that he at first questioned his own sanity. Then the thoughts started to make some sense to him. They formed a half shaped plan, soon evolving into something more definite, urging him to take concrete actions to make it a reality. That's why he recently put in a request to transfer into the role of the 101st Airborne's Nuclear Tactical Officer. This would involve him taking custody and control of the Divisions half dozen B 61 Tactical Nuclear weapons, each with a yield of 10 kilotons, slightly less powerful than the one used on Hiroshima. For his little plan one of these would be enough…not that he had yet told anyone about these bizarre machinations going on in his head. He couldn't tell the wrong person about this outlandish plan-after all-the idiots now in power could easily send him to a military prison or psychiatric hospital for even mentioning such a thing. No, he needed to move slowly, but he had time, lots of time, all the time in the world. In fact, right now that's pretty much all he had left. If successful at getting his transfer the next step would be to assemble a small cadre of trusted officers he could confide in, who could assist in the mission of getting even with the bastards responsible for keeping him and other good men down in the dirt. He knew someday he would make it happen, would make them pay... would make them all pay...

For the first time in Mankind's long troubled history, a human made object orbited another world in an alien star system. The USS *Hornet* circled the red sandy surface of Optimus 4 at a high orbit of approximately four hundred kilometers. In the first two hours after reaching her position the *Hornet's* digital spy cameras had mapped every inch of the alien planet, assembling a highly detailed holographic visualization now floating high above the Bridge. If they managed to win this coming battle the invaders from Earth would inherit a very dry world. Actual oceans were non-existent with three large inland seas being the extent of visible moisture on this barren looking planet. The officer in charge of explaining the holo-display to the Bridge Officers detailed a small area on the planet that contained the Grays largest city. Called something completely undecipherable in the alien's ancient Sumerian sounding native language, it had instead received the far less linguistically challenging code name "Capital City." The zoom view of this metropolis showed millions of the insect like Grays scurrying about to and fro from their primitive looking buildings made out of a rocky material appearing to be similar to limestone. The majority of the creatures looked to be simple pedestrians but some possessed a type of wheeled commuter vehicle. "Capital City" was situated close to one of the inland seas; in fact all six of the major

Gray population centers were located on the shores of these bodies of foul, brackish water.

General McLellan took the floor of the Bridge War Conference, explaining the simple strategy he of course took credit for coming up with. Rance could tell the old man, now a hyper bundle of energy, probably hadn't slept in days. Most likely an effect of the stimulants his "doctors" gave him.

McLellan explained how he immediately ordered a Combat Air Patrol or CAP of fifty F-72's to be established, protecting the USS *Hornet* from enemy attack. During the first three hours in Optimus 4's orbit no hostile actions had occurred. In fact sensors could not detect any enemy military action, the only air traffic on the planet seeming to be lower speed commercial transports. Since the Grays appeared undefended and ripe for the picking, General McLellan issued orders for the immediate commencement of Operation Sledgehammer, involving two successive waves of two thousand F-72 fighters hitting the alien population and transportation hubs with every weapon they possessed including the ultra-advanced Zinger 1 Kiloton tactical nuclear weapons. In the Dictators astute and compelling words of strategic brilliance, "they needed to hit the mothers and hit the mothers hard!"

After attaining complete air supremacy, hopefully within three days, they could then start Operation Anvil, the landing of ten Army and Marine Divisions on the planet's surface. Strategically landed near the main population centers, this army group would encircle these areas in a huge pincer movement. Once the encirclement had been completed, the remaining military units on the *Hornet* would be transferred to the planet, eliminating any enemy resistance in these pockets and setting up internment camps for the surviving Grays.

As soon as the military phase of operations neared completion the shuttles could then transfer support units such as engineer battalions and Seabees to set up some infrastructure for the rest of the colonists. The USS *Hornet* would continue to perennially circle their new world acting as a supply and support hub to the colony. At least that was how the plan McLellan presented to them was supposed to unfold, simple and brazen in its overconfidence, ignoring any inconvenient possibilities like strong enemy resistance. The General raised his arms almost like some minor mythological Greek God figure, expecting adulation for the genius of getting them to this spot, his boldness guaranteeing them an easy victory over these inferior aliens. His audience didn't disappoint, with everyone other than Rance and his aide screaming their praise to their Glorious Grandfather General.

The first fighter-bomber sorties soon began, all five of the ship's flight decks being kept continuously busy with F-72's taking off and returning. Even though technically barred from leaving the Bridge during battle conditions, Rance needed to be in one of the fighter pilot ready rooms, giving words of encouragement and support to the fighter jocks. He wished he could have been one of the pilots seeing action on this first day of battle but knew from experience sometimes a clap on the back or smile from a good officer could do wonders for aircrews facing death. Besides, Rance felt confident leaving Major Mitchell on the Bridge to answer any questions the Staff Officers might have.

Although smaller, the visual display in the ready room showed more than enough detail of all the carnage the *Hornet's* fighter-bombers were causing down on the planet's surface. Facing only light and sporadic Gray fighter disc resistance, the major population centers and roads were being blasted into submission. Almost one hundred of the Zinger battlefield nuclear weapons had already been used on the large cities, close to the upper limit of radioactive contamination deemed acceptable by certain eminent environmentalists. That limit of course was established only to protect the future colonists, not out of concern for the innocent alien civilians on the planet. Actually no one really gave a damn what those "small" nukes were doing to the unprotected Grays in the blast zone. No one except for Rance who said a small prayer every time one of those flashes indicated another detonation and more resulting deaths.

Although the Grays only proffered a very light resistance thus far, it didn't mean that the Alien discs hadn't caused the *Hornet's* fighter pilots some concern. During the first few hours of battle, twenty seven F72's had been shot down with another forty receiving some type of battle damage, three returning fighters so badly shot up they would probably be beyond repair. By early afternoon the second wave of two thousand fighters began their sorties, shooting at anything the first wave missed. Many returning pilots told tales of their exploits, many bragging about shooting down the lumbering and defenseless civilian craft, apparently not realizing or caring how these contained nothing but large numbers of helpless Grays. The fighter jocks were keeping an unofficial tally of who had shot down the most enemy fighters. So far an African American Colonel named Wayne Bruce and his wingman Captain Robin Burgess held the scoring title, downing 56 alien discs between them. They quickly became minor celebrities.

After most of the second assault had left the *Hornet*, Rance made his way back to the Bridge where the mood could only be described as jubilant. General McLellan concerned himself with trivial invasion details feeling as did every other Senior Officer the war had already been won.

"I want the SS100 loaded on a Galaxy shuttle. Right now! If things continue the way they're going we'll have to advance the timetable and start the ground invasion tomorrow. I told you those damn aliens wouldn't have any fight in em! They're nothing but weak, spineless cowards!" Rance noticed from the visual display of stats above them that the number of F-72's lost in action now reached forty eight, a relatively acceptable number out of almost four thousand sorties flown so far today. Acceptable or not, he didn't want to think about what the Grays may be doing to any captured pilots at this very moment. Search and rescue of downed pilots was yet another "trivial" detail that no one thought of during the planning phase.

    The General, after conferring with several of his most senior officers announced a revised battle strategy. The ground attack sorties would continue all night with the next phase of the invasion, Operation Anvil, the landing of troops on the planet's surface, to begin at 06:00 local time. The first three elements landed by shuttle would be the US Army 1st Infantry Division (the famed Big Red 1), the US Marine 5th Infantry Division and the 101st Airborne Division (The General's old division). Army Ranger Units would be first on the ground, preparing landing sites for continuous shuttle landings expected to take about twelve hours to unload all of the troops. These three divisions would then expand their perimeter outwards, waiting until the remaining seven divisions (including two armored divisions) built up their strength before starting their encircling pincer movement. Fighters would fly uninterrupted sorties providing air cover to this first and most vulnerable phase of the ground war. Since a few pointers on fighter tactics and a word of encouragement were things every pilot could use, Rance left the jubilant atmosphere of the Bridge to visit the three pilots who crash landed their shot up fighters on the flight decks. Although the *Hornet's* glide beam normally guided a battle-damaged fighter to a safe landing, the system failed in these three cases, apparently having something to do with their flight-positioning units malfunctioning. In spite of the injuries and Hyper Drive failures they all did a magnificent job of landing their mangled craft, only causing minor damage to the flight decks. Even so, the atmosphere in sickbay remained a little more subdued than on the Battle Bridge. Two of the injured pilots were in surgery having dead tissue removed from areas of the body where their space suits had been punctured by shrapnel. These small holes, although immediately sealed by their smart suits advanced technology, allowed the exposed flesh in these regions to die from the deadly cold airless environment of space. Some of these dead patches could affect an area a few centimeters across and a few centimeters deep.

Rance spoke to the less severely injured pilot, a young female Captain by the name of Naomi Fehr. The medics were just finishing the painful patch job, a triangular piece of gauze on her shoulder covering a wound where a needle size piece of shrapnel penetrated her spacesuit.

"I know what it's like Captain," said Rance with compassion in his voice. "Unlike me however, you actually brought your damaged fighter back to your ship. From one pilot to another I just wanted to say I think you did some damn incredible flying today. Good work!" Rance clasped her hand. Captain Fehr had tears in her eyes as Rance left the sick bay following a few supportive words to the doctors and nurses. This great man truly deserved to be called an officer and a gentleman.

After relieving Major Mitchell on the Bridge so his aide could snatch a few hours' sleep, Rance watched fascinated while the feverish preparations for the morning's troop landings began. Extreme magnification of the holo-display of the planet's surface showed sortie after sortie from the *Hornet's* F-72's devastating the Grays large population centers. Smoke rose in huge columns from vast areas in the cities, now reaching the stratosphere where it spread around the globe. Preliminary estimates of the Grays casualty level had just gone above five million out of a probable total population of about five hundred million. The *Hornet's* fighters still enjoyed an overwhelming superiority over the Grays fighter discs but during the last few hours' resistance had unexpectedly stiffened, leading to a fighter loss rate of eighty-six since the war started. Even so, the attrition rate definitely remained in the *Hornet's* favor with pilots claiming three thousand, two hundred and seventy Gray ships shot down. Several hundred of the aliens commercial transport ships were also downed. The fighter sorties continued all night, apparently completing the destruction of Optimus 4. High Command directed many of the missions to suppress the region where troops would soon be landing. This small center, located about one hundred kilometers south of Capital City was some sort of transport hub with all the Gray's major roads intersecting it. With flight after flight blasting the landing zone it didn't seem like anything could still be alive, let alone provide any opposition to the Army Rangers slated to be the first to go in. They would secure the stretches of highway designated to act as landing strips for the shuttles. The Bridge crew, although still happy, showed less energetic enthusiasm than they displayed earlier. They all must have been extremely tired except for the now manic General McLellan who showed no sign of needing sleep or of even slowing down for that matter.

"It's a freakin' turkey shoot boys!" he exclaimed as he danced a little jig, looking somewhat ridiculous because of his age. "The Rangers go in soon, then my old Division, the 101st. After that we secure the area, land the rest of the army and begin the pincer movement. Rommel and old General Patton would be in their element. We cut off their escape, and then we finish off the scum trapped in our pocket. Once that's done she's all over. The whole sick rotting Gray infrastructure will collapse. We win, they lose, and then we kill off the ones we don't need." Iron Maiden's

"Run for the Hills" set the appropriate backdrop to his tirade.

The General noticed Rance standing stoically at his battle station, displaying a noble bearing similar to his aristocratic Native American and Prussian ancestors. Rance didn't seem to be enjoying this triumphant moment, at least not enough to please the Dictator.

"What's wrong with my Christian friend? Too many Grays dying to suit your bleeding heart? You better decide whose side you're on pal, ours or theirs," he said, pointing at the holograph of Optimus 4's arid landscape. The General acted like he was on the upper edge of some drug induced high and couldn't stand anyone not sharing his passion. Rance of course felt no fear at anything any mere man could say or do to him. He knew his Father God, Creator of the Universe was the only one anyone needed to have a healthy respect for and this second rate despot certainly did not fit that category.

"Sir, just because I don't share your love of war or its resulting victims doesn't mean I'm not a patriotic American who's prepared to die doing my duty. If you think otherwise you are a fool."

The Bridge suddenly became silent. During the past half-century many good Americans found torture and death to be the brutal consequences for doing much less than this. The General glared at Rance before responding to this annoyance. Apparently nothing, not even such a glaring insult would be allowed to tarnish the General's moment of ultimate triumph.

"Everyone, I want you all to take a good look at the pathetic former war hero General Rance Edwards. He's the man who threw away a promising life because of some outmoded, phoney God. Have a good laugh."

The General turned his back on Rance and focused his attention on one of the tactical workstations. A few of the Bridge officers did titter a bit, some probably out of relief that none of them would be caught in the indirect crossfire of the General's legendary wrath. Rance knew he was now, even more than before, a marked man. The General would punish him, probably with the death penalty when these more pressing invasion concerns were taken care of. He honestly didn't care. None of it mattered in comparison to always staying true to his Lord and Savior, something that although difficult, he had done his best to do. After Major Mitchell returned to the Bridge, Rance went back to his quarters for a couple hours of sleep before the ground invasion began. In spite of the Generals antagonism towards him, he wanted to be at his battle station at such a crucial time. Now, more than ever, he needed to focus on his duty, both to his country and to the pilots and soldiers risking their lives. That thought still remained on his mind as he woke at 04:30 local time.

Rance made it back to the Bridge in time to see holo views of shuttles landing several hundred US Army Rangers into the target zone. They quickly secured a perimeter and set up radar-guided landing strips on the undamaged sections of highway for the coming waves of troops. Everything went well with the only mishap being a crashed shuttle, flipping over after hitting a shell hole while landing on one of the improvised highway landing strips. Even so, only three Rangers died in the crash. In fact those three were the only casualties in the entire opening maneuver of the ground war, the Rangers facing no enemy opposition, not even seeing one living Gray.

Soon after elements of the 101st Airborne, 5th Marine and 1st Infantry Divisions started their non-stop shuttle landings on the makeshift runways. Transport after transport landed, disgorging their cargo of troops and then heading back to the *Hornet* for another load. During the entire time F-72's flew constant air cover for the invasion. Opposition to the landings could only be considered light, a few alien fighter discs trying to break through the protective fighter cordon and immediately being shot down in the futile attempt. The fighter-bombers assault on the cities also continued unabated, killing untold millions more of the Grays.

Finally, after about twelve hours of nonstop shuttle flights, the last of the soldiers needed for the preliminary action were unloaded. On the Bridge, the jovial mood continued since the difficult and dangerous job of transporting over thirty thousand troops went off literally without a hitch. "Call Me Maybe" by Carly Rae Jepsen played over Comm-Rad 1, reflecting that lighthearted spirit.

The General, very pleased with himself, became less hyper. Everyone started to relax a bit as the most vulnerable phase of the whole operation was now over. Without warning that calm attitude evaporated instantly as if someone threw a glass of ice cold water into all their collective faces. One of the tactical analysts pointed to the holo-display, so shocked by it the man could only shout out "Oh my God!" even though he usually professed to be an atheist. Everyone on the Bridge now stared in complete disbelief, the holograph showing a horde of ten thousand gray fighter craft sitting calmly in an odd and precise geometric formation at a distance of only three kilometers from the USS *Hornet*…

CHAPTER 14

"This is Captain Dan with all the greatest hits of twentieth century Earth. You just heard "Go West" by the Pet Shop Boys followed by Green Day with their enormous hit "Basket Case." That one was goin' out to all you millions of Grays in the blast areas now slowly and painfully dyin' of radiation poisoning. Hope you're enjoyin' the weather down there on Optimus Four! Don't go away now! I've got some really special songs comin' up for you alien creepy crawlies... you're gonna love the Offspring with "Self Esteem," "What's the Frequency Kenneth" from REM and "Buddy Holly" by Weezer, but first, some Smashing Pumpkins with "Today"... Yes, today's the day all right... the day you're gonna die...take it and like it you filthy gray bastards..."

Things were starting looking up for Colonel George McLellan the last week of October 1995. He now approached his second anniversary of becoming the 101st Airborne's Nuclear Tactical Officer and almost a year had gone by since he had been promoted to full Colonel. Best of all, he actually enjoyed his job of managing storage and security of the B61 tactical nuclear weapons. George now had eight of "his babies" as he fondly called the 10-kiloton nuclear devices. Better yet, the asshole Generals thought they had finally found the perfect place for George, somewhere they could shove him to play out his career in obscurity without any chance of causing any...embarrassments. After all, they told themselves, there were so many safeguards on the nukes there could be absolutely no chance of "crazy George" doing anything stupid like selling one of his babies to Arab terrorists or detonating one when he wasn't supposed to. Such reassuring thoughts helped the Generals get back to sleep after occasionally waking up in the middle of the night with a terrifying nightmare, usually involving a maniacal, laughing Colonel George McLellan pressing "the button" on his nukes. Of course George's superiors ordered many covert reviews of his performance in the role of Nuclear Tactical Officer and each time he passed with flying colors. Upper Command all agreed that although Colonel McLellan could definitely be categorized as different, he really had an enthusiasm for his new role, so for the most part the Generals left him alone.

Mimicking the lead actor in the 1995 film *Richard III*, George smiled his evil little smile, the one that came over his face when he thought about his "ideas." Those mothers had one hell of a surprise coming to them when all elements of his plan unfolded the way he had envisioned it for at least the thousandth time. He even found one other junior officer who shared his ideas. Captain Wilbur Pattinson, the officer who directly supervised the various warrant officers and NCO's in the Tactical Unit, idolized Colonel McLellan.

During some casual discussions with the young man over a case of beer, George had carefully and systematically brought up the "theoretical concept" of how a small group of officers could take back the military from the incompetent civilian and military administration and put the United States back on the road to glory. Captain Pattinson agreed that the Clinton Administration debacle in Somalia pointed to the urgent need for someone in the military to do *something* although he didn't exactly know what. George hadn't quite reached the point of telling the Lieutenant everything about his plan but he would only when absolutely certain the man could be trusted. These preparations could take years, even decades but he forced his usually impatient personality to look ahead at the long-term objective. Similar to the North Vietnamese Army challenging the more powerful American military, he needed to be patient and slowly assemble all of his pawns for the sudden, decisive move, just like the Tet Offensive. For the plan to work properly, he needed the participation of at least a dozen officers of the rank of Colonel or Brigadier General. George estimated that it could take a decade; possibly more to assemble a cadre of highly trusted officers. Of course, he wouldn't tell his subordinates everything, especially the part about them being eliminated when no longer necessary. All of it so many years in the future…but he could wait. After all, he liked his job and even his personal life recently started to look up. He thought he had finally found true love (whatever that was) with his third wife, Lisa Castallano. A few years younger than George, she happened to be seven months pregnant with their first child. Such domestic bliss at home even caused George to drastically curtail (but not completely stop) his extramarital philandering. Yes, he thought as that sick smile came on his face again, things looked pretty good right now. He only needed to achieve one little thing to really complete his life…nuking Washington DC back into the freakin' Stone Age…

    Everyone on the Bridge stood transfixed by the holographic view showing the ten thousand alien fighter craft arranged in a neat geometric pattern of every three craft forming a pyramid shape, all being connected to each other. Rance had the absurd thought that the design actually looked like some bluffing attempt to make their numbers appear larger but with such an immense superiority of ships they really didn't need to bother. The sheer numbers of their craft were stunning enough all by themselves, leading Rance to pray to God, asking for His hand to be on this coming battle, whatever the outcome.
    One of the communication techs broke the stunned silence. "The CAP commander, Colonel Gibson is asking

for instructions Sir. Sir...?" General McLellan for probably one of the first times in his life appeared to be speechless, his mouth gaping in disbelief. His elderly mind needed to absorb this sudden shifting of gears, going from being on the verge of complete victory one moment to facing this unexpected and massive threat the next.

Finally after a few seconds, like some aging, drunken street brawler briefly knocked down but then staggering to his feet, he got himself together with the old Fighting General reappearing and apparently ready for the struggle of his life.

"Tell Colonel Gibson that I want the CAP to engage the enemy. Now damn you!" The tech, knowing full well that this order would be a death sentence for the pilots of the fifty fighter CAP Group did something brave, but very stupid. He dared question a direct order from the General.

"But Sir! The CAP is outnumbered two hundred to one! They are going to die if you...wait...no please don't ..." His voice became very high pitched, turning into a girl like scream which abruptly stopped when the General finished pulling out his old Mauser model 1896 machine pistol from a shoulder holster and fired off two bullets both of which hit the man in the chest. Rance watched in disgust but not surprise as McLellan walked up to the still twitching body and put another slug into the technician's head at close range. Incongruously, "Never Let You Go" by Third Eye Blind set an audible backdrop to the sickening scene.

"Anybody else want some?" he yelled out. "No? Good. Now you" he pointed to another communication tech, "send that damn message!" The man didn't need to be told twice. General McLellan sprung to action. "All gun crews! Fire at will! Activate main shields! How many fighters do we have deployed on Optimus right now?" It took a few seconds for him to get the answer. "Two thousand, one hundred and fifteen fighters are providing air support to our troops sir," said a frightened officer. McLellan didn't hesitate before making a decision. "Leave two hundred fighters on Optimus to provide cover for the landing force. I want the other eighteen hundred fighters recalled to protect the *Hornet*. Launch all remaining available fighters! I want to smash these dickheads!"

As an afterthought he added, "Tell the galley to send up some strong coffee and turkey flavored battle sandwiches." All the officers on the Bridge including Rance and his aide looked up to the holo-display and watched the fifty fighter CAP group courageously take on the ten thousand enemy fighters. They ripped into the pretty geometric pattern of the alien formation, blasting large gaps into their ranks as Comm-Rad 1 played a cover of Poison's "Talk Dirty to Me" by the old punk band Jughead's Revenge. Even though the aliens were outclassed both by the quality of the Earth pilots and ships they flew, it wasn't long before the overwhelming numbers of discs took a devastating toll on the attackers. Within a minute only about twenty of their number remained in the fight.

By this time some of the American fighters recalled from the planet's surface had joined the battle. The aliens soon started to break up their neat geometric pattern. On the Bridge, it quickly became apparent what the grays were up to.

"General!" called out the tracking tech, "It appears that about half of the enemy force is breaking off and proceeding at high speed towards the landing zone on Optimus 4. The remainder of their group is attempting to break through our fighter cordon and attack the *Hornet*!" The Dictator was livid. "Shit! Tell those gun crews to blast 'em! I don't give a damn if we hit our own fighters... just nail 'em with everything we've got! Quick! Give me a holo on the situation down below!"

General Wilbur Pattinson actually got off his fairly large seat and now at last seemed to be taking an active interest in the battle. "Gun crews are firing at will Sir! Holo being displayed now." Everyone looked up at the split screen, one side showing the large number of enemy fighter discs attacking the *Hornet*, being harried by F-72's and now starting to be targeted by defensive plasma blasts. The beams hit a lot of the attacking aliens but also took out a number of their own protecting fighters, unfortunate victims of friendly fire. The other side of the screen showed the two hundred F-72's providing air support to the ground forces being ripped apart by close to five thousand alien ships. Rance watched their display of bravery with quiet admiration, saying a prayer for the souls of those being lost. Even though these pilots must have known they were doomed, not a single one cut and ran back to the comparative safety of the *Hornet*.

It wasn't long before the tremendous weight of alien numbers led to the complete loss of all two hundred F-72 fighters. With all fighter opposition eliminated, the aliens started methodical strafing and bombing of the thirty thousand cut off American soldiers on the hostile surface of Optimus. Rance and everyone else on the Bridge now focused their attention on the other side of the display however. Like thousands of tiny cuts, alien energy beams assaulted the *Hornet's* shields, some even penetrating and causing decompression of affected areas. Close to four thousand of the *Hornet's* F-72's carried on the defense against the alien ships, taking many out but also taking heavy losses themselves.

Rance, recognizing the urgency of the situation and frustrated by being able to do nothing except pray for the *Hornet's* overwhelmed fighter force, approached the General. "Sir!" demanded Rance. "I request permission to launch my fighter and take part in the defense." Major Mitchell stood behind Rance, adding "Me too Sir!" The General didn't even look away from the visual display as he dismissed their requests. "No! I need all my staff officers here on the Bridge. Now get back to your posts!"

Rance briefly considered disobeying a direct order but knew it would adversely affect his young assistant. He forced himself to go back to his station and helplessly watch the deaths of many young Americans. The stranded troops on the planet's surface were being slaughtered, wave after wave of enemy fighters coming in at low altitude with energy beams blazing. American antiaircraft fire took its toll on the grays because of these suicidal tactics but the aliens still had several thousand operational fighters left for their reckless offence.

Rance realized the majority of those brave soldiers on Optimus 4 would probably die if somebody didn't immediately take action. "General McLellan," he called out, not waiting for a response. "Requesting permission to organize a rescue attempt for those three divisions on Optimus. We can use Galaxy shuttles with fighter escorts, at least save some of…"

"Permission denied!" grunted the General. "No one leaves Optimus. The original plan will still be carried out. Not only is there going to be no evacuation, I want the remaining seven divisions of the first wave on standby ready to board shuttles. Send the order! " He pointed to one of the Liaison officers who immediately transmitted the command. Rance had that sick feeling again. The name Stalingrad suddenly came to mind. If the dictator attempted to land more troops without complete air superiority…well he didn't want to think about that gruesome possibility. Their present circumstances soon became all he could think about anyway. The tactical reports indicated at least two thousand of the alien fighter discs still pressed their vicious attacks on the USS *Hornet*. More and more of the alien energy beams, apparently of a newer generation of design, and much stronger than originally anticipated by the Americans, now blazed through the vessels defensive shielding. Damage reports flooded into the Bridge, telling tales of explosive decompression, lost lives, and heroic rescues of severely injured crewmembers. Nearly all of the *Hornet's* available F-72 fighters had now been launched, engaged in bitter combat with the attacking aliens. Rance could only watch the carnage, pray for the victims and wish that he'd been given more time to teach tactics to these young pilots.

Another problem became apparent as the fighting raged. Quite a few damaged American fighters were stranded in space with no way to bring their ships in for a landing on the *Hornet's* flight decks. The defensive shielding acted like a one-way door, allowing fighters to be launched but not recovered. With the savage alien assault continuing, they could not afford to drop the shields, even for a moment. Many just floated in space, helpless, more than a few being picked off by the aliens as easy targets. Rance found it difficult to resist the impulse of jumping into his F-72 and coming to the aid of his stricken comrades.

General McLellan couldn't have cared less about the plight of a few abandoned pilots. He could only focus on the larger war strategy, how to hold onto his dream of conquering the planet they orbited. "We're winnin' people!" he called out to no one in particular. "What's the fighter count at? Thirty two hundred for us to eighteen hundred for them? Good! Keep those plasma cannons firing. The fifty calibers too." In actual fact, the lethal combination of the plasma cannons and the dated but still deadly fifty caliber gun stations meant the USS *Hornet* now slowly started to turn the tide on the alien onslaught. The aliens may have been losing but apparently somebody forgot to tell them as they pressed attack after suicidal attack at the USS *Hornet*.

The situation for the soldiers still surviving on Optimus was much more desperate. Dug into whatever shallow trenches they'd been able to improvise while under fire, the alien attacks killed or wounded fifty percent of their original strength. These brave men and women, from

Divisions with a long illustrious history of warfare could never be referred to as quitters however. Facing low level air assault from the aliens, they used every weapon at their disposal, the new generation of SAM's, 150 MM cannons, 20 MM antiaircraft guns, 50 caliber machine guns, their personal M30's, even in the case of the commanding General, his own pearl handled model 1911 Colt .45 once used by an ancestor in the Second World War. The sandy hills surrounding the landing zone eventually took on a shiny metallic hue because of all the shot down Gray fighter craft. Still they came, shooting their fingers of fire, the smell of burning flesh filling the Americans makeshift trenches, with even the wounded and dying firing back, taking down ship after ship. It looked as if they were now engaged in some ghastly war of attrition, the Americans cut off from evacuation or support and the aliens fighting for their home planet with a tenacity that would have made any Japanese Samurai proud. The *Hornet*, orbiting high above, seemed to have turned the gray tide, there now being less than three hundred alien fighters still attacking. Many of these had received some battle damage, mainly from the fifty caliber machine guns, making them an easier target for the now veteran *Hornet's* fighter pilots. Even though Rance still regretted not having enough training time with the pilots the education they did have now paid massive dividends. The grays didn't seem to understand tactics or strategy, merely hoping overwhelming numbers would carry the day, which in fact they almost had. But now that the odds were in the favor of the American pilots, strategy compounded the weakness of the grays. The aliens did show a form of bravery, continuing to press their attacks even when it was becoming obvious they were beaten. Finally when less than a hundred alien fighters remained, they tried something radically different, a massed attack. Recognizing the *Hornet's* flight decks as a crucial element of the ship, all eighty-seven survivors, energy beams blazing, rocketed at high speed towards the K Deck #4 main flight deck. Eighty-six of these alien discs impacted and detonated against the shield. The eighty-seventh, following a fraction of a second behind, made it through the weakened shield and flew into the flight deck, crashing at near light speed and causing a huge explosion, which completely destroyed the hangar and flight deck. The impact was so great that even some officers on the Bridge were knocked off their feet.

"Bloody Kamikazes!" screamed the General. "Give me a report!" The details of the attack took a few minutes to compile, probably due to the massive area impacted by the blast and large number of casualties. Rance, although fairly sure that Christine St. James quarters and workplace were both located in more protected parts of the ship still found himself involuntarily concerned for his former fiancés safety. He prayed for her along with the other members of their small Church congregation. Rance also knew Christine's husband, Rick had been designated as one of the shuttle pilots ferrying troops to the planet's surface and that young Marine Eddy Furlong belonged to the heavily decimated 5th Marine Division.

While they waited for detailed information on the damages, the General ordered five hundred fighters to relieve the beleaguered troops fighting for their very lives on the sandy surface of Optimus. As a small concession to the large number of casualties reported he also ordered four Galaxy shuttles to be launched from one of the undamaged flight decks to evacuate the more severely wounded. The General, exhibiting his famous stubbornness, still insisted the healthy troops remaining on Optimus would not be pulled out.

Finally a female Colonel announced she had finished compiling a battle impact statement. "Sir! Damage report is ready." Her monotone voice remained calm in spite of the horrors she now needed to relay. "Apparently one alien disc impacted at high velocity against the Air Boss Control location in Hangar #4. The resulting blast completely destroyed the entire flight deck and hangar including three F-72 fighters, two hundred and twenty four X-52 shuttles and nineteen Galaxy class shuttles. Two decks above the impact area and three decks below experienced decompression effects and warping. Fire suppression systems did function according to design specifications. A very high loss of life has been reported in the affected areas, best estimates at this time putting deaths from this single event at one thousand nine hundred and forty eight, with several thousand others severely injured. In addition, prior to this final attack, alien energy beam impacts caused damage and decompression of thirty-two other sections of the ship adjacent to the outer skin. The total number of dead and missing crewmembers recorded on the *Hornet* since the beginning of the campaign now stands at five thousand, eight hundred and fifty five. That is my report Sir."

    The General didn't say much, just muttered "shit!' a few times under his breath. The events of the last few days were finally catching up to him. Rance said a brief prayer out loud asking for the Lord to watch over them and protect them. He asked for God to help the wounded during their painful recoveries and requested that discernment and wisdom be given to General McLellan as he guided them through this costly war. No one, including the General made any vocal objections to Rance's prayer. The time had now arrived for the USS *Hornet* and her exhausted crew to lick their wounds and prepare for the next phase of the conquest of Optimus 4. One thing was sure. The little misconception about the war being some laughable cakewalk had been cleared up…once and for all…

CHAPTER 15

"Okay you alien dicks. This is the USS *Hornet* and I'm telling you were gonna make you pay for what you've done. Oh yeah…but before you die I'm gonna play you some more music. That song you just heard was Third Eye Blind…"Jumper" following "Counting Blue Cars" from Dishwalla, and Billy Idol's "Dancing with Myself" as performed by Blink 182. Comin' up I've got one you're really gonna love, "Hypnotize" by The Notorious B.I.G, then some Wallflowers with "Heroes" and "Cubicly Contained" from the Headstones. This next song is something you all should hear before our fighters blast the living shit out of ya…The Foo Fighters with their famous cover of Gerry Rafferty's "Baker Street"…"

By June of 1998, George McLellan found himself single again. Third wife Lisa recently came home early from a shopping trip and discovered him in a compromising position with his latest extramarital conquest. Lisa, although suspecting George hadn't always been faithful, couldn't stomach the humiliation of this blatant affront to her dignity, especially since the woman in question also happened to be another officer's wife. In such a closed knit group like her extended military family she knew the juicy gossip about such a sensational event would soon get out and be salaciously recounted by everyone at Fort Bragg. She calmly told George the marriage was finished; she would be leaving and taking their two and half year old son George Junior with her. A determined woman once making up her mind about something, she also told him he would never see his son again. Lisa explained that if he tried to stop them, or ever attempted to contact his son, Lisa would tell her father, Salvatore (Big Sal) Castallano, better known as under boss of the Kansas City Cosa Nostra all about his sordid infidelity. She didn't need to say more. Castallano, violent rage always simmering just under the surface of his large frame, was probably the only man George ever respected as a possible threat. Following their ostentatious Italian Wedding, Sal took him aside and made something very clear: if George ever hurt his little girl in any way, he would regret it. Then he pulled George into a smothering bear hug, welcoming his new non-Italian son in law into the family. Afraid of no man, George still had enough sense to understand he couldn't fight the entire KC mob on his own. So another wife had left. That pain still paled into insignificance when compared to losing his little boy.

At least his professional life continued to go well, the job of protecting the 101st Airborne's eight tactical nuclear weapons now becoming routine to the point of boredom.

The progress towards the methodical fulfillment of his real ambition, the secret plan of nuking Washington DC, continued to inch along, albeit at what seemed like a snail's pace. Young Major Wilbur Pattinson continued to worship his superior like some Adonis, in spite of George sharing more and more of his plan with the young man. George also found a small nucleus of support from three other Airborne Colonels who shared some of his radical ideas. It would soon be time to divulge more of the "plan" with them, once he could be one hundred percent assured of their loyalty. The next step in his preparations would involve George's promotion to Brigadier General and transfer somewhere higher up in the 101st Airborne's Command structure. He could then rig things to ensure his young protégés advancement to Lieutenant Colonel, automatically making him the most logical best candidate to fill the role of Nuclear Tactical Officer. He knew this would happen sooner or later, but a war, any war leading to more rapid promotions could really move things along. As George walked across the base and looked up at the contrails of a highflying commercial jet, he knew fate would somehow provide that conflict. He could sense it...

Rance and Major Mitchell had just been dismissed from the stricken *Hornet's* battle Bridge with orders to return in two hours for an important Command Battle Conference. Before heading back to his quarters however, Rance stopped by Sickbay, its capacity strained to the limit by the thousands of severely wounded from the *Hornet* now being supplemented by shuttle loads of injured troops from the planet's surface. He said a few words of prayer with some of the more grievously injured. As he tried to give comfort to a male NCO with a shattered face, Rance noticed that the postoperative patient now being brought into the room looked familiar. He quickly realized the sedated man with the stump of a left leg covered by dressings was none other than his fellow Christian PFC Eddy Furlong. Rance prayed with Eddy, giving reassurance that for him at least, the war was now over. Before he left to go back to his quarters, a distraught Corporal Heather Calloway had taken Rance's place at the bedside of the injured Marine. Obviously the two of them had recently formed a strong personal bond in addition to their shared Christian faith. Rance checked his messages as soon as he got back to his billet, crying out with relief when he read the text from Christine saying she was okay. She went on to add that Rick had survived flying non-stop shuttle flights for the past twenty-four hours. Another message came in from Lieutenant Dennis Crowder telling everyone that he too had lived through the battle. Praise the Lord! , thought Rance before he grabbed an hours' worth of shuteye. Their little group of believers had survived, although God only knew what the next phase of the war would bring.

Rance made it back to the bridge conference room just as the briefing began. General of the Fighters, James Cross was conspicuous by his absence. The spineless hedonist was probably trying to forget their reversal in the war by surrounding himself in a soothing environment of beautiful women, priceless art and fine whiskey.

General Wilbur Pattinson started his discourse, accompanied by some rather bizarre motivational music, "We're Not Gonna Take It" by Twisted Sister.

"I just wanted to give tribute to the members of our brave forces who not only met but also defeated the greatest challenge our military has faced in the last three centuries! We still aren't sure where these Gray fighters came from, but it appears that it must have been a last gasp assault on the part of their defeated fighter force, an onslaught that we stopped cold! We broke their back similar to the way the Marines stopped the doomed Japanese Banzai charges in World War Two. They're done. The invasion can now proceed according to plan. Any questions before I continue?" A young General, Rance didn't catch his name, did have a rather unsettling comment. "Sir, what if… instead of being the last of the alien fighter force, these were only the beginning of a general recall of their military strength back to the threatened home world, you know, the way the ancient Romans would summon the legions from the provinces if barbarians threatened to sack Rome?" Quite a few faces went white at even the hint of such a thing. General McLellan jumped out of his seat to personally dismiss this outrageous statement. "Ludicrous!" he snarled. "Listen, I'm getting downright sick and tired of the traitorous and defeatist attitudes I've heard from some of you officers today. If it continues there will be summary executions of anyone daring to subvert my authority in a time of war. Is that clear?" Not everyone nodded agreement but no one disagreed either. "Okay, time to get this little invasion back on the rails. We still have, how many fighters left?" the General asked an aide. "Three thousand one hundred and twenty? Good. That should be enough. What we're going to do is start immediate shuttle landings of the remaining seven divisions needed for the ground offensive to continue. Three thousand F-72's will provide air support to the shuttles, the remaining one hundred or so fighters will act as a CAP to the *Hornet* even though our sensors have picked up negligible enemy fighter activity. General Pattinson is right. We have destroyed the last of their organized fighter resistance so our three thousand fighters should be more than adequate to take on any alien threat. Since our fighter losses now prevent us from carrying on both the support of the landings and the continued air strikes on the cities I am ordering our two trillion watt plasma cannons to hit the alien population centers." There were a few gasps at this from some of the assembled officers. "I realize the immense power of these weapons presents some hazards to air crews who venture too close but I'm afraid we don't have any choice. Landings will proceed in fifteen minutes. Now…General McClane, our Psychological Warfare expert would also like to say a few words. General…"

The pale, bald and colorless fifty something scientist stood up, activating the holo imaging. "Thank you General McLellan. From studying the Grays we have come to the conclusion that their societal structure is similar to certain social insects such as bees or ants on Earth. That would explain the geometric pattern their fighters assumed at the beginning of the battle and also the "hive" like strategy of mindlessly attacking the two threats to their planet, the USS *Hornet* as well as the troops landed on their soil. The troubling mass suicide attack at the end of the battle is the only variation of their behavior that we have not yet been able to understand. A moot point however since we have destroyed their entire fighter force." He smiled. "We will have many years to study and fully understand the unique, fascinating psychology of the Grays, before we finally exterminate their genetically redundant race…when of no further use. One other mildly disturbing development from a psych ops standpoint has to be the images on your holos, showing the impact point on Optimus 4 of the concentrated radio beams hitting the major urban area of the planet. Although the massive strength of these ancient musical signals at first proved toxic to the Grays, it appears they have now begun to adapt to it and are in fact congregating nearby the beams impact area. This adaptive ability could be similar to that demonstrated by insects on Earth when exposed to pesticides. If they weren't an inferior form of life I would say they are now even enjoying the music, which means we must make an immediate format change to Comm-Rad 1. We will begin transmitting the style of twentieth century music our studies showed had the next greatest adverse effect on the aliens, something called old style country music and bluegrass".

He noticed the negative facial expressions of his audience. "I know I know very vile stuff indeed. Anyway, that is my presentation Sir."

The old General had regained his former confidence. "You all know what you need to do. Now get on with it and good luck."

As everyone got up to leave, the Dictator narrowed his rheumy eyed gaze on Rance. "General Edwards! Hold on for a moment. I need to talk to you."

Soon only the two of them remained in the immense conference space. "Rance I've been doing some thinking about your role here and about the request you made to personally do some fighting. I'm starting to think that might be a good idea. I want you and your young aide to form an elite fighter unit. Have that test pilot Gary Nguyen volunteer, along with whomever he selects as his wingman. You can provide fighter protection to the Hornet but are forbidden to enter the atmosphere of the planet. Understood?"

When Rance agreed, McLellan gave a snappy salute and left the room. He realized the General never changed his mind about anything, instead was probably deviously planning to eliminate a potential embarrassment by targeting Rance's F-72 with a plasma blast once fighter protection of the *Hornet* became unnecessary. He knew he didn't have a choice but to follow orders in spite of whatever his commanding officers true motives might be. In any case, he welcomed the chance to see some action and quickly proceeded to the Bridge to share the orders with his aide and now wingman, Major Mitchell. On the way he also text messaged Gary Nguyen, explaining the orders and asking him to select a wingman and meet them on flight deck #2.

As the legendary BLMD test pilot explained to Rance when they all met in the ready room, until now he also had been barred from flying even though he made several desperate requests to use his personal fighter. He introduced his wingman, a fellow BLMD test pilot by the name of Captain Mario Andries to Rance and Major Mitchell. They all donned space suits and waited for their turn in the flight deck rotation to get into their fighters, something that only took a few minutes. The Air Boss launched their F-72 fighters seconds after they strapped themselves in and put the bubble canopies down. Launch efficiency now became a matter of survival. After all, several hundred more fighter pilots waited in line to be launched. Only Rance's rank and their units "elite" status got them bumped to the head of the line. Rance welcomed the opportunity to be flying again, finding the helplessness experienced the last two days as he watched the epic battles unfold, probably the closest thing to "hell" he would ever know. Rance cruised at a moderate speed waiting for the other three pilots in his unit to form behind him in a textbook finger four formation. The space around the *Hornet* now became so congested with traffic that several times only his on board collision avoidance system prevented a fatal crash. Most of the fighter traffic now headed to the planet's surface to provide cover for the huge Galaxy class shuttles conducting the transport operation. Loaded down with bulky consignments of troops and tanks, they would quickly discharge their cargo then turn right around to come back to the ship for another load.

Rance took his formation of four fighter craft out a few kilometers from the ship, cognizant of the danger the *Hornet's* plasma beams, continuing to zap the cities of Optimus meant for any fighter craft straying too close to their blinding brilliance. He couldn't help occasionally looking towards the awe inspiring thirty-five cannon array of two trillion watt plasma cannons vaporizing the various atmospheric layers before they pulverized the planet. Rance didn't envy the fighter pilots assigned to fly cover for the invasion, as the beams would be causing wild, unpredictable wind shear effects over much of the alien ecosphere. The death toll in the already devastated Gray population centers must have also been horrendous. Rance couldn't let the fate of the poor aliens down below distract him as his unit had only one mission, to protect their mother ship, the USS *Hornet*.

All of a sudden a silvery disc shape flashed like an apparition, an alien ship trying to break through the protective fighter cordon. Rance pushed the stick, accelerating his fighter and quickly getting in behind the Gray. A second later he pressed the firing button which launched a missile, destroying the disc in a brief but blinding blast. Out of the corner of his eye he registered the flash of three other Gray ships going past him, his flight mates following in hot pursuit. As they each successively took out an alien, Rance realized the brief battle allowed them to stray much too close to the USS *Hornet*. Every nearby gun placement on the ship opened up on the discs, seemingly not caring at all if they also hit one of their own fighters. In fact, only by executing a series of blinding maneuvers did Nguyen avoid getting hit. Rance led his flight back to the relative safety of circling their ship at a range of approximately five kilometers. Other than the four alien fighters they had destroyed there were no signs of any opposition. Quite a few other fighter units circled the ship at different ranges and altitudes, all looking for any possible enemy threats. No one could spot anything other than the constant stream of shuttles traveling back and forth between the *Hornet* and Optimus 4, now limited to operating from the three remaining main flight decks and one emergency flight deck.

    As they circled for hour after hour, Rance thought the destroyed flight deck looked like some jagged scar, the explosion having blown a huge hole in the side of the ship. The four decks still operating were launching every available shuttle of both the Galaxy types and the smaller X-52 variety each probably jam packed above capacity with troops and supplies to make up for this unanticipated shortfall in flight facilities. Rance resisted becoming prideful but the sight of such a huge vessel, final product of centuries of American inventiveness and ingenuity engaged in launching an invasion of another planet couldn't help but emotionally affect any true patriot. Rance inexplicably had the inane impression that the USS *Hornet* resembled some huge beehive in space, the stream of X-52's similar to worker bees with the gigantic Galaxy shuttles appearing to wallow like huge bumblebees, looking almost too big to fly. Rance absently wondered if the insect like grays would even understand such an analogy.

    The answer to his trivial question would forever remain unknown since Rance understandably became much more concerned with the twenty thousand Gray fighter discs instantly appearing only a few kilometers distant from their position. One second only empty space existed in front of him, the next a vast geometric pattern of triangularly arranged Gray fighter discs of what would have been an incalculable number were it not for his ships on board sensors. *Rome recalling her legions* thought Rance before he decided on a course of action for his elite fighter unit. The cowardly action of running back to the *Hornet* would of course be unthinkable, leaving him with only one option. Attack and take any initiative away from the Grays who were somewhat limited by their collective consciousness. On some subconscious level, Rance realized he and his flight mates were about to die in a spectacular *"Wild Bunch"* finale kind of way but also knew that those three men would follow him into hell had he ordered it. Something he then literally commenced to do by transmitting the "tally ho, engaging the enemy" signal, driving his fighter into the midst of the overwhelmingly superior enemy force. All weapons blazing, Rance immediately took out six Grays, punching a hole in their neat symmetrical design. After this aggressive opening attack, there could be no time to think or to even maintain formation, every man was now on his own and desperately trying to survive. All four of the Americans destroyed large numbers of enemy craft.

Captain Mario Andries was the first to die. At least a dozen alien craft had him in their sites as he continued to weave frantically through the enemy ranks, screaming into the voice mike, keeping his firing button locked down and killing untold numbers of Gray ships before his F-72 exploded. Rance couldn't pause to take notice as he put his own F-72 through a series of mind aided twists so severe he was surprised they didn't rip his fighter apart. Dozens and dozens of the enemy fell to his weapons, nothing interrupting his intense concentration until Major Mitchell called out on the emergency voice channel, interrupting "Bro Hymn (Original)" by Pennywise on Comm-Rad 1.

"General! I'm in trouble! They..." Rance caught his aides last moment out of the corner of his eye, literally hundreds of aliens blasting him at once with their energy beams and instantly vaporizing his ship. Rance didn't have time to grieve the loss of his friend and fellow believer, as now only he and Gary Nguyen remained to carry on the fight. The former BLMD test pilot put on a show of combat mastery that would never again be equaled. Truly skilled in the visualization concepts needed to fly the F-72, he almost transcended this dimension as he zipped in and out of the enemy formations taking a huge toll on the Grays. He seemed unstoppable until a random energy beam from a Gray fighter hit the propulsion unit on his F-72, disabling his hyper drive. Even then with only conventional thrusters operational, his flying skills still allowed him to take out several more of the fighter discs until suddenly the propulsion unit failed completely, leaving the undisputed master of the F-72 floating helplessly in space. Rance tried to come to his comrade's aid but found himself tangled up with dozens of enemy ships. The Grays made no mistake on such an easy target, killing Nguyen instantly.

Rance could now see only one option. He needed to draw the enemy ships that were now firmly stuck on his tail closer to the *Hornet* so the defensive weapons of the large ship could take them out. Since death was now inevitable he reasoned he might as well take as many of the Grays with him as possible. He said a brief prayer as he gunned his ship towards the USS *Hornet*. He thought of Christine; how he still loved her and would never see her lovely face again, at least not in this corporal existence.

Sure enough as he drew closer to the large ship, every gunner still alive opened up on the dozens of enemy fighters trailing him, too good a target to turn up. Many slugs hit his fighter as well. Almost instantly all of his pursuing aliens were blasted into oblivion, but one of them took out both his propulsion units a millisecond before being destroyed. Rance found himself helplessly floating in space, the battle now moving closer to the *Hornet* and leaving him far behind. He watched the horrific yet fascinating scene as thousands of energy beams assaulted and penetrated the *Hornet's* shields. Even though he had been spared death for the time being he knew that his chances of making it back to the *Hornet* in a disabled ship were practically nil. Given the present circumstances, there could be only one course of action. He proceeded to pray to God as the battle in space raged all around him…

CHAPTER 16

"You just heard Gob with "I hear You Calling," "Bohemian like You" from the Dandy Warhols and prior to that we played some good ol' Metallica with "Whiskey in the Jar." Last hour you listened to some classic Buckcherry, "Low" by Cracker and Bif Naked with "Rich and Filthy." Okay…I've got some big news for you alien freaks. Since I've been told you now kinda like those tunes, were gonna go and change it all. Whaddya think of that? Huh? You dirty rotten, lousy dick wad Grays…anyway; here's something we call Old Time Country Music. Comin' up we've got vintage George Jones… "The Race Is On" not to mention the unforgettable "San Antonio Rose" from Bob Wills and his Texas Playboys. Also you're gonna hear "East Bound And Down" from Jerry Reed, some legendary Buck Owens and his Buckaroos with "I've Got A Tiger By The Tail" but first, a song that apparently made an early childhood impression on our Glorious Leader General McLellan, Marty Robbins… "A White Sport Coat"… I hope you filthy sons of bitches get real sick from listenin' to this shit…"

Even though the 101st Airborne Division had been put on full alert, deep down inside, Colonel George McLellan felt ecstatic. On the outside he needed to remain angry, agreeing with everyone he spoke to that they "would get the bastards who did this" and how "those damn terrorists were going to pay." After all, September 11, 2001 was an emotional time for everyone even though secretly, George couldn't have cared less about the innocent victims of this tragedy. It only meant one thing to him. The war would soon begin, the war that meant promotion and advancement, bringing his little "plan" one step closer to fruition. He now had five co-conspirators willing to do anything to help him achieve his aims, so power hungry they would gladly sell their souls to the devil if it meant getting a small piece of George's future empire. He'd already heard rumors the Division might be deployed to Afghanistan, maybe even Iraq or Iran. George didn't give a shit. The President could send them to Mars as long as it meant him getting his promotion to Brigadier General and his protégé Wilbur Pattinson getting the Nuclear Tactical Officer position. The rest of the plan could then leisurely fall into place. He only needed seven or eight more officers willing to help him achieve power, leading to the next phase of picking a suitable day for implementation. He needed to abscond with one of the nukes and its triggering device, replacing it with a dummy so realistic an expert might be fooled. Put it into a specially modified cargo van and get within a thousand feet of an event where the President, Vice President and most other senior Government officials needed to be in attendance, an inauguration or presidential funeral would do, and then set the timer. Bang! Let the surviving high ranking government and military commanders fight it out for a while and then seize control of key military bases by dropping in select units commanded by his men. George planned on setting up an interim military Junta (he always liked the sound of that Latin American term) of course planning on eventually eliminating all of his co-conspirators, leaving him as sole American Dictator. He hadn't quite decided about young Wilbur Pattinson but at this point sort of leaned towards letting him live. The man really didn't have an ambitious bone in his body and would probably make a good lifelong flunky and assistant, something every true Dictator needed. Personally things weren't going that great, since he hadn't seen his five-year-old son George Junior for several years. The boy was healthy and happy though, at least according to the periodic reports from George's private investigator. He knew he couldn't let that or any other personal tragedy deter him from his goal. That's why today's events encouraged him so much. Yes, September 11th had been a good day, actually one of the best days in George's life... now only one nagging, unpleasant thought kept bothering him. Why the hell did the network have to go and cancel the *"Steve Landesberg Show"* all those years ago? Now that was truly ground-breaking television...

Rance sat in his damaged fighter watching the dramatic war in space, listening to "We'll Burn That Bridge" by Brooks & Dunn. From his clear vantage point it became evident the USS *Hornet's* remaining three thousand fighters had been recalled from their original mission of providing support to the troops on the planet's surface. They fought tenaciously, tearing chunks into the enemy formations but after less than an hour the overwhelming numbers of aliens took their toll on the American forces. Every so often Rance winced at a telltale flash as another F-72 cooked up in an explosion. Eventually he couldn't see any friendly fighters at all. With the *Hornet's* protective fighters gone, the Grays concentrated their attacks on the huge ship, cutting through the shields and sometimes right into its skin, causing explosive decompression to many areas. Locked in a fight to the death, the warship's plasma beam defenses took a toll on the alien discs and the more powerful weapons still pummeled the Gray's population centers.

Finally the Grays started using their destructive massed suicide attacks, this time sending hundreds of ships towards the aft section of the *Hornet* somehow knowing that to be the location of main engineering and the crucial hyper drive. Rance estimated the Grays sent nearly a thousand of their flying discs pummeling into the shield and armored skin of the ship before a blinding flash indicated that some of them found their target. The plasma beams emanating from the USS *Hornet* instantly stopped and the massive warship appeared to take on a slight list. Surprisingly, even though the still numerous alien discs could now have delivered the coup de grace to Earth's invading ship, the attack stopped. A few thousand of the discs remained close to the ship while almost ten thousand others dove at high speed for the surface of Optimus 4. To destroy our troops on the planet, thought Rance with a grim realization. Once they finish that little job they'll be back to finish our ship. Since the *Hornet's* offensive ability had now been fatally crippled, the madman still in command of the ship ordered a last ditch attempt to destroy the alien planet, launching nearly five thousand remaining large nuclear tipped cruise missiles. If even a few hundred of them detonated they would make Optimus 4 uninhabitable for centuries. If the General couldn't have the prize, it appeared he was now determined to make sure the Grays couldn't have it either. The alien discs surrounding the *Hornet* easily intercepted and harmlessly destroyed the torrent of slower cruise missiles as they entered the planet's atmosphere. None made it down to the surface of Optimus 4, causing no further harm to the already devastated alien population centers. These much-vaunted "wonder weapons" had proven to be useless without protection from a close fighter escort. Those fighters now no longer existed.

Now that McLellan's last throw of the dice had failed, Rance knew that somehow, someway, he needed to get back to the dying ship. He wanted to see Christine one last time. After playing around with the attitude controls, he found he could use the little gas jets to push his F-72 towards his target at the phenomenal rate of three or four kilometers an hour. He just hoped he could make it back before the alien main force returned. The *Hornet's* list also seemed to be worsening as he slowly approached. Some of the ships fifty caliber gun stations might still be operational so Rance keyed the voice mike to alert flight deck #2 he was coming in for a "landing"…eventually. He dispensed with the now pointless formality of using his "Dog 12" call sign. "USS *Hornet* Air Boss Number Two: this is General Rance Edwards. I'm coming in for a landing, propulsion off line, attempting to use attitude jets to push me in towards the deck."

The voice of the Air Boss sounded genuinely happy, Rance's miraculous survival probably the only good news he had heard since the Grays lethal massed attack.

"Yes sir General Edwards. Alerting gun crews to give you cover if those asshole aliens give you any trouble." The aliens didn't intervene to stop him even though he passed quite close to some of the discs. Rance received an odd impression of confusion, possibly some sort of telepathic chatter from the Grays, making him believe the aliens were probably told to remain inactive until their comrades returned from destroying the Earth troops on Optimus 4. They didn't seem capable of individual thought or action.

Finally after what seemed like an eternity, he passed through the glowing blue doors of the flight deck, the armored doors closing behind him. His heavily shot up F-72 stopped on the slanting deck. Stepping out, he realized that with the hyper drive off line, the gravity backup system left a lot to be desired. He seemed to float rather than walk into the ready room. Christine and Rick waited there for him. They gave thanks to the Lord for their temporary deliverance from death. Rick was fortunate enough to have been loading troops on one of the *Hornet's* flight decks when the devastating attack came. Other than his, most of the other shuttles and crews were lost.

Christine started to cry. "They're all dead Rance." She gestured towards Optimus 4, the tragic planet they still had the misfortune of orbiting. "All of our poor troops. The aliens have killed most of them and from what we've heard, as soon as the Grays finish the few survivors, they're probably coming back to destroy us."

Rance had to admit things did not look good but as he reminded Christine and Rick, with God all things are possible. He felt the Holy Spirit pushing him to take action as a plan formed in his head. "It just might work," he said more to himself than to his companions. "Rick, how many Galaxy shuttles are left?" Santchez only thought for a second before snapping off the response. "Three or four including the Generals two command shuttles on Flight Deck 1, why do you ask?"

Rance made it brief. They didn't have much time. "Listen to me closely. We're going to take the General's personal shuttle. We can't save everyone Christine but we might be able to save the children in your pilot project. Can you get them and their surrogate parents loaded up on one of the shuttles in fifteen minutes?"

Rick answered for both of them. "We'll do it Rance, no matter what objections we get from that old bat Dr. Vandenburg, but what about you? Where are you going?" Rance was already out the door. "I'll be there in fifteen minutes, but first the General and I need to have a little talk." During his run towards the Battle Bridge, he used his micro mobile to try calling Dennis Crowder even though seriously doubting the genial man still lived. The Seabee's offices and warehouse were located right next to the five hundred meter cavernous hole where main engineering used to be. Not surprisingly, Rance couldn't get any response, not even the Seabee's voice mailbox. At least the end came mercifully quick for his Christian Brother. Nearly out of breath, he burst onto the Bridge. The former command center of the *Hornet* looked to be a shambles with General McLellan nowhere to be seen. The holo array displayed several bright red system failure warnings with a synthetic female voice calling out "Alert! Life support primary and backup systems are off line! Alert!"

In jarring contrast, several other secondary holos were playing the original 1981 music video of "Just Can't Get Enough" by Depeche Mode. General Pattinson lay dead on the metal deck, a pool of blood under his head, a gun still clenched in his hand. *Coward*, thought Rance as he quickly searched the room with his sharp eyes, only a few dazed officers still present.

"Where's McLellan?" he shouted out to one of them. "Try his quarters," said the man. He didn't even look up from his workstations pornographic holo-display.

Rance ran to McLellan's stateroom, ready to take out any security guards, but even they had abandoned the Glorious Leader in his moment of greatest need. As he approached the door, the primeval sounds of "Rock and Roll All Nite" by KISS could be heard emanating from the Dictator's private quarters. Rance found the General at his work area, the room completely dark except for flashes of light from a movie playing on his holo-comm. The dictator wore a hooded robe and seemed to be ignoring the very old films playing on a split screen, yet another holo screening of two of his perennial favorites, *The Wanderers* and *Dazed and Confused*, instead intently studying the Walther PPK handgun resting on the desk in front of him.

Noticing Rance, General McLellan looked up. "You know I really thought it would work. I honestly did. But maybe fate intended it to be this way all along, my whole life, all my ambitions leading up to this final dramatic moment. What better noble end for the cream of American Civilization than to die in battle. Don't you agree?"

He stared at Rance with a puzzled expression on his face, recognition suddenly fading. "Who are you...what do you want?"

Rance wanted him coherent, at least for a few moments longer. "Sir, I needed to do the right thing and request your permission on an urgent matter. I'm going to use one of your shuttles to take the orphans from the pilot project down to the planet's surface. If we use non-violent subliminal messaging attached to classical music maybe they'll accept our surrender and have mercy on us. All I know for sure is that we can't just let those innocent kids die!"

The old man snapped back into reality, waving his arms. "You can't have any of those brats, they're mine damn you. In fact one of them is my great, great grandson, why else would I care so much about a bunch of snot nosed orphans? Don't you understand? They need to die, we all need to die since we failed in our mission, failed to achieve our destiny…" his eyes became glassy. "Now get the hell out!"

Rance shook his head, realizing nothing, not even the lives of innocent children could reach this pathetic madman. It didn't matter anymore. He had done his duty but now he needed to help those who still might survive, God willing. He turned on his heels and ran towards his quarters to retrieve some essential gear before making it to the sickbay, fortunately located quite close to the shuttle deck.

Entering the medical center, he heard two gunshots, apparently more suicides. Terrified and abandoned patients lay in despair waiting for their imminent end. For some unknown reason the cool jazz sounds of Duke Ellington blared from the now vacant Nurses station. All of the medical staff had long since fled, not that any place on the USS *Hornet* could now be considered safe. As a last, futile afterthought before fleeing, someone must have thought some old jazz would keep these dying people serene. One of Rance's famous ancestors had been a friend of Duke Ellington but right now he found himself a little too busy to recall the details.

Rance quickly found those he sought, Marine PFC Eddy Furlong and Corporal Heather Calloway. He threw the still very unwell Eddy into a wheelchair and rushed the two of them towards the exit. Rance then directed all ambulatory patients to help those with mobility issues and to follow him towards the shuttle deck; knowing only mere moments remained to make their escape. Even though he wanted to rescue everyone, lack of time now dictated that saving all others would be impossible. Rance pushed two wounded soldiers in wheelchairs towards the shuttle deck but needed to turn his back on all of those other lost souls in the sickbay. This was so extremely difficult he knew it would haunt him the rest of his life, assuming of course he lived through this. At this point that was a rather big assumption. They ran with difficulty down the slanted deck, the USS *Hornet's* list definitely worsening in the short time since Rance landed his damaged fighter. It was also becoming difficult to breathe.

They found McLellan's well stocked command shuttle, the *Ronald Reagan* sitting on deck ready for takeoff with Colonel Rick Santchez behind the controls, Christine in the back with the children and surrogate parents. Christine focused on calming the nervous and frightened innocent youngsters as they had never before been out of their simulated circa 1958 neighborhood. "It's okay kids! We're all going on a grand adventure starting with a plane ride to Disneyland! Remember how we talked about Disneyland during your studies last week?" Several children started chatting about that fabled place in Anaheim, excitement evident in their voices, all thoughts of fear now gone.

Rance put Furlong into a jump seat and told Corporal Calloway to strap him in and prepare for takeoff. Somehow they also managed to cram the remaining survivors from the sick bay into the overloaded shuttle.

The takeoff didn't happen. Rick called back from the cockpit. "We've got a problem Rance. The Air Boss isn't going to open the flight deck doors; he's saying the General forbids it."

Rance felt like swearing but instead prayed to God as he and Christine ran forward from the cargo area up to the cockpit. Rick paused before saying anything. His eyes appeared to be welling with tears. "I love you honey..." He said to Christine, and then turned to Rance. "Here take the controls. I'm going to ride shotgun." Rance yelled out an order forbidding whatever crazy plan Rick was considering but it was falling on deaf ears.

Rick jumped out the side door and secured it behind him before running over to General McLellan's other command shuttle, the *Richard M. Nixon*. As he started it up, Christine started to get emotional.

"Tell me what he's doing Rance! Tell me he's not going to..." Christine didn't need to say anything more as they both now knew what Rick intended on doing in order to ensure their survival. Rick Santchez turned to look out the side glass of the *Richard M. Nixon*, smiling and giving them a thumbs up signal before launching his huge galaxy shuttle at full speed into the flight decks heavy armored exit. The resulting explosion ripped a jagged hole in the doors, all of the debris being immediately sucked out into the cold vacuum of space.

Christine could only say "Oh my God! Rick! No...," in complete shock as Rance powered up their shuttle and guided it through the gap, an escape only made possible because of Rick's courageous sacrifice. Rance found the appropriate classical music Johann Strauss's "The Blue Danube" with a peaceful subliminal message attached, broadcasting it to the several hundred alien discs still shadowing the USS *Hornet*. As they passed by, none of the Gray's silvery craft made any attempt to intercept them. They were ignored as their shuttle started entering the upper atmosphere of Optimus 4, the aliens radiating a telepathic aura of indifference, nothing more. Rance praised the Lord for their apparent deliverance, also silently thanking Rick Santchez, a true hero. Back in the shuttle cargo bay a small child broke free of his surrogate mother and ran to the ancient dark blue automobile, jumping up on the rear step and then into the comfortable, red stained back seat, waving and pretending to be President Eisenhower...

The warship USS *Hornet* last will and testament to the once great nation of the United States of America began her final fiery plunge into the atmosphere of the planet she journeyed so far to conquer. Somewhere deep inside the bowels of the disintegrating monument to human idealism, a gnarled old finger pushed a button causing two final song selections to be broadcast, Kate Smith's stirring rendition of "God Bless America" followed by Jimi Hendrix's version of "The Star – Spangled Banner."

AUTHOR'S NOTES

Optimus 4 is not meant to predict the exact or even approximate time frame of certain key end-time prophecies. My novel is intended to be an entertaining chronicle that also just happens to feature a character of uncompromising Christian faith set in the general time period of the Great Tribulation. The Bible clearly states that only God the Father knows the day and the hour of these events and the physical return of Jesus Christ. For a more accurate and in depth explanation of Biblical prophecy I direct the reader to the classic, *The Late Great Planet Earth* by Hal Lindsey.

Although there is no definitive Biblical reference to the possible existence of extraterrestrial life, some evangelical Christian authorities believe that the alien abduction phenomena and UFOs are actually caused by Satan and his demons in an attempt to mislead non-believers. The following scripture from 2 Thessalonians 2:9-11 is sometimes used to support this opinion: "the one whose coming is in accord with the activity of Satan, with all power and signs and false wonders, and with all the deception of wickedness for those who perish, because they did not receive the love of the truth so as to be saved. For this reason God will send upon them a deluding influence so they will believe what is false ..."

Given the quite often horrific accounts of many individuals claiming to be abducted by aliens, this very well may be the case. In this regard, *Optimus 4* should only be viewed as mere entertainment and not a definitive statement on the possible existence or source of extraterrestrial life.

This is a work of fiction and not intended to provide any actual United States Military or United States Military Academy at West Point operational procedures.

Optimus 4 Sources and Notes

OPTIMUS 4 SONG TITLES REFERENCES LIST*

The Beastie Boys. "(You Gotta) Fight For Your Right (To Party)." *Licensed to Ill.* Def Jam/Columbia, 1986. Record, Audiocassette.

Better Than Ezra. "Good." *Deluxe.* Elektra, 1995. CD.

Martin, Dean. "Volare." *This is Dean Martin.* Capital Records, 1958. Record.

The Ronettes. "Be My Baby." *Presenting the Fabulous Ronettes.* Philles Records, 1963. Record.

Sinatra, Frank. "Strangers in the Night." *Strangers in the Night.* Reprise, 1966. Record.

Eve 6. "Inside Out." *Eve 6.* RCA, 1998. CD.

Harrison, George. "What is Life." *All Things Must Pass.* Apple, 1971. Record.

Jethro Tull. "Aqualung." *Aqualung.* Chrysalis/Reprise, 1971. Record.

Cat Stevens. "Wild World." *Tea for the Tillerman.* A&M, 1970. Record.

Bacharach, Burt & David, Hal. "The Look of Love." (Instrumental). *Casino Royale Soundtrack Album.* Colgems, 1967. Record.

Blue October. "Hate Me." *Foiled.* Universal Records, 2006. CD, Digital Download.

Presley, Elvis. "Suspicious Minds." (Single). RCA, 1969. Record.

Bowie, David. "Suffragette City." *The Rise and fall of Ziggy Stardust and the Spiders from Mars.* RCA, 1972. Record.

T-Rex. "Bang a Gong." *Electric Warrior*. Fly/Reprise, 1971. Record.

Deep Purple. "Smoke on the Water." *Machine Head*. EMI/Warner, 1973. Record.

Bread. "If." *Manna*. Elektra/Rhino, 1971. Record.

Looking Glass. "Brandy." *Looking Glass*. Epic, 1972. Record.

Black Sabbath. "Paranoid." *Vertigo*, 1970. Record.

Carly Simon. "You're So Vain." *No Secrets*, Elektra, 1972. Record.

Jackson, Michael. "Ben." *Ben*. Motown, 1972. Record.

Living Colour. "Cult of Personality." *Vivid*, 1988. CD, Record, Audiocassette.

Bacharach, Burt, David, Hal. "I Say a Little Prayer." (Instrumental). Sceptre, 1967. Record.

Steely Dan. "Rikki Don't Lose That Number." *Pretzel Logic*. ABC, 1974. Record.

McCartney and Wings. "Jet." *Band on the Run*. Apple Records, 1974. Record.

Nazareth. "This Flight Tonight." Loud 'N' Proud. Mooncrest/A&M, 1973. Record.

Pilot. "Magic." *Magic*. EMI, 1974. Record.

Sweet. "Barroom Blitz." *Desolation Boulevard*. RCA/Capitol, 1973. Record.

Parliament. "Give up the Funk (Tear the Roof off the Sucker)." *Mothership Connection*. Casablanca, 1976. Record.

The Sex Pistols. "Anarchy in the UK." *Never Mind the Bollocks, Here's the Sex Pistols."* EMI, 1976. Record.

Foghat. "Slow Ride." *Fool for the City*. Bearsville, 1975. Record.

Thin Lizzy. "The Boys Are Back in Town." *Jail Break*. Vertigo/Mercury, 1976. Record.

Del Shannon. "Runaway." Single. Big Top, 1961. Record.

The Diamonds. "Little Darlin'" Single. Mercury, 1957. Record.

Danny & the Juniors. "Rock 'N' Roll is Here to Stay." Single. ABC/Paramount, 1958. Record.

Young, Neil. "Heart of Gold." *Harvest*. Reprise, 1972. Record.

Frampton, Peter. "Show Me The Way." *Frampton*. A&M, 1975. Record.

Sweet. "Fox On The Run." *Desolation Boulevard*. RCA/Capitol, 1973. Record.

Chicago. "If You Leave Me Now." *Chicago X*. Columbia, 1976. Record.

The Bay City Rollers. "Saturday Night." *Rollin'*. Arista, 1975. Record.

The Floaters. "Float On." *The Floaters*. ABC, 1977. Record.

The Fugees. "Killing Me Softly." *The Score*. Ruffhouse, 1996. CD.

The Spinners. "Rubber Band Man." *Happiness Is Being With The Spinners*. Atlantic, 1976. Record.

The Runaways. "Mama Weer All Crazee Now." *And Now...The Runaways*. Cherry Red, 1979. Record.

Rafferty, Gerry. "Baker Street." *City to City*. United Artists, 1978. Record.

Elliman, Yvonne. "If I Can't Have You. *"Saturday Night Fever: The Original Movie Soundtrack*. RSO, Polydor, 1977. Record 7" 45.

Sid Vicious. "My Way." Single. Anarchy Music, 1978. Record.

Welch, Bob. "Ebony Eyes." *French Kiss*. Capitol, 1977. Record.

Joel, Billy. "My Life." *52nd Street*. Columbia. 1978. Record.

Boz Scaggs. "Lido Shuffle." *Silk Degrees*. Columbia, 1976. Record.

The Cars. "Just What I Needed." *The Cars*. Elektra, 1978. Record.

Seger, Bob & the Silver Bullet Band. "Still the Same." *Stranger in Town*. Capitol, 1978. Record.

Kansas. "Carry on Wayward Son." *Left Overture*. Kirshner, 1976. Record.

Heart. "Barracuda". *Little Queen*. Portrait Records, 1977. Record.

Soul, David. "Don't Give Up On Us Baby." Private Stock, 1976. Record.

Elton John & Kiki Dee. "Don't Go Breaking My Heart." Single. Rocket Records/MCA, 1976. Record.

Stewart, Al. "Year of the Cat." *Year of the Cat*. RCA/Janus, 1976. Record.

Berlin, Irving. "Puttin' on the Ritz." *Puttin' on the Ritz (Film)*. United Artists, 1930.

Harlequin. "You Are The Light." *Victim of a Song*. CBS/Epic, 1979. Record.

Collective Soul. "Run." *Dosage*. Atlantic, 1999. CD.

Jackson, Joe. "Is She Really Going Out With Him?" *Look Sharp!* A&M, 1979. Record.

XTC. "Making Plans for Nigel." *Drums and Wires*. Virgin, 1979. Record.

The Knack. "My Sharona." *Get the Knack*. Capitol, 1979. Record.

Stewart, John. "Gold." *Bombs Away Dream Babies*. RSO, 1979. Record.

The Doobie Brothers. "What a Fool Believes." *Minute by Minute*." Warner, 1979. Record.

Lowe, Nick. "Cruel To Be Kind." *Labor of Lust*. Radar, 1979. Record.

Journey. "Any Way You Want It." *Departure*. Columbia, 1980. Record.

Alice Cooper. "Clones (Were All)." *Flush the Fashion*. Warner, 1980. Record.

Jackson, Michael. "Rock With You." *Off the Wall*. Epic, 1979. Record.

The Human League. "Don't You Want Me." *Dare.* Virgin, 1981. Record.

Depeche Mode. "Just Can't Get Enough." *Speak & Spell*. Mute/Sire, 1981. Record.

The Ramones. "Rock 'N' Roll High School." *End of the Century*. Sire, 1979. Record.

The Psychedelic Furs. "Pretty in Pink." *Talk Talk Talk*. CBS, 1981. Record, Audiocassette.

Osbourne, Ozzy. "Crazy Train." *Blizzard of Oz*. Jet/Epic, 1980. Record.

Split Enz. "I Got You." *Tru Colours*. Mushroom Records, 1980. Record.

Eddie Rabbitt and Crystal Gayle. "You and I." *Radio Romance*. Electra, 1982. Record, Audiocassette.

A Flock of Seagulls. "I Ran." *A Flock of Seagulls*. Jive Records, 1982. Record, Audiocassette.

Devo. "Whip It." *Freedom of Choice*. Warner, 1980. Record.

Sheriff. "When I'm With You." *Sheriff*. Capitol, 1983. Record, Audiocassette.

RUN-D.M.C. "Christmas in Hollis." *A Very Special Christmas*. A&M, 1987. Vinyl, Audiocassette.

Berry, Chuck. "Run, Run Rudolph." Single. Chess, 1958. Record.

Berlin, Irving. "Cheek to Cheek." *Top Hat*, Film, RKO, 1935.

Simple Minds. "Don't You (Forget About Me)." *The Breakfast Club Soundtrack*. A&M, 1985. Record, Audiocassette.

The Outfield. "Your Love." *Play Deep*. Columbia, 1985. Record, Audiocassette.

UB40. "Red Red Wine." *Labour of Love*. A&M, 1983. Record, Audiocassette.

Animotion. "Obsession." *Animotion*. Mercury, 1984. Record, Audiocassette.

New Order. "Blue Monday." Single. Factory, 1983. Record, Audiocassette.

The Thompson Twins. "King for a Day." *Here's to Future Days*. Arista, 1985. Record, Audiocassette.

Motley Crue. "Kickstart my Heart." *Dr. Feelgood*. Elektra, 1989. CD, Audiocassette.

O'Connor, Sinead. "Nothing Compares to U." *I Do Not Want What I Haven't Got*. Chrysalis, 1990. Record, CD, Audiocassette.

Whitesnake. "Here I Go Again." *Saints & Sinners/Whitesnake*. Geffen, 1982 & 1987. Record, Audiocassette.

House of Pain. "Jump Around." *House of Pain*. XL Recordings, 1992. Record, CD.

EMF. "Unbelievable." *Shubert Dip*. EMI, 1990. CD, Record, Audiocassette.

Guns N Roses. "November Rain." *Use Your Illusion I*. Geffen, 1992. CD, Record.

The Cure. "Friday I'm In Love." *Wish*. Fiction, 1992. CD, Record.

The Proclaimers. "I'm Gonna Be 500 Miles." *Sunshine on Leith*. Chrysalis, 1988. CD, Record, Audiocassette.

The Gin Blossoms. "Hey Jealousy." *New Miserable Experience*. Fontana/A&M, 1993. CD, Record, Audiocassette.

The Counting Crows. "Mr. Jones." *August and Everything After*. Geffen, 1993. CD.

Haddaway. "What is Love." *Haddaway*. Cocoanut, 1993. CD.

Nirvana. "Smells Like Teen Spirit." *Nevermind*. DGC, 1991. CD, Record, Audiocassette.

Iron Maiden. "Run For The Hills." *Number of the Beast*. EMI, 1982. Record, Audiocassette.

Jepsen, Carly Rae. "Call Me Maybe." *Curiosity, Kiss*. 604/Schoolboy/Interscope, 2011. CD Single, Digital Download.

Pet Shop Boys. "Go West." *Very*. Parlophone/EMI, 1993. Record, CD, Audiocassette.

Green Day. "Basket Case." *Dookie*. Reprise, 1994. CD, Record.

The Offspring. "Self Esteem." *Smash*. Epitaph, 1994. CD.

Radiohead. "Creep." *Pablo Honey*. Parlophone/EMI, 1992. CD, Record, Audiocassette.

REM. "What's the Frequency Kenneth." *Monster*. Warner, 1994. CD, Record, Audiocassette.

Weezer. "Buddy Holly." *Weezer*. DGC, 1994. CD, Audiocassette, Record.

The Smashing Pumpkins. "Today." *Siamese Dream*. Virgin, 1993. CD, Record, Audiocassette.

Third Eye Blind. "Jumper." *Third Eye Blind*. Elektra, 1998. CD.

Third Eye Blind. "Never Let You Go." *Blue*. Elektra, 1999. CD.

Jughead's Revenge. "Talk Dirty to Me." *Punk Goes Metal*. Fearless Records, 2000. CD.

Dishwalla. "Counting Blue Cars." *Pet Your Friends*. A&M, 1995. CD, Audiocassette.

Blink – 182. "Dancing With Myself." *Before You Were Punk*. Vagrant 1997. CD.

Notorious B.I.G. "Hypnotize." *Life After Death*. Bad Boy, 1996. CD, Record, Audiocassette.

Wallflowers. "Heroes." *Godzilla: The Album*. Epic, 1998. CD.

The Headstones. "Cubicly Contained." *Smile & Wave*. MCA, 1997. CD.

The Foo Fighters. "Baker Street." Roswell Records, 1997. CD.

Twisted Sister. "Were Not Gonna Take It." *Stay Hungry*. Atlantic, 1994. Record.

Pennywise. "Bro Hymn Original." *Pennywise*. Epitaph, 1991. CD, Record.

Gob. "I Hear You Calling." *The World According to Gob*. Sony/BMG, 2001. CD.

The Dandy Warhols. "Bohemian Like You." *Thirteen Tales from Urban Bohemia*. Capitol/Parlophone, 2000. CD, Record.

Bif Naked. "Rich & Filthy." *Essentially Naked*. Her Majesty's Records, 2003. CD.

Metallica. "Whiskey in the Jar." *Garage Inc*. Elektra/Sony/Vertigo, 1998. CD.

Jones, George. "The Race Is On." *The Race Is On*. United Artists, 1965. Record.

Bob Wills and his Texas Playboys. " San Antonio Rose." OKeh, 1944. Record.

Reed, Jerry. "East Bound and Down." *Smokey and the Bandit Soundtrack*. RCA, 1977. Record.

Buck Owens and his Buckaroos. "I've Got a Tiger by the Tail." *I've Got a Tiger by the Tail*. Capitol, 1964. Record.

Robbins, Marty. "A White Sport Coat." Single. Columbia, 1957. Record

Brooks & Dunn. "We'll Burn That Bridge." *Hard Workin' Man.* Arista, 1993. CD Single, 7".

KISS. "Rock and Roll All Night." *Dressed to Kill.* Casablanca, 1975. Record.

Strauss, Johann. "The Blue Danube Waltz." 1866 op.314.

Berlin, Irving. "God Bless America" 1938. Sung by Kate Smith.

Hendrix, Jimi. "The Star Spangled Banner." Woodstock 1969.

*Note: Only song titles and artists names were used in *Optimus 4*. No lyrics were used in the novel.

The following hymns used in the book are public domain:

What a Friend We Have in Jesus
Standing on the Promises
In the Garden
Rock of Ages
O Sacred Head, Now Wounded

Other Solstice Horizons titles you might enjoy...

How Evil Works
By: C.S. Groendal

Owen Black is wealthy, powerful, and deadly. His sole purpose for existence is
to infiltrate the human mind, deaden the human heart, and keep it hostage for an
eternity. He slithers his way into every human life at one point or another... but today he has been given an assignment...Rory Analise McClelland. Fourteen-year-old Rory McClelland doesn't know it yet, but she has a destiny ordained by God. It is because of this destiny that she finds herself fighting for her life against the unseen force of Owen Black.
Rory stared at her phone in horror. Her assault had been immortalized on the Internet for everyone to see. The mob of zombie cheerleaders and quarterback Marcus White encircled her crumpled, half naked body, like a tribe of cannibals looking down at their next meal. A warm sensation washed over her arms and belly. Rory watched with shame as a river of crimson flowed from her self-inflicted wounds. Would she ever find redemption for her broken spirit? Will she ever break free of the black shroud that blinds her to her Creator's open arms? Rory's parents Will and Miriam are doing everything possible to help Rory recover from a viscous assault suffered at the hands of a mob of sadistic cheerleaders and the Grafton Junior High quarterback. When Miriam is offered the opportunity to leave Detroit and open a new hospital in Southern California, she seizes the chance to offer her daughter a new beginning.

Alatya Earth Cleanser
By: Charles Arien

Alatya encounters a poacher pack in the protected White Mountain Reserve led by a dangerous mercenary and the trail leads to a destructive and powerful corporation based in Centre City. She travels on Bonna Venture to the slave planet Vocta and there becomes involved in an attempted assignation of a high Councilor before returning to Earth and battling mercenaries attacking the Daphes fishing fleets on coastal Los Angeles with the Kuji. Join her environmental battle to prevent the corrupt Sturmundrang Corporation from felling the surviving Denver forests, and then a blow by blow battle through all levels of the Sturmundrang Tower to confront and destroy its evil creator and the machines that protect him. Alatya battles to save the last remaining natural resources of planet Earth in this action packed novel.

Adventure in the Secret City
By: Chuck Kelly

On his first day at the Learning Center, on the enchanted planet Otherland (not far from planet Earth) thirteen-year-old Bunker Charles' personal flying Zoomer is borrowed by a student named CJ, who takes off and flies to the mountains. Bunker and his friend, Gittel, take a Cobacycle, turn it into a Cobaplane, and follow him. After a few misadventures along the way, they come across the mysterious Secret City hidden among snowcapped mountains. Bunker and Gittel meet Victor, a tall silver man who shows them around the Secret City. Snooping on their own, Bunker and Gittel soon discover a startling secret about the Secret City! In their search for CJ outside the city, they find two Azanos Indians who are half human and half lizard have kidnapped CJ. To add to the excitement, the dreaded Dogg Bolesto lands his huge spaceship on top of the Secret City and demands the return of his daughter, Orisha, who plans to marry Victor. He has brought along his Doggers to back him up. (Doggers are men and women whom he has turned into human zombies.) CJ and the Azanos Indians appear and frighten Dogg Bolesto, who runs away to his spaceship. An impending catastrophe is about to happen in the Secret City (from taking in too much oxygen) and Bunker and Gittel leave just in time. On their way home, safely in the Cobaplane, they look at the coins Victor gave them earlier and written on the coins they discover the real treasure of the Secret City.

Made in the USA
Charleston, SC
13 July 2014